John Harris was born in 1916. [...]
Sea Shall Not Have [...] and
Mark Hebden an[...] ax Henn
journal[...]
the Se[...]
navies. [...]
adventure stories and created a sequence of crime novels
around the quirky fictional character Chief Inspector Pel. A
master of war and crime fiction, his enduring fictions are
versatile and entertaining.

JOHN HARRIS

FLAWED BANNER

HOUSE OF STRATUS

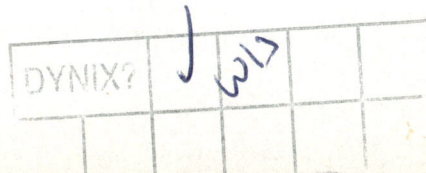

This edition published in 2001 by House of Stratus, an imprint of Stratus Holdings plc, 24c Old Burlington Street, London, W1X 1RL, UK.

www.houseofstratus.com

Typeset, printed and bound by House of Stratus.

A catalogue record for this book is available from the British Library.

ISBN 0-7551-0239-8

'Dead scandals form good subjects for dissection.'

Byron

Author's Note

Parts of this book are true. I am indebted for details to William Clive's *Fighting Mac* (Macmillan, 1977).

Part One

one

'Ever heard of Fighting Mac?' Pullinger asked.

James Woodyatt shook his head. 'Who's he? An up-and-coming prize-fighter?'

Pullinger frowned and lit a cigarette. 'Not exactly,' he said. 'He died thirty-seven years ago – to the day almost. March 25, 1903, to be exact. Just about the time when I first went to infants' school, when Hubert James Woodyatt was making his debut in his mother's arms, and not very long after distinguishing himself in a far better war than the one we've got now.'

Woodyatt glanced through the window. In his line of sight, hanging over the roofs, was a barrage balloon fat and floppy, tugging at its wire in the breeze. Below it, every door and window in Whitehall was 'bricked up' with sandbags, and all the passers-by wore ineffectual-looking little cardboard boxes on string containing their gas masks. Unless they contained their make-up or lunch, which they all too often did.

Pullinger was right. In the early spring of 1940 the war in England still had a shockingly amateur look about it. After Poland had been invaded British troops had taken up positions alongside their French allies on the continent but, with the Germans between them and the Poles they had promised to save, there was little they could do and, as though baffled, they had simply sat down to wait for something to happen.

Woodyatt prodded. 'This Fighting Mac,' he reminded. 'Who is he?'

Pullinger looked up. 'He was a soldier,' he said. He was inclined to be self-important and loved to make mysteries. His was one of the multifarious little departments connected to Intelligence that had sprung up since hostilities had commenced in September the previous year. It seemed to exist on a shoestring, with two or three rooms and one or two intellectuals drafted into the job against their will. There were also one or two women to do the typing, make the tea and provide dalliance for the intellectuals. And there was one very smart piece of work, who looked like a female staff officer in mufti, who acted as Pullinger's liaison with somebody at the War Office. She was divorced and, Woodyatt believed, was Pullinger's companion on jaunts to the country on weekends when nothing was happening. Her name was Almira Hannah and Pullinger always referred to her by her surname. Woodyatt felt she probably encouraged it.

The department seemed to exert a surprising amount of pull. Woodyatt put it down to the fact that British Intelligence was bad, that nobody knew a damn thing about anything, and that the creation of these little enclaves was the reaction to the fact that they possessed nothing in the way of weapons and nobody was doing much to provide them.

'Hadn't you better tell me more about this Fighting Mac?' he suggested.

Pullinger nodded. 'Take a pew. Cigarette? I think we'll have a drink while we're at it too. It'll help us digest it.'

'Is it that indigestible?'

'On the whole, yes, it is.' Pullinger picked up the telephone and a minute or two later the elegant Hannah appeared with a tray. She smiled at Woodyatt and gave Pullinger a look that obviously meant a lot to them both but was supposed to mean nothing to anyone else.

Pullinger leaned over the table as she vanished. 'Sherry? Whisky? Gin?'

While Pullinger was busy at the tray, Woodyatt glanced at the situation map on the wall. The bomber attacks which had been expected to wipe out half London had not materialised and the cardboard coffins stacked in swimming baths 'closed for repairs' had not been needed. On the other hand the months, like the year the Prime Minister – Chamberlain – had gained through the Munich agreement with Hitler, had been wasted in lethargy and inactivity. The attitude among the woolly minded men at Westminster seemed to be that an inefficient army was more moral than an efficient one, and there had been a feeling that if they didn't bother about it too much the war would go away.

Unfortunately, it hadn't. While nobody was looking, German troops had descended on Denmark and Norway; and Britain and France, rushing to help, were at that moment trying to avoid being flung back into the sea. A Norwegian politician called Quisling was making it more difficult by proclaiming himself Prime Minister and telling the Germans he was on their side.

Though press hand-outs and a sacrificial naval engagement had seemed at first to indicate victory, in fact the British had been caught totally unprepared. The magnificent weather had aided and abetted the impression. It had been one of the best holiday periods ever for seaside landladies. Eager visitors to the East Coast resorts sat on the front and cocked their ears hoping for the sound of naval gunfire from the North Sea, where they imagined the Royal Navy was knocking spots off the Germans.

The invasion of Scandinavia had thrown the government – mostly old men who had gone to war worried about shedding blood – into confusion. Yet even now, with the allied troops backtracking towards the Norwegian coast as fast as they could manage, Parliament still maintained its leisurely debates, people still went to the theatre and football matches, and the newspapers still seemed more concerned with the approaching cricket season than they were with the progress of the fighting. It was a lousy war really.

Pullinger was pushing a glass across to Woodyatt. The two men might almost have been brothers, both tall, lean-faced and intelligent looking, the only difference being that Pullinger was older, smoother and more self-satisfied. He was a Regular Army Officer who had served in France as a youth in the other war. Woodyatt had been recruited from Fleet Street and had donned uniform willingly enough because his marriage had collapsed and the secretive nature of the job suited him down to the ground.

'During the last war in the trenches,' Pullinger remembered, 'instead of a little whisky and a lot of water, we drank a lot of whisky with a little water. It took the taste away.'

'My brother Tom's up near the Belgian border,' Woodyatt said. 'He's billeted with a couple of elderly ex-prostitues. He says they feed him well. He's having the time of his life.'

'Tell him to make the most of it.'

'You think something's coming?'

Pullinger smiled. 'Spring, I reckon.'

'You were talking about Fighting Mac.'

'Yes. Make yourself comfortable. This is going to take quite a while. Fighting Mac – ' Pullinger drew a deep breath ' – real name Sir Hector MacDonald. Not a very popular man with his contemporaries.'

'Martinet?'

'No. Sound enough with the troops. But he was the son of a Scottish crofter who enlisted in the Gordon Highlanders and by sheer merit and totally without influence or help, rose to the rank of major-general and was eventually knighted and appointed aide to Queen Victoria. She loved chaps in kilts.' Pullinger paused. 'As a commander not outstanding,' he went on. 'But then, with a few exceptions like Roberts and Wolsely, neither was anybody else in that day and age. In the second Boer War he was given the Highland Brigade when their commanding officer was killed. As a hero, he duly got his portrait on cigarette cards, and in newspaper headlines and boys' magazines.'

Woodyatt wished he would cut out the sarcasm. As a newspaperman he was certain a story was about to come up but it seemed to be taking a long time to surface.

'Around 1903 he was given command of all British troops in Ceylon,' Pullinger continued. 'Good jumping-off place where things could go sadly wrong. You see, he'd developed a few odd tendencies over the years and it reached the ears of the authorities that he was involved with a known homosexual. Enquiries were made and, rather than face the music, he committed suicide.'

'And this affects us?' Woodyatt asked. 'In 1940?'

'Hold your water. We'll come to it eventually.' Pullinger frowned. He seemed to find the story wearing because he filled his glass again and pushed the bottle across. 'The body was brought home and buried in Edinburgh and that was that. People have argued about it ever since.'

'Why?'

Pullinger's shoulders moved. 'People refused to believe he was dead. You know the way it goes. People like their heroes alive. It was said he'd gone on a secret mission for the government, that he'd been murdered, even that he'd been seen at the unveiling of a monument to him in Dingwall in 1907. Other people claimed to have met him as a general in the Japanese army. In 1916 Scottish soldiers on the Somme said they saw him in French uniform. One story was that he'd turned up as the German Field Marshal von Mackensen.' Pullinger waved a languid hand. 'Rubbish, of course. All of it. But now we get to the nub of the matter. There was another.'

'Another what?'

Pullinger's face changed. 'Another Fighting Mac,' he said sharply.

'What's that supposed to mean?'

'Well, he wasn't called MacDonald and he wasn't a Highlander. But there *was* another case. About the same time, too. Very off-putting.'

'Soldier?'

'Oh, yes. Very much so. These people aren't all greenery-yallery types like Oscar Wilde. Take Richard the Lionheart, for example.'

'And this other one?'

'Obliterated, of course. Deleted. Rubbed out. The Army List doesn't show his name after 1904. But you'll find him all present and correct until then. Because it came so soon after MacDonald, the case was hushed up. Even Edward VII co-operated. He was very worried, of course. His assistant equerry, Lord Arthur Somerset, had been linked to a homosexual scandal in 1889, you see; and so had his son, the Duke of Clarence, so he wasn't very keen to have these cases exposed. And like MacDonald, this other chap had also been an aide to the old Queen, and two in eighteen months was just too much. People were going to start wondering what these types were doing in the army and what the Royal Family were doing to choose them as aides.'

Pullinger sat back, sank his whisky, shoved a few papers around on his desk and looked up. 'You'd have thought he'd have been a bit more careful, wouldn't you?' he went on. 'But perhaps it's part of the character. There was that chap, Redl, Chief of Austrian Intelligence in 1913. Sold secrets to the Russians because he was being blackmailed as a homosexual. He felt he could get away with it but they caught him over something quite trivial.'

'Was our chap – this chap you're talking about – being blackmailed?'

Pullinger lit another cigarette. His frown had grown deeper.

'Hang on,' he urged. 'Take it in the right order. Like MacDonald – like Redl, come to that – he was good-looking, caused a few sighs in London boudoirs.'

'How do you know?'

Pullingers face was blank. 'I heard,' he said.

Woodyatt was wondering where it was all going to lead.

'Hadn't we better have a name?' he suggested. 'Instead of arsing about talking about "this chap" and so on.'

Pullinger frowned, then he shrugged. 'You can find that out for yourself,' he said. 'I've dug out the files on the affair for you to look at. Took a bit of getting, but they eventually gave permission.'

'Who did?'

'High altar. Chief of Staff. Prime Minister. Take your pick.'

'Why did it require so much weight?' Woodyatt asked. 'For God's sake, it took place thirty-six years ago, you said. Why are *we* so interested all of a sudden?'

Pullinger gestured. 'Suppose you go and sniff through them, then I'll tell you.'

Woodyatt frowned. 'Do I expect to find something?'

Pullinger gave a bark of mirthless laughter. 'I reckon you might,' he said.

two

Major-General Sir George Surtees Redmond.

For the first time, Woodyatt had a name. It meant nothing to him and he could only assume that, apart from his disgrace, Redmond hadn't made much mark on the world's tapestry. But a man who had enlisted as a private soldier, served through the first and second Boer Wars and on the North-West Frontier, to say nothing of a host of minor wars before finally reaching senior rank in the days when influence counted more than skill, could hardly be said to be of no account. It was all there. He had been born near Harrogate in Yorkshire in 1861, into the family of a farmer, but had immediately been taken into the home of a family possessed of a minor title. The inference was obvious. Redmond had been sired either by the owner of the title or one of his sons. He had been educated privately – doubtless to avoid wagging tongues – by a governess and then by a tutor; but then, following some dispute with the family, had cut himself off from them and enlisted in one of the country's regiments. He had risen quickly through the ranks and been granted a commission just before the first Boer War in which, having distinguished himself – one of the few who had – he received a quick step up in promotion.

About this time, because his childhood governess had happened to be half-German and he had developed an ability to speak that language, he found himself eligible for an interchange German language course through the German staff college at Potsdam. He applied for it and got it. He was obviously clever with a gift for languages and, in addition to German, he had also learned to write and speak French. By the outbreak of the second Boer War in South Africa in 1899 he had become a brigadier and the early disasters there and the subsequent sacking of senior officers had made him a major-general.

He had done well. One senior officer had written of him: 'Highly intelligent and well read. A born staff man.' Another had said 'In action, very reliable.' But there was one other, who disagreed. 'Too clever by half,' he had said.

As Pullinger had suggested, it hadn't been a vintage period for British generalship but it seemed Redmond had always had the ability to inspire the ordinary rank and file to stand fast when standing fast was important, and to go forward without hesitation when that was the order of the day. In 1904, still a bachelor, he was appointed commander of all British troops in Upper Burma with a seat on the Legislative Council.

Those were the facts according to the copy of the entry for *Who's Who* of 1904 which lay on top of the file. So far, it was all straightforward. After that point, however, the file entries seemed to consist of copies of reports, newspaper cuttings, and comments. In March, 1904, Redmond had been asked to report to the office of the Governor of Upper Burma who had sent to the Foreign Office a report indicating in close detail exactly what had been said between them. A copy of it now lay in front of Woodyatt.

'It has come to my knowledge, Sir George,' the Governor had said to Redmond, 'that a very grave accusation has been made against you. So grave I find it hard to decide exactly what to do.'

There had been more in the same strain, with the Governor, a gentleman by the name of Sir Horace Varah, showering clichés and platitudes about failing in his duty if he didn't allow the accused to make some comment. Apparently, Redmond had not answered and Sir Horace had produced a sheet on which he had written down all the details of the accusation. 'I found them most unpalatable,' he had commented in his report to the Foreign Office.

Until a short time before, according to Sir Horace, Sir George Redmond had had on the staff of his quarters a young soldier by the name of Ma-Ling from one of the Burmese regiments that had been raised. This youth had acted as servant-cum-batman and it was he whom the charges concerned. Confronted with the allegations, Redmond had said that the soldier had already left his house and been returned to regimental duties.

'I felt obliged to disagree with this,' Varah went on, 'because I had been informed that the man had *not* been returned to regimental duties. He had been removed from the army and returned to his village. I urged General Redmond to consider the accusations very seriously.'

Redmond had continued to remain silent, and Sir Horace had pressed on. 'The accusation,' he had said, 'is that while this man was employed at your house, you behaved with him in a manner that could not be said to conform to the proprieties we live by.' He had been careful not to put in plain words what had happened but it was pretty clear what he meant.

Shifting his position, Woodyatt now shuffled the papers. He was finally beginning to grow interested in the long-dead Redmond.

It seemed there had been an outbreak of smallpox and, as a precaution, all troops in the area had been vaccinated. But a junior army medical officer, a Lieutenant Arthur Thomas Witkins, had noticed that somehow Redmond had not been among those treated and had made arrangements for him to appear at the hospital. When Redmond had failed to turn up, Witkins had supposed perhaps he was ill in his bungalow and had felt it his duty to check up on him. With a Captain Wilfred Nicolson, one of Redmond's aides, he had gone in the evening after duty with the excuse that he was bringing reports.

'There,' Sir Horace's report continued, 'these two men – both officers in the British army and men of good reputation – claim they found Sir George Redmond in a situation of a most unnatural nature with the soldier, Ma-Ling. They retired at once – in silence.'

But one of them had not been able to hold his tongue and gossip had reached the ears of a reporter of an English-language newspaper, the *Upper Burma Gazette*. Not unnaturally his editor had decided it would be wiser to leave the matter well alone.

'Not so,' Sir Horace wrote, 'the native-language newspaper.'

It seemed the General's servants were well-aware of what was happening and had passed it on to their friends. The paper had not hesitated to let it be known by means of a discreet paragraph hidden among reports of minor native events.

It would probably still never have been noticed by any but Burmese because the British did not normally read the native papers, but the Native Affairs Officer, going through them as a means of keeping his finger on the pulse of the country, had spotted it. The story had not taken long to spread.

'There seemed,' Sir Horace Varah reported in an magnificent understatement, 'to be a crisis before me.'

Following Varah's report, there were several Roneoed sheets about the law. Homosexual offences, they pointed out, were not considered punishable under the Burmese legal code, but under British civil and military law they most certainly were. After all, it was only nine years since Oscar Wilde had been sent to prison. How far the Governor should have acted in this case was doubtful, but a deputation of officers – and Woodyatt wondered how many of them had disliked or envied the ranker risen to major-general and had seen in the situation a chance to be rid of him – had requested that the formalities of a court martial be set in motion. Sir Horace, however, had preferred to refer the matter to Whitehall.

Redmond had complained that the accusation consisted of nothing but hearsay and gossip, that the two officers concerned might have been drunk, and that the gossip might even have been part of a campaign to embarrass him. He had had no illusions, it seemed, about how he was regarded by the wealthy officers to whom he had once been subordinate.

'I went over all these points,' Sir Horace reported. But he had also indicated to Redmond that there was a factor that could not be avoided. The soldier, Ma-Ling, had been returned to his village not by Redmond but by the aide, Captain Nicolson, *after* the incident at the bungalow. If an enquiry were placed on an official basis, he would have to be brought back to give evidence.

'This,' Sir Horace wrote, 'was greeted with silence.' He had pointed out to Redmond, his report continued, that he would probably feel the need to consult with people in London, even that he might find in necessary to seek a command elsewhere. 'I urged him, in fact,' Varah announced, 'to depart at once as if he were going on leave, on the SS *Omshah*, which was due to sail in three days' time.'

At this point Sir Horace Varah retired from the fray and his place was taken by a man with the unusual name of Captain Albert Aimable Slough, who seemed to have been some sort of aide to the Adjutant-General.

'Sir George was know aboard the *Omshah*,' he reported, 'and there were many awkward moments. *Why was he going to London?* He was asked. *When was he returning to Burma?*' A young nobleman by the name of Lord Seley, who was also an officer in the army as well as a fellow-

Yorkshireman and an ardent admirer of Redmond, was an eager questioner. He had joined the ship at Aden. His questions had been answered evasively.

In London, the Adjutant-General, an old friend of Redmond's, had already received a coded telegram which had startled him. He had immediately gone to see the Commander-in-Chief, the last incumbent of that high office before it had been discontinued that very year. At the time it had been held by the legendary Lord Roberts of Kandahar, the man who had regained Kabul after the British disaster there in 1848, a man who had won a Victoria Cross during the Indian Mutiny and whose son had posthumously been awarded another during the Boer War.

He had been shocked by the information he received and couldn't believe it of Redmond whom he knew well. 'However,' Captain Slough wrote, and it wasn't hard to believe that the comment came from Captain Slough not Lord Roberts, 'Sir George Redmond *was* a bachelor and it had been noticed that he was always friendly with the Burmese and had been seen to offer sweets to their children.'

When the Adjutant-General had met Redmond and listened to his account of the affair, there were, according to Captain Slough, areas of hesitation in Redmond's replies which did not help to render his version of the story credible. Added to the report was a copy of army law, which covered the whole area of homosexual activity under one simple Victorian heading – 'Sodomy' – an act calling for a prison sentence of anything up to life.

Perhaps, Woodyatt decided, it would have been different for a major-general who was a known hero. In such a case an admission of guilt would probably have meant only a demand for resignation. In the unlikely event of a refusal, cashiering for conduct unbecoming an officer would inevitably have been the result, and would have been followed by the removal of the guilty party's name from the army list with a loss of pay and pensions. There would have been the slamming of doors in his face, unpleasant publicity in the cheap newspapers, comic songs in the music halls, social ostracism, expulsion from clubs and ill-mannered comments from shopkeepers.

During his interview with Redmond, the Adjutant-General had not offered a chair and had remained on his feet himself. He had informed Redmond that it was his unpleasant duty to order his return to Burma to face a court martial. He had shown no indication of his old friendship and had not offered to shake hands.

Leaving the Adjutant-General's office, Redmond had apparently wandered round London for some time. He had been to his club but his story had already become known and he had not stayed long. First he had been recognised in Hyde Park by a policeman who had seen him walking alone, his hands behind his back, his head down, deep in thought. Then it emerged that he had spoken for a minute or two to an old soldier from his regiment who had spotted him lighting a cigarette in the street near the side door of the German Embassy at the Duke of York's steps.

It seemed an odd place to be, and Woodyatt wondered what he was doing there. By this time he was deeply involved and even beginning to feel sympathy for the wretched Redmond. The drama was building up and he could feel the tension coming from the scrawled lines on the dog-eared papers in front of him.

There was a photograph of Redmond in the next batch of papers, and one or two drawings of him reproduced from journals. Woodyatt wasn't sure what he had expected but it was nothing like what he saw. Somehow he had pictured a tall slender man with a soft face, an intellectual soldier perhaps. But here was a good looking man of strong physique, fair-haired with a straight nose, a smiling mouth and large handsome eyes. He was in uniform and, in the manner of the day, looked stiff, formidable and arrogant, but there was no getting away from the intelligence and humour in his face.

When Redmond subsequently caught the ferry across the Channel and then the train to Paris, the story there was taken up by a Major Albert Francis Cummings Darby, who had been Assistant Military Attaché at the Embassy.

Darby's first comment indicated that Redmond had taken a small apartment in a Hotel Angleterre in the Rue Jacob. 'Unostentatious,' Darby's report pointed out. 'Genteel clientèle.'

Attached to the report was the copy of a clipping from a Burmese English-language newspaper. It referred to a meeting of the Legislative Council of Upper Burma at which an unexpected question had been put to the Governor. The questioner had read in a Reuters' report that General Redmond was to return to Burma and wanted to know why. Like everyone else he had clearly heard the rumours and had believed the affair would blow over quietly with the general replaced and the scandal allowed to die.

The question had brought a long reply from the Governor and Woodyatt could well imagine the expressions on the faces of the Members of the Council – the disgust, the indignation, the surprise of those not in the know. Yet it was a reply which had not satisfied the questioner, who had insisted on knowing what Redmond's status would be on his return. This time the Governor was more sharp. 'Officers about to be tried by court martial,' he had said, 'are considered to be under arrest.'

That was the end of the report from Burma but, judging by what followed, the press, up to that point largely kept in the dark, had not waited long to get the story on the wires to Delhi, London, Paris and the rest of the world.

Woodyatt sat back and lit a cigarette. He could see headlines among the piles of papers – 'Grave Charges Against Sir George Redmond' read the *New York World*.

Laying down the cigarette, Woodyatt reached for the next batch of papers. They began with a hurried note from Major Darby. 'Sir George Redmond,' it stated, 'planned to take the night train from Gare de Lyon to Marseilles.' Attached to the report were the ticket and the reservation for a sleeper. 'He intended,' Darby continued, 'to pick up SS *Howadah*, bound for India. Guests at hotel unaware of identity.'

Woodyatt could well imagine the dread with which Redmond must have faced every new day's journals. The fact that he was prepared to return to Burma indicated that he had been expecting to be acquitted. Whatever the two officers, Witkins and Nicolson, had seen, when it came to the trial they would inevitably agree, willingly or otherwise, that they might have been mistaken. The whole thing would be treated with discretion, the general would leave Burma and quietly drop out of sight. The army would never permit gossip to continue and up to that point there had been no publicity.

But now, there it was in bold type with Redmond's face staring out from the front page. Woodyatt picked up the newspaper account gingerly. It was by-lined 'Rangoon' and it made no attempt to hide anything.

'It seems,' Darby reported, 'that the general was in the habit after breakfast of collecting all English-language newspapers from a kiosk near the Church of St Germain des Prés and carrying them back to the hotel to peruse. After reading the story in the *New York World*, he sat in the salon, quietly smoking a cigar. Then, after a while, he went to his room, took a gun from his luggage and shot himself through the right temple. He was found by a maid going to clean the room.'

The manager of the hotel had telephoned the police and the British Embassy. By the time Major Darby had reached the scene with the British Consul General, the corpse was already being examined by a British medical man, Dr Angus McVicar, and a Paris police surgeon. The shocked Darby had returned to the Embassy to inform the ambassador who had telegraphed the Under Secretary for Foreign Affairs in London. A copy of the telegram was included.

Woodyatt was just sitting back staring at the papers when Pullinger appeared. 'How are you getting on?' he asked.

Woodyatt passed a hand across his face. 'He's just shot himself,' he said.

'Come and see me when you've finished. I'll still be here.' As the door closed, Woodyatt returned to the papers. It was obvious by this time that Darby, the attaché, was well out of his depth. Reading between the lines, it seemed that the ambassador, heavily engaged with a projected visit by a British military mission, had not been very helpful.

Woodyatt lit another cigarette, frowning, and picked up the next sheet. The news had clearly thrown the War Office and the Foreign Office into uproar. The British newspapers were all wary and backed away from being explicit. All of them expressed the wish that the dead man would be laid to rest in his native Yorkshire soil.

That their hopes were in vain was obvious from the notes that must have been whirling between London and Paris. The War Office had quickly made up its mind that it wasn't going to be involved. A funeral in England would mean problems over the removal of the body, newspapermen with their questions, military honours, and a lot of very difficult publicity.

'A quiet interment in one of the Paris burial grounds should be quickly arranged,' went the note from the Adjutant-General to the ambassador. 'A whisper in the ear of the next of kin about the situation should make it possible. The family would never wish to face the adverse publicity.'

'The next of kin,' the telegram ended, 'is Mr Henry Howard Redmond, JP, of Pinder, Yorkshire, where the deceased general was born.'

From then on, it seemed a whole snowstorm of telegrams had passed between London and Paris. Within hours Mr Henry Howard Redmond, JP, had been unearthed and had very sensibly given his consent for the funeral to take place in Paris the following day. Darby, the unfortunate attaché saddled with the affair, was obviously very nervous and had contacted a firm of British solicitors in Paris to help him prepare a statement. 'They helped to arrange the funeral of General MacDonald a year ago,' he'd commented. 'They should know what to do.' There were letters making arrangements for carriages and wreath, and a copy of the death certificate for the Director of the Cemetery of Père Lachaise. There was also a note from Darby to the British doctor, McVicar, reminding him that he would be expected to attend.

Wondering how it all worked out, Woodyatt closed the file on the last of the papers. There were no reports of the funeral.

Nothing. And, having come to the conclusion that Major Darby was a careful and sensible person, he wondered why not. Surely he would have made certain his report ended with the indication that the dead soldier had been placed under the soil, duly blessed by a priest, and that the family had returned home, if not exactly content, then at least satisfied that all the proper rites had been attended to.

But there was nothing.

Frowning, Woodyatt looked at his watch. It was nearly dusk and he wondered if Pullinger were still in the building. Rising, he headed down the corridor. Pullinger's light was on and he was dozing in his chair, his feet on the desk, alongside a thick file of papers. The rest of the building was silent.

As the door opened, Pullinger's eyelids lifted and he became awake and alert at once. 'Finished?'

'I don't know. I suspect not. I think there's more. It isn't wrapped up properly.' Woodyatt gestured at the file on the desk. 'Is that the rest of it?'

Pullinger nodded. 'Yes,' he said. 'That's the end of the story. Or is it?'

'You're behaving as if it's a major puzzle.'

Pullinger's eyebrows rose. 'But that's exactly what it is,' he said. 'From here on, we go through the thing together.'

'Why?'

'Because that's how it's got to be. You'll see why eventually.' Without opening the file, Pullinger waved at the whisky bottle. He seemed in a dour mood. 'Help yourself. Have a cigarette. Make yourself comfortable. You got to the point of the funeral, I assume?'

'Yes.'

'Read everything?'

'Everything.'

'Right. Let's get on with it. The chaps in Paris, of course, were unaware that across the Channel in Yorkshire the announcement of Redmond's death had already started a wave of anger, disbelief and shock at every level of society. It spread to London, the rest of the country, and even the Dominions where there were similar reactions because Redmond had commanded Australian troops in South Africa.'

'So why didn't Darby finish his report with a note about the funeral at Père Lachaise?'

Pullinger frowned. 'Because there wasn't one. It didn't take place.'

'*What!*'

'Well, not at Père Lachaise. You see, unknown to Henry Howard Redmond, JP, and the rest of the family, unknown to the army, the Foreign Office, the War Office, the Paris Embassy, and the Legislative Council in Upper Burma, Redmond was married.'

'*What!*'

Pullinger looked angry suddenly. 'Oh, yes. There was a Lady Redmond, and she now enters the ring. On your left in the blue corner. And she wasn't going to have any funeral in Paris. She was going to have it in Redmond's native Harrogate – a place, I might add, that has great importance in Yorkshire, that most independent and bloody-minded area in the British scheme of things. She wasn't having it where it wouldn't be noticed. She wanted it where it – and she – would be seen.

'Redmond had married her in 1882 and there was even a twenty-one-year-old son.'

'Good God!'

'Exactly. She hadn't even known of the suicide until she read of it in the *Yorkshire Post*. I've looked it up.' Pullinger's hand moved. 'It's in the file here.'

'She didn't know about the charges against him?'

'The only thing she knew about him was that she received a regular allowance from him for herself and her son. Through a solicitor. It was a private allowance. Redmond was always considered tight with money. But he would have to be, wouldn't he, if he were supporting his family in style solely on his army pay.'

'Why did he do that?'

'Can only guess. Judging by the dates, it seems the boy was conceived out of wedlock and that the mother forced Redmond to marry her to make him legitimate. I imagine, in fact, the boy was the result of the one and only time Redmond and his wife found themselves together in the nest. Perhaps not the only time but, if his tastes were as they seem

22

to have been, there couldn't have been many other times. His name was never linked with a woman's and his movements are pretty well known, and none of them ever led to Harrogate. Yet here he is with a wife and child.' Pullinger shifted in his seat. His expression was unrelenting. 'Still,' he went on, 'Oscar Wilde was a married man with two sons. Anyway, she seems to have read of the suicide and the funeral that was to take place in Paris in accordance with the wishes of the next of kin, and began to wonder who the devil *were* these kin. As his wife, *she* was his next of kin.'

As Pullinger talked, Woodyatt sat silent, absorbed by this new twist.

Pullinger continued. 'Although she had never lived with him, she was still Lady Redmond and she was determined to have her little hour. It seems the son had often wondered about his father and when the story appeared he had just, at twenty-one, officially become an adult. She made up her mind to tell him and between them they decided it was time to claim the relationship.

'You can imagine how it startled the relatives, three brothers, one a lawyer, one a JP, and two sisters, all married.' Pullinger was silent for a moment, his face sombre, then he went on briskly. 'Having been told the story, they doubtless welcomed the funeral in Paris and, to make it appear they had been close to their brother, two of them, the lawyer and the JP, arranged to cross the Channel. But by the time they set off it was becoming obvious that the people of Yorkshire were not only rejecting the allegations against their hero but were even demanding that he be brought home to be buried in style. In the end, Henry Howard Redmond decided to telegraph their objections to the War Office.'

Pullinger gestured at the file. 'It's in there. "Yorkshire most anxious Sir George should be buried here. Postpone funeral arrangements until my arrival Paris." '

Pullinger pushed the whisky across again. He seemed curiously affected by the ancient scandal. 'That evening,' he went on, 'a Yorkshire solicitor, a Mr Joseph Halcro, appeared at the War Office with a twenty-one year old who said his name was Geoffrey Surtees Redmond. They produced the young man's birth certificate and indisputable evidence of his mother's marriage to Redmond. On behalf of the widow, they claimed possession of the body with all effects. The funeral, the solicitor announced, would be in Harrogate.'

Pullinger was silent again, frowning. 'You can imagine the Adjutant-General's face,' he said. 'He had personally known Redmond throughout his career and he'd never heard a murmur about any marriage. It had been kept a secret for twenty-one years.' He fished among the papers on his desk and tossed across a faded letter. 'From the Adjutant-General,' he said. 'To a friend.'

Indignation blazed from the letter. 'Just when we thought everything was sorted out,' Woodyatt read, 'this damn solicitor and the son appear! I did all I could to dissuade them from holding the funeral in England. We had this business only last year with MacDonald. But there's nothing we can do because we have no claim whatsoever to the body now that the heir claims it on behalf of the widow. I have written to the Lord Lieutenant and expressed regret at the course insisted on. When I explained that in no case could a military funeral be allowed, I was informed – thank God! – that the funeral would be private. I have now wired the assistant military attaché in Paris to comply with their wishes but have informed Sir Harding Hereward, Commander of the Northern District, in Richmond, Yorkshire, that there must be no kind of patriotic demonstration. That we cannot be doing with. We must try to arrange it that the funeral takes place early in the morning. If we get it on the night train and have it met on arrival the body could be interred before anybody is about.'

'He had to inform the Commander-in-Chief, of course,' Pullinger said. 'Roberts was in Manchester. There's a reply from him insisting that there must be no hint of a scandal.'

Woodyatt was frowning. 'Why has all this been brought up now?' he asked. 'What's so special about it that we're going through it all again?'

Pullinger's eyebrows rose. 'The fuss hasn't really started yet,' he snapped. 'They were still hoping to persuade the family into a Paris funeral. But the Foreign Office, the War Office, the Embassy in Paris, the Lord Lieutenant, Members of Parliament for Yorkshire seats, and all the national and local newspapers were being deluged with demands for the military funeral to which Yorkshire thought it was entitled. The Prime Minister and the Foreign Office were dragged into the controversy. For Whitehall it must have been rather a wearing weekend.'

Pullinger sighed and Woodyatt realised he looked tired. 'When the solicitor and the son appeared,' he continued, 'they had to be made to understand thoroughly that, on taking possession of the body, they would become entirely responsible for all arrangements and expenses connected with its removal and interment. There were to be no gun-carriages, drums, flags on the coffin, last posts, or graveside firing parties.'

Pullinger paused. 'Not, I think, that the widow was all that bothered. The two brothers who'd intended to represent the family arrived in London to learn they were no longer the centre of attention. To save face, they pretended to know all about the widow and claimed she preferred to remain anonymous. Doubtless they went into a heavy huddle, wondering who the hell she was.'

'Who was she, anyway?'

'A Miss Mabel Pendle. Her family owned property in and around Sheffield. How she squared the arrival of her son to her family I don't know. She acquired a house near York and lived quietly under her own name as a married woman, claiming nothing until the point when she obviously felt she wanted at last to be part of any glory that was going.'

Woodyatt was still trying to work out what all this had to do with 1940 and why Pullinger considered it of such importance.

Pullinger was watching him closely – almost too closely, it seemed to Woodyatt. 'You'd better read the rest for yourself,' he said.

'Why?' Woodyatt asked.

'I'll tell you all in good time. But you need to know first what it's all about.'

three

As Pullinger vanished, Woodyatt huddled over the desk again. It was all there. In letters, press cuttings, photographs, telegrams.

When Redmond's brothers had reached Paris they had found that what was to have been a tidy solution to an awkward problem had descended into a macabre farce. The body had been taken to the Gare St Lazare by the French undertakers who had sealed the coffin in a plain deal crate with the dead man's initials scrawled on it, with the destination, 'Harrogate, England,' written underneath. It was to travel as normal freight on the nine p.m. express to Dieppe. The solicitor and the son had left ahead of it, together, it seemed, with a discreet official observer. His instructions were attached. The War Office wasn't going to have any more mistakes. An officer was instructed to attend the funeral but he was *not* to wear uniform. The orders had clearly come from Intelligence. The scrawled signature was unreadable but seemed curiously familiar. A last telegram had been sent to the Adjutant-General. There it was, now, in front of Woodyatt, signed by Darby. 'Body leaves Paris tonight via Dieppe–Newhaven due London Bridge 7.30 Sunday morning. Stop. Arrangements made for transport to King's Cross and from King's Cross to Harrogate.' It seemed there was nothing for Redmond's brothers to do but accompany the body.

The widow had been waiting at King's Cross. She was accompanied by her son, the solicitor, Halcro, and the two brothers, who were still determined to have a share in the affair. As soon as it had dawned on the reporters who she was, her compartment had been besieged but she had refused to speak. All they could say of her was that she had seemed to be 'a lady of noble appearance, her features lined with grief'. The son was not described. As the doors slammed and the whistles shrilled, the train eased out. According to one newspaperman a band had played 'The Dead March in Saul' and tears had streamed down the onlookers' faces.

The sentimental overwriting of the period was beginning to wear a little heavy on Woodyatt. But he pushed on, determined to get the rest of the story.

Despite the fuss that had been made about a ceremonial burial, when the train had arrived in Harrogate the following morning there was nobody on the station. A closed hearse and three closed carriages were waiting but they contained no one in uniform. The officer commanding the area had apologised by wire for his absence, claiming that he wished to respect the widow's privacy, an excuse that was clearly the result of explicit instructions from the War Office.

It was at this point that the widow finally gave an interview. There had been a delay – obviously, it seemed to Woodyatt, to allow people to learn what was happening – before she had consented to talk to a reporter from the *Yorkshire Post*. She had given the impression that there had never been a separation between herself and Redmond, and that when she wasn't visiting him in London he had met her at a secret rendezvous in Harrogate.

'All rubbish!' The comment on the side of the report was in Darby's writing. 'They never met again.'

When the cortege moved off it was followed by a stream of unofficial mourners, and hats had tumbled as it had passed through the streets. The reporters were still there, of course. Short of facts, they went to town with descriptions of the weather. They also made great play of the widow's beauty and her iron control of her emotions. She had commanded as much of the coverage as Redmond himself. She must, Woodyatt decided, have enjoyed her moment of glory.

With the funeral out of the way, Woodyatt stretched, wondering what came next. The cuttings which followed were all about the nationwide storm of fury over the hurried interment. The protests and accusations raged over months, blaming everyone from the widow to the Prime Minister. They seemed to go on until the start of the Great War in 1914 which turned out to be big enough to sweep away all other concerns as it took centre stage. During the whole time the War Office did not make a single statement in answer to the requests for enlightenment.

There was little left to read now. Redmond's will left heirlooms to his son – mostly caskets containing the freedom of this city or that, a signed photograph of Queen Victoria, a sword presented by the officers of his regiment on his leaving for higher rank, and many other things. But there was little money. The widow died in 1915 and was buried close to the general. Her son, killed on the first day of the Somme in 1916, was buried near Thiepval in France.

Closing the file, Woodyatt sat back, wondering what the hell it was all about and why Pullinger kept insisting there was more to come. What more could there be?

He was still sitting there, smoking and staring thoughtfully at the pile of papers, when Pullinger returned. He sat down at the opposite side of the desk.

'Finished?'

'Yes. They made sure he was put away for certain, didn't they? Darby even included the written instructions from Intelligence for the War Office observer. Why *written* instructions? Was it that important?'

'They were anxious that it should be done properly,' Pullinger said stiffly.

'Who was he? – the type in charge.'

Pullinger was silent for a moment then he drew a deep breath. 'Major J D C Pullinger,' he said harshly. 'My father.'

Woodyatt couldn't think what to say. No wonder Pullinger was keen to sort out the mystery, whatever it was. No wonder the scrawled, almost illegible signature had seemed familiar.

'He was in Intelligence at the time,' Pullinger explained, speaking slowly as if every word hurt. 'He went into it after he was wounded in South Africa. He caught the backlash for what happened.'

'What did happen?' Woodyatt was anxious to move away from talk of blame. It was obviously a very delicate subject for Pullinger. 'I'm still baffled. What's it all about? I've read everything. Every newspaper cutting. Every report. Every telegram. Somebody did a good job of collecting and copying it all. Who was it? Darby?'

'Yes,' Pullinger rapped. 'He passed it over to the archivists in 1914.'

'Why so long afterwards?'

Pullinger leaned back in his chair. 'In 1914 there was good reason.'

Woodyatt began to lose patience. He could understand Pullinger's dislike for the case but they were treading around it as if on eggshells. 'Look,' he said. 'I don't know what all this is about but if I'm to be involved with this bloody Redmond I think it's about time you came clean and told me all there is to know.'

Pullinger studied him for a moment then he nodded. 'Yes,' he agreed. 'It's time. But you had to know everything that's definite first.'

'What do you mean – *definite*?'

'Well, after the point when he was buried at Harrogate it all became a bit – well – indefinite.'

Woodyatt still felt angry but somewhere beneath the story, he sensed there was a wound that pained Pullinger and he didn't press the point too much.

Pullinger gestured. 'Reminds you of Crown Prince Rudolf, doesn't it?' he said. 'Heir to the throne of Austria. He shot his mistress in her bed at Mayerling in 1889 and then committed suicide. To conceal the fact that a girl was involved, she was dressed and walked out to a closed carriage by two of her uncles. She rode back to Vienna held upright between them as if she were alive. It was a bit like that.'

He poured whisky and squirted soda into the glass.

'The passing of a national hero,' he said when he was seated again, 'is always accepted with reluctance. You'll remember what happened when Lawrence of Arabia killed himself on that motorbike of his five years back. National mourning. Usual service of remembrance. Everybody there. But, in spite of it all, people still insisted he wasn't dead. They said he'd been withdrawn from circulation to take on a secret mission in the Middle East for the government. With Hitler beginning to grow stroppy, it had a grain of sense in it.' Pullinger paused. 'When Kitchener died in 1916, people insisted he'd also gone on a secret mission. It's a reluctance to see a great name vanish from the scene, I suppose. Same with MacDonald. Same with Redmond a year later. North-Country people insisted he couldn't have committed suicide, that he'd been withdrawn.'

'What evidence could they have had?'

'Plenty. They pointed out quite correctly that the only people who saw him after death were Doctor McVicar; the French police surgeon; a variety of French policemen of various ranks; the French undertakers; the solicitor the widow sent and her son. Not one of them had ever met him.

Not one of them would have been able to identify him. Even the widow didn't see the corpse, and no fingerprints were taken. Everybody just accepted the maid's story that the dead man was Redmond.'

'I'd have thought the Paris police would have demanded more than that.'

'Ah!' Pullinger frowned. 'But that was a bad period for the Sûreté. They'd led the world up to the end of the nineteenth century with their crime detection. But unfortunately, at this time, while everybody else had gone over to fingerprints for identification they were still using a weird system invented by a chap by the name of Alphonse Bertillon, who called himself an anthropometrist. It consisted of measuring parts of the human body – head, fingers, feet, forearms – which he claimed remained unchanged during the whole of a man's adult life so that he could be identified by them years after they'd been recorded. Obviously it wasn't much use for this kind of identification, and since Redmond was known to have occupied the room and to have been seen going there by the maid, the Paris police just accepted that it *was* Redmond. It was reasonable enough to do so.'

Was it? Woodyatt wondered briefly why Pullinger's father had not noticed the discrepancies which had already become clear to him. It seemed to have been an opportunity that had been missed.

Pullinger was gesturing at the file again. 'After all,' he pointed out, 'it was a pretty complicated affair and it was to be the cause of a lot of legends and a few damaged reputations – my father's among them.'

'Why?' Woodyatt was still puzzled.

Pullinger held up a hand. 'Wait a minute,' he said.

'Redmond's admirers were quick to notice there had been no inquest. Some even claimed the coffin was filled with stones. Others claimed to have met him as a general with the Russian army after the Russo-Japanese war, the same stories that followed the death of Fighting Mac – MacDonald. North-Country soldiers who had served under him and were taken prisoner in the last German push in 1918 swore they saw him wearing the uniform of a German officer.

Woodyatt was becoming intrigued again and Pullinger waved a hand. 'The most persistent theory suggested that Redmond had become a German general called Georg von Rothügel, that he'd been spirited away by the German High Command and substituted for an officer who'd died. It was claimed, in fact, when Kitchener was drowned on his way to Russia that he was heading for a meeting with Redmond who had contrived to join the German army as a British agent and was acting as an intermediary for the ending of the war. And, in a way, that made some sense because there had always been suggestions that Kitchener, who was a bachelor, had the same sort of tastes. Another version was that Kitchener was on his way to see MacDonald. That hadn't the faintest glimmer of truth to it, but – '

'But what?'

'But in the Redmond version there *could* have been an element of truth.'

In the silence that followed Pullinger fished in a drawer and produced a couple of photographs. They were old, grainy and faded, and he placed them side by side facing Woodyatt. One was of a man in the uniform of a British general of the turn of the century, wearing a bicorn hat, with gold braid on his collar and a row of decorations across his left breast. The face was heavily moustached in the fashion of the day, with the same straight nose, firm jaw and deep-set eyes that Woodyatt had noticed on the photograph among the file papers. 'Redmond,' Pullinger said.

He pushed the other one forward. This time the photograph was of an older man, wearing the busby and frogged uniform of a German Death's Head Hussar. The nose seemed identical and so did the deep-set eyes. Though the moustache was similar, it had acquired the upward twist so beloved of the Kaiser and his generals.

'Von Rothügel,' Pullinger said. 'Look at the eyes. The nose. The mouth. The lobes of the ears.'

Two more photographs were pushed across the desk. One showed a British general shaking hands with Edward VII. The other showed an older man – also shaking hands, but this time with the Kaiser. These photographs showed the features of the two men in profile, and the noses, jaws, eyes, and ears were clear. Apart from the difference in age, they were identical.

Woodyatt looked up. 'They could be the same man,' he said.

Pullinger's face was hard and set. 'They *are* the same man,' he said. 'For once the great British sporting public had got it right.'

'Redmond didn't shoot himself?' Woodyatt jerked his chair forward. 'What in God's name are you trying to tell me?'

Pullinger removed the photographs. 'It was a put-up job. Doubtless the suicide of MacDonald the year before suggested it.'

'So what happened?'

'Redmond *was* von Rothügel.' Pullinger gestured again. 'Redmond's reputation wasn't just based on his record as a fighting soldier. He had another based on his command of languages and that period he spent in Potsdam. Just before the Boer War he had been attached to Intelligence, and was considered to be very thorough. There's a story that once, when he searched the house of an officer suspected of passing secrets and found nothing, he took the man's six-year-old daughter aside and got her to show him a secret drawer she knew about in Daddy's desk. The officer was sent to prison and the child lost her father. After that Redmond became

Chief of Staff to the Reserve Army which, of course, would be incorporated in the event of a major war.'

'This is all certain?'

'Files exist. But they were reviewed in 1905 and stripped of anything that was considered dangerous. A lot of nonsense was put out about Redmond's suicide being due to overwork and neurasthenia, but unpleasant evidence of his sexual proclivities had turned up by then. Nothing was proved.'

Again Woodyatt wondered why only Darby had thought to collect the material on the case, why Pullinger's father had not spotted the potentials. Had he, he wondered, been one of the people who had been concerned to avoid a scandal and had destroyed the files?

'Go on,' he said.

Pullinger took his time. 'When war broke out in 1914,' he said, 'they remembered the stories that had gone round and started looking into them again. This time they found they were true. The German High Command had arranged everything.'

'But there *was* a body.'

'Oh, there was a body all right. But it wasn't Redmond's. Who it was, God only knows. That's something that was never found out. The bullet through the head and the absence of fingerprints saw to that.'

'So how did *we* find out that Redmond was alive?'

'When this chap Rothügel turned up, somebody noticed it was a free and easy translation of Redmond. "Rot" – red. "Hügel" – hill, mound; Red mound. Redmond. I suppose the similarity in the name is what led people to think Mackensen was MacDonald. In his case he wasn't. In Redmond's case he was.'

'A name's not much to go on.'

'No. But it was decided afterwards that the Germans had got on to Redmond's habits when he was on his language course at Potsdam – which, of course, would be very likely because they'd have been sure to watch him. The enquiry at the War Office after it was all over decided he'd been working for them for some time, but the business in Burma brought things rather suddenly to a head so that something had to be done quickly.'

Pullinger pushed the papers on his desk about thoughtfully. 'In the last war,' he said, 'the Germans out-thought us all along the line. Because they were cleverer? It wasn't an age of clever generalship anywhere. But think of the first day of the Somme. They were ready for us. They'd built deep dugouts where they sheltered from our bombardment. Why? Could they have known we were going to throw the biggest barrage ever at them?'

Pullinger ran his fingers along the edge of the desk, thinking. 'We went over in straight lines and, because they'd survived the barrage and knew we were coming in straight lines, that's how they mowed us down. I was there. I was eighteen. They carted me off the field with three bullets in me.' He sounded bitter. '*I* think they knew. We all thought they knew. So how? Was it because some swine who knew British generalship told them? For instance someone who'd known Haig, who was running the show.'

Pullinger paused again. 'What about Passchendaele? Cambrai? We often thought there was someone on the other side of the lines who knew exactly what we'd do. It adds up. As a senior British Intelligence officer, Redmond must surely have known how the army was thinking after the Boer War. I dare bet he told the Germans all the top jobs were held by cavalrymen so that they worked out their machine-guns-and-barbed-wire defences to stop them.'

Again, Woodyatt couldn't help feeling that Pullinger was making excuses for his father's lapse of judgement thirty-six years before. By this time, in fact, he was convinced that Pullinger senior, who had failed to connect the possibility of blackmail with a reported sighting of Redmond near the

German Embassy in London, had badly failed in his duty; and his son, now that the opportunity had arisen, had dredged up the old scandal in an effort to produce something that would soothe the family conscience.

'A newspaper would ask for better proof than that,' he said stubbornly.

'We *have* better proof,' Pullinger said stiffly. 'A man called Karel Pichurek. Captain on the Austrian staff. He crossed the lines in 1917 and gave us the story from that side. Redmond was taken to Berlin and later turned up on the Eastern Front as General von Rothügel who pulled a few German chestnuts out of the fire at a place called Gumbikunen.'

'*Why* did he go over?'

'Have you heard of Benedict Arnold? He was an American who changed sides in the American War of Independence. He felt he wasn't appreciated because other officers of less skill had been advanced ahead of him. There was a worm of bitterness in his mind about it. Perhaps Redmond was the same.' Pullinger produced a sheet of paper, yellow with age and printed in old-fashioned German script, all spiky ends and unnecessary curlicues.

'Read German?'

'Not very well.'

'It's a propaganda pamphlet that came out just before the Somme. It was issued by the German Foreign Office.' A typed sheet followed the pamphlet across the desk. 'That's a translation.'

'Is it not marvellous,' the translation said, 'that one of our most famous commanders was born a poor man in the North of England? General Georg von Rothügel, conqueror of Gumbikunen, joined the British army as a common soldier. Disliking the powerful British hierarchy, he sought service with the Kaiser and was given the name of another officer who was on the point of death.'

Woodyatt examined the pamphlet carefully. 'It doesn't mention Redmond by name,' he said.

'It gives his birthplace and the date. It also hints, you'll notice, at the bogus suicide. And, you'll notice, it says that in 1894 a certain Colonel Maximilien von Schwartzkoppen, at the time serving in the German Embassy in Paris, contacted a senior British officer. For your information, Schwartzkoppen was the German officer involved in the spying that started the Dreyfus case.'

Pullinger gestured at the pamphlet. 'A chap called Georg von Rothügel, aged fifty-one, is mentioned on the German staff list at manoeuvres in 1904,' he said. 'We know he died of cancer in a Dresden clinic that year. But his name remained firmly on the German army list. When Intelligence started to check the story all they drew were tantalising blanks. There's no longer a record of Redmond's career in the War Office files. Not a scrap. A file on his suicide? It doesn't exist. The Paris Prefecture of Police lost everything they had. Biographies of von Rothügel? Two came out just after the war. They don't even touch on his early life. Everywhere you look you meet dead ends. Why, our people asked themselves, was everybody so anxious to prevent anybody knowing anything if there was nothing to know? That pamphlet confirmed what they'd already guessed. Pichurek brought the final proof when he came over.

'This is a hell of a story,' Woodyatt said. 'Is it generally known?'

'*I've* known about it all my life.'

'What happened to him in the end?'

'He left Germany in 1936. When the Nazis came to power Hitler wanted to gain control of the armed forces, so in 1938 General von Fritsch was accused on fabricated evidence of being a homosexual and Field Marshal von Blomberg was brought down by accusations against his wife. You're a newspaperman. You surely remember those Stories.'

Woodyatt nodded and Pullinger pressed on. 'I expect,' he said, 'that, being cleverer than most, von Rothügel/Redmond had seen the writing on the wall and got out ahead of it.'

'What happened after he left Germany?'

'According to the Germans, he died in his bed at the age of seventy-six.'

'So that's that.'

'That is by no means that,' Pullinger snapped. 'I've told you. He didn't die.'

'You mean he's *still* alive.'

'Why not, for God's sake? It's 1940 now. Thirty-six years since it all happened. He was a contemporary of Marshal Pétain, the hero of Verdun. *He* was born in 1856 and at the moment he's French ambassador to Spain. My father's still active at eighty-two in spite of wounds he got at Spion Kop in 1900, and in spite of being ruined by this damn business. If he can be active at eighty-two, if Pétain can be active, why can't Redmond?'

Pullinger fished into his drawer again and produced another photograph. He brought them out as if they were rabbits out of a magician's hat. This time the man in the picture was in civilian clothes and was very old. The hair was white but the moustache was still there, less cared for now and drooping a little, but still thick and strong.

'Same chap,' Pullinger said. 'It was taken secretly by one of our chaps in Lucerne. That's what he looks like now. Or roughly. We aren't sure because soon afterwards, in 1937, he slipped into France.'

'So?' Woodyatt was still puzzled. 'Are we trying to contact him or something?'

'Of course.'

'To bring him back and charge him with high treason?'

Pullinger's smile was hard and mirthless, 'We would have done a few years back. It's different now. He could help us.

39

If the Germans could turn him, can we? We're willing to offer an alternative.'

'What good can it do now?'

'If Redmond was on the German staff as General von Rothügel and worked with their Intelligence Service he'll very likely know the route they intend for their attack in France when it comes. So we want him. We've always wanted him. I've always thought *I* might get him. It would give me a lot of pleasure.' Pullinger's face was like granite.

Woodyatt studied him. How much vindictiveness was there in the decision to bring Redmond back? How much of what was being planned sprang from spite? Pullinger, he knew, was a man who had fought his way up not always by fair means. It wouldn't be out of character for him to feel the need for a little revenge.

Pullinger was speaking again. 'A few years back when he was younger,' he was saying, 'we'd have charged him if we could have got our hands on him. But it's been talked through and it's felt now that to drag back a man of eighty to face charges of selling secrets forty years ago would make British Intelligence – the British army, the British government, if you like – seem to the world to be monsters. However – ' he drew a deep breath as though struggling to control himself ' – it would come to the same thing in the end, wouldn't it? He'd be given a house but there'd be a permanent guard. He wouldn't be referred to as "the prisoner" but that's exactly what he'd be.' Pullinger seemed to derive considerable pleasure from the thought.

'So we're going to dig him up and transport him back here?'

'Since he very likely has a shrewd idea what the Germans are intending, he might well be looking for an opportunity to use it to change sides again.'

Woodyatt couldn't resist a comment. 'What a cynical lot of shits we are, aren't we? Imagine dealing with a man who changes sides as he changes his shirts.'

Pullinger's face twisted into a thin smile. 'We're at war and Redmond's suddenly become important.'

'He'd hardly be called Georg von Rothügel.'

'He isn't. Not any more. He became Georges Montrouge. Notice the name again? "Rouge" – red. "Mont" – same as Mond. Montrouge. Rot-hugel. Red-mond. People who take an alias often try to keep something in their new name from their old one. Ask any policeman. His family – '

'He's got *another* family?'

'Well, a wife – '

'He married *again*?'

'Yes. And he was unwise enough to marry a Jewess.'

'He really did do for himself, didn't he?'

'He did indeed. Name of Jeanne Picard. But she died and the last we heard of him was in Metz in Lorraine. We want him to come to England. Willingly if possible. If not, unwillingly. It shouldn't be impossible to dig him out.'

'And if we do?'

'First we identify him.' Pullinger smiled grimly. 'At some point in his career, our friend, Bertillon, of the body measurements, came to England to demonstrate his methods to the British police. He was allowed to try his hand on a group of soldiers. Redmond was among them. We have Bertillon's findings. Which means that if we can just get our hands on the bugger we can apply Bertillon's system. All it requires is someone to go and find him.'

'Who gets the job?' Pullinger's smile was a little malicious. 'You,' he said.

PART TWO

o n e

It was a staggering prospect. Woodyatt was being asked to leap nearly forty years back into the past to persuade some old soldier – a treacherous old soldier into the bargain and by now doubtless crotchety and unwilling – to return to the scene of his humiliation. It seemed a hell of a job. He was going to have to find out a great deal more about him first.

He learned that two of the major participants in the drama were still alive. Sir Horace Varah was living in a set of London flats occupied largely by old people. He was now eighty-nine and widowed but was willing to see Woodyatt. The other was the army doctor who, it was alleged, had caught Redmond in the act in Burma. He was now Brigadier Witkins and living in Winchester. There was one other man worth seeing – Field Marshal Sir Martin Gerrit, who had been a major in the 51st Foot when Redmond had first been commissioned and had known him well. All three might be able to contribute something that would help identify him when he was found.

Sir Horace Varah turned out to be a total blank. He was very old and wasn't clear in his thoughts and, what was more, behaved as he had in 1904 and avoided committing himself to an opinion.

'Funny chap,' he said. 'Couldn't make head or tail of him.'

Sir Martin Gerrit was willing to help but also didn't have much to offer. 'Odd chap,' he said, echoing Varah. 'Lots of people tried to make him feel easy. These men who come up through the ranks are sometimes a bit touchy at first and in those days it was harder for them than it is now. But everybody – except a few damn fools, and there are always some of those – tried to put him at his ease. But he had a bit of a chip on his shoulder.' The Field Marshal frowned. 'Yet he was intelligent and a very likeable chap in many ways in spite of all that. Sense of humour. No end of a brain. Not surprising he did well. Could never understand why he did what he did.'

For an army man of the old school he was remarkably broadminded. He listened to Woodyatt's next question and shrugged. 'Well, the case in Burma was never proved, was it?' he said. 'Because there was never a trial. But he *might* have been that way inclined. I have to admit there were little things that could make you suspicious.'

He couldn't remember a lot about Redmond or any of his habits that might identify him, but he remembered that he had a trick of rubbing his nose with his finger when asked an awkward question.

'To give him time to think of the answer, I suppose,' he said. 'Getting it right was important to a man who'd come up from the ranks. Why all the questions, anyway? Is he still alive?'

Woodyatt smiled. 'It seems very much, sir,' he said, 'as if he might be.'

Despite his age, Brigadier Witkins was in uniform again, running an army hospital near Winchester, and Woodyatt found him in his office. He was a brisk helpful man but he hadn't known Redmond long.

'I'd only just arrived out there,' he said. 'And of course, soon after that Redmond went home to confer with his superiors. He didn't come back, so I never saw him again.'

'According to the reports, you actually caught him in the act.'

Witkins smiled. 'Let's say, I seemed to arrive at an inopportune moment.'

'There couldn't have been any mistake?'

'I'd already been in the army two years and I'd served all of it in the Far East. Funny things happened in the Far East. Men developed strange habits. However, I only described what I saw, not what I *thought* might be happening.'

'Did you ever speak to Redmond about it?'

'Briefly. At the hospital. He claimed he was suffering from a recurrence of malaria and must have been in some sort of coma.'

'Did you believe him?'

'Not really. But I wasn't the one who started the rumours. It must have been his aide.'

'He saw what you saw?'

'He said he did.'

'What the two of you said carried a lot of weight.'

'I suppose so. But *I* didn't say a word beyond a discreet report to my senior officer because I felt that as Senior Medical Officer he should know. He insisted I tell the Governor what I knew. I knew quite a lot as it happened, because I questioned the orderly before he was sent away. He was a nasty piece of work. Dangerous. Redmond should have got rid of him at once. I certainly would have. He insisted it had happened before.'

'Did you believe him?'

'I never said I did. Or that I didn't. I was asked to report on what had taken place and what the orderly told me. That's what I did. I questioned him carefully. I didn't want to be involved in the downfall of a chap as brave and able as I knew Redmond to be.'

'Do *you* think Redmond was guilty?'

Witkins smiled. 'I was asked that many times,' he said. 'I always simply told what I'd seen. I never gave an opinion. I'm not giving one now.

Woodyatt accepted Witkins' attitude. He was clearly a man of some honour and he didn't try to push him.

'I suppose you know what happened next to Redmond?'

'Yes, I know. He went to England and according to the newspapers, he shot himself in Paris on the way back.'

'Is that all you've heard?'

Witkins smiled again. 'Oh, no,' he said. 'I've heard a lot more than that. Around 1907, and again in 1914, they questioned me very closely at the War Office. You'd have thought I was the guilty party. I learned later there were suspicions about what he'd been up to in London when he arrived from Burma, because he was seen near the German Embassy.'

Witkins paused for a moment, thinking. 'It seems there were suggestions that he should be watched,' he went on. 'But with the impending trial it wasn't considered urgent and nobody did anything. Somebody slipped up, of course, and they were looking for a scapegoat.'

'You heard what happened to him afterwards?'

Witkins smiled and sat back in his chair. 'I heard Hitler sacked him. I suppose he's dead now.'

'On the contrary,' Woodyatt said, 'he seems to be very much alive. Which raises the next question. Did you know him well enough to notice anything special about him by which he might be identified?'

Witkins didn't ask why. He seemed a very restrained type. Instead he simply sat musing for a while and Woodyatt was driven to prompt him. 'Habits?' he suggested. 'Marks? You were a medical man. Did you ever examine him?'

'Once,' Witkins said. 'When he got malaria. After that I spoke to him again only once, briefly, before he returned to England.'

'Notice anything special about him?'

Witkins smiled. 'Have you found him?' he asked.

'We're hoping to.'

'Then, in that case, I can't be of much help. It's difficult to face a man who's about to fall from grace because of something you've noticed. I'm afraid, being young at the time and him being older and powerful and famous, I was very embarrassed about the whole business and kept my eyes on the blotter on my desk throughout the whole interview.'

'Was there *nothing* about him you noticed? Something that would help me identify him.'

'Why?'

'It's hoped we might persuade him to return to England.'

Witkins gave a little laugh. 'You've a hope.'

'It might be possible. They're prepared to wipe the slate clean.'

'Are they, by God? Why?'

'The Germans got him to talk about us. It's thought we might be able to get him to talk about the Germans.'

Witkins frowned. 'Well, I suppose there's that,' he admitted. 'You know where he is?'

'Not exactly. I'm hoping to. But I suspect he'll need a lot of persuading to come back here. Even to admitting to who he is. That's why I need things which will prove he's the man I want. If he doesn't come back willingly, he has to come back unwillingly.'

Witkins smiled. 'Well, I suppose that's fair enough. He asked for it, doing what he did.' He paused, sitting silently for a moment. 'Let me see. Things that might identify him? Blue eyes. Fair hair. Straight nose. He was a handsome devil.'

'What else?'

'He had a slight limp. Favouring his right leg.'

'I'd not heard of this.'

'It was almost unnoticeable. But doctors spot these things at once. A bullet hit him at Majuba and it gave him trouble.'

'Any marks on him I'd be able to see? Things you noticed. Scars for instance.'

'He had one or two. He took a bullet through the hand. There was a scar. In the fleshy part between forefinger and thumb. It was still pink when I saw it, though it'll have changed now. It was a sort of indentation. Quite deep.'

'Anything else?'

'A scar along the line of his jaw. Very slight. He got it in some scuffle on the North-West Frontier somewhere. Just a line and the marks of two or three stitches. Barely perceptible. But it was there. I can't think of anything else. But if I do I'll pass it on. On the other hand –'

'On the other hand – what?'

Witkins studied his hands for a while. 'Well,' he said, 'it occurs to me there might not be time. It's just an idea that might not have occurred to anybody else.'

'What's that?'

'If he's suddenly become valuable to us, won't he be just as valuable to the Germans?'

The thought that they had been wasting time suddenly began to worry Woodyatt and he headed back to the office as fast as he could. Pullinger met him in a determined mood.

'It had occurred to me, too, of course,' he maintained. 'We certainly want him before the Germans get him. For more than one reason.'

'Isn't treachery enough?'

'Not this time. There's been a leakage of information probably from Cabinet papers. The man who's responsible seems to be known as "Charlie". We've suspected something of the sort for some time. We code-named him "X". Then yesterday MI5 picked up a German agent called Camorgis. Part-Greek. Works in the Foreign Office. Minor post. He's been blackmailed into working for the Germans. He confirmed what we know. But he doesn't know the name. Apparently he's code-named "X" by the Germans, too, so we got that right even if only by accident. When you find Redmond you could ask about him.'

'Will he know him?'

'There are a lot of things he might know. We've had a memo from the Chief of Staff's office. They know about you and why you're going to France. Hannah keeps in touch. They've suggested you do a bit of questioning. Immediately. They're very keen.'

'About what?'

'You ever heard of pilotless aircraft? They were thought up during the last war by a Frenchman who was considering guiding them by radio. We used the idea for a target plane. But that was an orthodox piston engine. We're thinking now of jet engines. It's a new form of propulsion that does away with propellers. The Germans are on to it. The Oslo report confirmed it.'

'What's the Oslo report?'

'British naval attaché there was offered a statement on German technical developments. It was anonymous and to this day we don't know where it came from. It said the Germans were developing large rockets.'

'What sort of rockets?'

'Not the sort you light on Bonfire Night or fire at sea when you're in distress. These are big ones. Probably weighing sixty tons. With warheads as big as a torpedoes.'

'How are they aimed?'

'With a target as big as London you don't need to aim them. We know a type called Hermann Oberth has developed a liquid fuel for them. We also know the Germans have set up a branch to develop the idea under a general called Walter Dornberger.'

'And will Redmond know all about this?'

'He was working on the development of the Luftwaffe at Lipezk in Russia in 1922. In 1918 the Germans were deprived of an air force so they persuaded the Russians to allow them to train there. Redmond was one of those who went, so he might.'

'Isn't he a bit too old to know about this sort of thing?'

'He wasn't old in 1922. He wasn't old in 1931 when Dornberger was appointed, or in 1929 when Oberth published a book on his ideas.' Pullinger seemed elated. 'If we pull this off,' he said enthusiastically, 'it'll be a real feather in our caps. You've seen everybody who knew Redmond. Well, not everybody. Hannah's actually turned up Darby, the Paris military attaché. He's living in France. It would be well worth while going to see him. Married a woman called Daphne Quennell. Lives near Bordeaux. I'll wire him to expect you. You'd better get moving. I take it you've nothing on.'

'I *was* due for leave this weekend.'

'Going anywhere?'

'Only to Truro to see my mother.'

'I'll get Hannah to contact her. How about your wife?'

'There's no need to worry about that.'

'No hope of a reconciliation?'

'None whatsoever. She's found a chap in the navy. She prefers a life on the ocean wave.'

Pullinger didn't argue. 'We've arranged for you to be flown from Hendon to Paris. After that, it's up to you. Contact the Transport Office there and arrange things. You can go wherever you wish. I've arranged documents that will open doors, and papers that will threaten anybody who's obstructive. They carry an impressive barrage of signatures. The Chief's. Mine. The CIGS's. Even the Prime Minister's. That ought to be enough. You'll have a car. Hannah's taken care of it. If you need anything – support, copies of papers, anything – arrange for a signal to be sent. Just remember we want Redmond.'

'What am I supposed to do if he's difficult? Club him?'

'Don't let that worry you. When you've identified him beyond doubt, just let us know and we'll arrange the rest.'

'The rest?'

'Ship. Aeroplane. Whatever's needed to get him back quickly. Escort perhaps. Just identify him and then leave it to us. If you need help, just contact me. Just remember –' Pullinger's last words remained with Woodyatt for some time ' – *I want him back.*'

t w o

Despite the size of the task ahead of him, Woodyatt found himself looking forward to the adventure. Since his wife's departure there was nothing to keep him in England. He knew France well because his parents had taken their children on walking tours in Alsace and Lorraine. They had got to know a French farming family called Maury with whom they had stayed regularly, and France was as familiar to him as England. He spoke the language fluently and being part of the British Expeditionary Force was a prospect that pleased him. Called up under the reserve of officers scheme, he had been whipped away at once on the order of Pullinger and had spent every bit of the war so far in and around Pullinger's little enclave. The thought of seeing something of hostilities at closer quarters intrigued him.

There was another attraction. The Maury family had a daughter, Nicole, who even at the age of fourteen, had seemed interested in him. Perhaps, he thought with pleasant nostalgia, she might be even more interested now that she had grown up. He hadn't seen her for four years but he remembered her as remarkably pretty. His mother had clearly thought the same and had even dropped strong hints that were blatant match-making. Following university, Nicole had started work as a library researcher in Metz, and happily his orders would take him to that city.

The aircraft waiting for him at Hendon was an Avro Anson which was a little like a flying greenhouse. He was given a seat next to the pilot, who was the only member of the crew.

'Ferry service,' he said. 'Deliver mail and odd bods like yourself. Not very fast. These things are hardly front-line machines. Wings flap in a strong wind. To get the wheels up you have to wind that handle there about three thousand times and, since it's stiff, I usually fly with 'em down. Bit slow at landing. Tend to float. Might have to ask you to stamp your feet a bit.'

The pilot was middle-aged and clearly quite happy in the humdrum job the Phoney War had thrown up for him, and he kept Woodyatt entertained until the Eiffel Tower appeared out of the mist ahead.

Paris wasn't very different from London. The statues in the Place de la Concorde were sandbagged and in the Rue Halévy they were selling tarred paper vests 'to keep the soldiers warm'. In one shop there were pottery dogs lifting hind legs over pottery copies of Hitler's *Mein Kampf*.

Compared with London's version, the black-out was blinding and the newspapers were full of official optimism and stories that the Germans were already starving. Theatres and dance halls were open and there seemed no limit to food, while the air was loud with emotional songs full of banal sentimentality. Even the soldiers you saw on the streets didn't seem to think the war was dangerous.

Signalled ahead by the Hannah woman, the Transport Officer had a car waiting. It was a little Morris with a hood and the usual camouflage of brown and green.

Woodyatt's first call was at the Préfecture de Police on the Quai des Orfèvres.

'Sir George Redmond?' The police officer he spoke to looked baffled. 'In 1904? That is a long time ago, Monsieur le Capitaine, and we are in the middle of a war.'

The policeman introduced him to the archivist. He was no more helpful. '1904?' he said. 'You wish a report on a suicide in 1904? I can't imagine where to look for such a thing.'

Woodyatt's first job now seemed to be to find Darby, who'd been assistant military attaché at the Paris Embassy at the time of Redmond's faked suicide. He had an address at a village called Bray-en-Basse in the Charente near Saintes. It was an attractive village that seemed to be full of anglers, either on the way to the River Charente or on the way back. He found Darby's house without difficulty, a low, ivy-covered building with a garden sloping to the river.

The door was opened by a tall woman. She was grey-haired but straight-backed and imperious. She must once have been elegant and, judging by her features, beautiful.

'Daphne Darby,' she said in English. 'You'll be Captain Woodyatt.'

She led him through the house to where a table and chairs stood out of the sun on a vine-covered patio. 'My husband's on his way,' she said and Woodyatt saw Darby heading up the garden.

He was tall like his wife, with thick grey hair and a moustache clipped so short it almost didn't exist. It was only after he watched him for a short while that Woodyatt realised he was minus one of his legs. But he had obviously learned to manage very well and there was barely a sign of a limp.

'Better have a drink,' he said immediately. 'Redmond,' he went on as he sat down. 'Bloody man! I'll never forget him. What happened over that weekend was enough to give me nightmares. It was desperately important, y'see, to avoid a scandal and we were all in such a hurry. King Edward was hoping just at that time to put the seal on the Entente Cordiale and he was livid. Anything that might throw a spanner in the works was most unwelcome, and here was this damn fool ruining everything by shooting himself.'

As his wife occupied herself with drinks, Darby went on with enthusiasm mixed with a touch of nostalgia. 'No one knew what religious denomination Redmond had followed, so the French police played safe by using the English Episcopal Church in the Rue d'Aguesseau. But then, of course, up popped this business of him having a wife and we had to start all over again.

Darby looked harassed even at the memory of it. 'Even when the funeral finally took place it was a total farce.'

'There was someone there from the War Office, wasn't there?'

'Not half!' Darby said. 'Me.'

'Were you the chap who accompanied the body from Paris?'

'Yes. Instructions had been received that it had to be accompanied to its destination. And as there wasn't anybody else available, it fell on me.'

'Were you on the same ferry?'

'Yes. It was a dreadful crossing – the Channel at its very worst – and when we arrived at London Bridge station it was deserted. Typical British Sunday. You couldn't even get a cup of tea. The crate was loaded into a Carter Paterson van for King's Cross. Not very dignified. Had *Typhoo Tea* on the side. His brothers – you'll have heard of the brothers – they followed in a hansom. But the word somehow got around and King's Cross was crowded. Mostly North-Country people they seemed to me, and a few ex-soldiers and their families.'

Darby looked as though he didn't know whether to laugh or weep at the memory of the confusion. 'You won't believe it,' he said, 'but the bloody crate containing the coffin stood on the platform all day just like an abandoned suitcase. The widow and son were in the Great Northern Hotel and everybody started making a lot of fuss over the demands of Redmond's Yorkshire admirers, trying to persuade her to change her mind about the private interment. There were at least three Members of Parliament and they all seemed to think the War Office had refused to meet the expense of a public funeral. She refused to listen.'

Darby sat for a moment, his eyes distant. 'When the evening train for the North arrived,' he went on, 'the crate was placed in the guard's van and immediately flowers and wreaths appeared. The bloody station-master even allowed it to be opened so that for half an hour there was an unofficial lying in state with people filing past. When I discovered what was going on, I played merry hell. The station-master said it was what the people wanted and I had to tell him very firmly that it wasn't what the army wanted. Fortunately, he had the lid back on by the time the family mourners appeared from the hotel.'

'Did you go all the way to Harrogate?'

'Yes.' Darby filled a pipe and took his time lighting it. 'The funeral was a shambles. A lot of people turned up at the cemetery and graves were trampled because nobody had thought to inform the police. The following day people came from all over Yorkshire – all over the country, in fact – and a whole battle array of bobbies was needed to keep them back. Mourners waited in a queue five deep to pass the graveside. There were so many wreaths the cemetery refused to take any more, so they piled up at the entrance until the street was blocked. It couldn't happen nowadays, of course, but in those days things like that were a form of entertainment. By the time it all ended I loathed the sight and sound of Redmond's name.'

The Darbys managed to laugh, but beneath the laughter it wasn't hard to see that for them the affair had been in the nature of a tragedy in the end.

'The most extraordinary thing about it, of course,' Darby said, 'was that it wasn't Redmond at all. They were seeing off someone they'd never heard of – a foreigner into the bargain.

For all I know, a German. God, that weekend I wished France could sink under the ocean! Funny I should come back here to live. I swore at the time I never wanted to see the place again.'

As the brandy and the syphon of soda went round again, they chatted about themselves. Daphne Darby had come from a wealthy family, but after her marriage had followed her husband everywhere he'd been posted, mostly – because of his lost leg – to dull commands and dreary rented houses.

'I remember the affair well,' she said in her high, strong voice. 'It just about finished poor Frank's career.'

'There seemed to be a suspicion in higher circles,' Darby explained, 'that somehow I ought to have been aware of what was going on and stopped it. It all started again in 1914. Then again in 1917 when that chap, Pichurek, appeared. That's why I'd begun to collect all the documents. Had a feeling they were trying to lay the blame on me. After 1917 I handed everything I'd collected over to Intelligence. That, of course, was after this happened.' He tapped his stiff leg 'I'd been given a battalion of Yorkshiremen in 1915. Miners every one of them. Superb chaps. And, my God, how they could dig! Very useful, the ability to dig in that war. Tragedy they were nearly all wiped out on the first day of the Somme. Which is where I got this.' He indicated his artificial leg again. 'Shell.'

'Redmond,' Woodyatt reminded him gently.

'Yes, Redmond,' Darby swallowed his drink. 'He had everything. DSO. KCB. Aide to the Queen. Can't imagine what he was up to, chasing that bloody Burmese. Forty years ago, that sort of thing was tantamount to the end.'

He paused, deep in thought, trying to recall things as they were. 'When you're involved in a drama of that size, with someone of Redmond's standing, you don't easily forget. Paris, of course, was still the city of light and delight. Bit looked down on by the British but no end envied just the same.' Darby's eyes glowed at the memory. 'I thought it was tremendous. Then this happened.'

'Why did he go to Paris?'

'They said it was to catch the train to Marseilles where he was booked on a ship to India. *I* think he went there to meet a German contact.'

The brandy bottle was offered once more. Woodyatt refused but neither of the Darbys hesitated.

'Did you see the body?'

'Oh, yes,' Darby said. 'I saw it. I was the only man, I think, who did see it who had met him and known him. He was lying on the floor by the bed.'

'Did *you* think it was Redmond?'

'Yes. But, of course, a bullet through the head makes a mess, doesn't it? People don't realise. It pushes things around. Eyes weren't in their proper places. Face was covered with blood. 'Fraid I just assumed it was him. After all, the hotel register said it was. Maid who found him said it was. Examining magistrate said it was. Thinking about it later, I must admit I thought the chap on the floor looked younger than I'd imagined Redmond to be. And I noticed that the trousers he was wearing didn't match the jacket, which was odd. In 1904 people always wore suits. And this was a suit jacket with trousers of a different colour and texture. In those days it would have been considered very infra dig. After that, I began to wonder if a body had been brought in – in one of those big laundry baskets they use in hotels for bed-linen.'

'But nothing was proved?'

'No. The whole thing was a bit hurried. One other curious thing: maids were on the landing below but they didn't hear a shot. And the gun found alongside him wasn't a British weapon. It was Italian – seven millimetres. Why use an Italian seven-millimetre when he already had a service revolver? It's known he did have one with him.'

Darby reached for the brandy bottle again. 'I questioned the police,' he said. 'They were most obstructive. I wondered at the time, in fact, if money had changed hands – money from the German Embassy. I was certain it had. That's why I started collecting everything into a file. Felt sure something wasn't right.'

He poured drinks all round once more and continued. 'Then the rumours started,' he went on. 'It was said that he spent his last night in the company of the German military attaché. Might well have done. I knew the German, of course. Used to meet occasionally socially – Embassy dos, that sort of thing. Clever type. Well able to work the sort of thing they said he did.'

Woodyatt produced the copies of Pullinger's photographs. The first two just showing the face, then the two full-length pictures in profile.

Darby nodded. 'I've seen those. When they called me in to ask what I could add to it. Scared stiff they'd accuse me of something. They would have done if they could have, because they were all covering their rears like mad. It was a chap called Pullinger who was in charge.'

'It still is.'

Darby looked startled. 'Surely not the same chap?'

'His son.'

'Good God! No wonder he's keen.' Darby was silent for a moment. 'The original Pullinger seemed to me to be a bit obsessed with the affair.'

'I think this one is, too.'

'The defection took a bit of swallowing, of course. He should have been stopped in London. God, I spotted that something fishy was going on straightaway. Why didn't they?' Darby sighed and shifted in his chair as if to make his artificial leg more comfortable. 'Wasn't easy for me. People began to avoid me. Amazing how little loyalty there is when people think their own position's threatened. Then the war came and Redmond's name was forgotten and the public found new heroes: Haig. French. People like that.'

'You'll know the story that he became a general in the German army?'

'Yes. Know that.'

'Why did no one ask where he went after 1918? Why wasn't he found by the Army of Occupation? Somebody must have looked.'

'*Somebody* did. Me!' Darby shrugged. 'But strange things were happening at the time. Germany wasn't allowed to have an army worth talking about and was forbidden aircraft, so they persuaded the Russians to allow them to train men on their side of the border. I got hold of photographs of some of the bastards. I'm sure he was one of them. Which makes him guilty of helping Germany to prepare the next round – this one – as long ago as 1922.'

Woodyatt pushed across the last of Pullinger's photographs. Darby stared at it then lifted his eyes to Woodyatt. 'This him?'

'Taken in Switzerland in 1937. He's still alive.'

Darby looked startled. 'Is he, by God?' He reached for the bottle hurriedly. 'I wondered why you were digging him up again. Good God! Alive!'

'We believe he's here in France. He calls himself Georges Moutrouge.'

'Is he going to be charged? He ought to be.'

'The powers that be have decided the situation would be best served with a sort of pardon.'

Darby looked disgusted. 'Ought to be shot, not pardoned,' he growled. 'The man was guilty of giving information to the Germans.

'It's thought now he could be made to give information the other way. That's why I'm here. I've been told to bring him back. You said in one of your letters that you'd known him.'

'Yes, I did. During the Boer War. I had a job on the staff in Cape Town. Got to know him pretty well. Didn't like him. Thought he was ruthless, devious, clever, self-interested. That's why I was able to believe the story of him going over to the Germans. Once met one of his brothers. Can't remember which. Bit of a shit.'

As Darby rose to find a fresh soda syphon, Woodyatt noticed that Mrs Darby was looking thoughtful. 'Did you ever meet Redmond?' he asked.

'Oh, yes,' she said. 'Many times.'

'What was *your* impression?'

'He was a very handsome man.'

'Did you think the same of him as your husband?'

She considered the question for a while, then she laughed. 'Not really,' she admitted. 'I was very young and I thought he was terrific. But it wasn't me he was interested in.'

Darby returned with the fresh syphon. He looked at Woodyatt. 'Are you going to arrest him?' he asked.

'Something of the sort. Once I'm certain.'

'Bring him here. I'll identify him for you. I'd never forget him.'

'I shall know pretty well who he is before I approach him, but I'd like a few details about him that would confirm it.'

Darby thought deeply. 'Hell of a long time ago,' he said. 'But – well, he had a nickname in the army: Gorgeous George.'

'Why?'

'Always spotless. Always well turned-out. Fetish with him, cleanliness. Insisted on his troops being clean, too. Even in the field when everybody else was scruffy. South Africa was hot, dusty and sweaty and, when it rained, muddy. Never seemed to affect him, though. Always smart. Came down like a ton of bricks on sloppiness.'

'He's pretty old now. About eighty. At that age, men drop food down their ties.'

Darby grinned. 'Yes. You want more than that. Well, he was a brave man. You have to admit that. *And* a dead shot. About the time of Omdurman one of the Fuzzy-Wuzzies sneaked into the camp. Redmond spotted him and shot him. At long range, too. And with a revolver, which takes some doing. Happened again in South Africa. Boer commando got among the British wagons and again it was Redmond who stopped it. Shot two of them and the rest bolted. Known as a sharp thinker and amazin' quick to act. Oh, yes. There was one other thing. He loved B and S.'

'B and S?'

'What we've been drinking. Quite a fashionable drink in those days. So, if you see some chap swigging brandy and soda, it's either me or Redmond. Bring him here. I'll know him at once.'

three

The Darbys provided Woodyatt with lunch and as they finished the wine the war situation was discussed.

'What will you do if they attack in France?' Woodyatt asked.

'They'll never come down here,' Darby said stoutly.

But after the goodbyes were said and the promises renewed to identify Redmond when he was found, he walked to the car with Woodyatt.

'Look after yourself,' he said quietly. 'And don't trust the bloody French. They're not the French of the last war.'

Woodyatt was thoughtful as he drove north. His job seemed difficult enough without the threat of a disaster hanging over his head.

His first duty was to make himself known at British Headquarters, which were at Arras. He had been told of their whereabouts by Pullinger's Hannah who said it was an official secret. But when he asked the way a French policeman told him without a moment's hesitation. There was a great deal more official secrecy inside. Nobody would tell him where the British Expeditionary Force was, though he'd already learned from Darby that it was along the Franco-Belgian frontier and, contrary to what British newspapers suggested, a long way from the Germans. Everybody in the area was aware of the fact and he had no doubt the Germans were, too.

However, Intelligence had been warned to expect him and he was seen by a brisk brigadier by the name of Douglas who produced documents to cover him in the event of an emergency.

'Any problems,' he was told, 'Contact me. Just be careful, though. We're hearing rumours that the Germans are on the move.'

The weather was warm and the soldiers of the BEF seemed to be moving about like bees drugged with pollen: slowly, happily, but with no great urgency. There appeared to be a lot of digging going on and a great many concrete works under construction. As Woodyatt moved further north and east, he saw more and more soldiers, but the ratio between British and French was noticeable. For every British soldier there seemed to be twenty Frenchmen.

It was something that appeared to bother the French, who clearly felt the British weren't prosecuting the war as ardently as they might. While the French had mobilised 6,500,000 men, disrupting all their manufacture and social amenities, the British had less than a quarter of that number under arms and still a million and a half unemployed. The French had even sarcastically offered to equip a few of them.

'They don't seem to like us a lot,' Brigadier Douglas admitted. 'They accuse us of looting and lechery. On the other hand, have you seen their chaps?'

Woodyatt had and, while many were smart, the reservists were often unshaven, with ungroomed horses, dirty vehicles and badly fitting clothes and saddlery. He'd also seen small incidents that indicated a great lack of discipline.

'Too many years of bloody awful governments,' Douglas said. 'It's made 'em a bit apathetic.'

Certainly the French seemed excessively casual. Only the French African troops seemed alert and Woodyatt grew tired of being stopped by black Senegalese who brooked no argument. While French air force officers, seeing him in

difficulties, shouted the password. *'Le mot est "Duroc"!*
Passez! Passez!' In the end, buying a large sheet of expensive
paper, Indian ink and sealing wax, he made himself an
impressive-looking document written in French. Signing it
with the name of Winston Churchill, which he assumed was
the only British name they would know, he placed a huge red
seal of wax at the bottom, marked with the coat of arms off
a key. It worked like magic.

With the clear spring weather, everybody seemed to be
looking over their shoulders and the atmosphere was one of
nervousness. The German attack in Norway had come as a
surprise and now that a few facts were emerging, people
were aghast that it was ending in disaster. They all knew
Hitler was coming and the British railed against French
indifference.

'Some of 'em would rather have Hitler than the Popular
Front,' an RASC officer told Woodyatt. 'I'd like to drop a
bomb or two on Paris to wake 'em up.'

On the outskirts of Metz Woodyatt ran into an RAF
squadron. They were confidently expecting something to
happen at any moment. The armaments officer seemed a bit
odd and had decided the area was full of spies and that they
were there for a reason. RAF radio messages, he said, were
being jammed by a woman with a large house nearby, who
owned fierce dogs to keep intruders off her land. He also had
his eye on a blind man who had been a professor at Nancy
University. He ran down the stairs to watch he said, every
time a car appeared.

'How?' he demanded. 'If he's blind.'

Newly out from England, to Woodyatt his fears and
suspicions seemed foolish but he remembered there had
always been a strange air of mystery about Metz. He had
known the place for years and its dark streets and mist-
shrouded islands had always seemed secretive and gloomy.

'People have been shot at,' the armaments officer said. 'And a couple of our despatch riders were found with their throats cut and their bikes and uniforms stolen. I should carry a gun if I were you.

The news from Norway remained bad. But the air was mild and still and the French tricolours hung limply.

It was possible to be reassured by the numbers of soldiers. They were everywhere: pilots of the French armée de l'air in their dark blue uniforms, some of them wearing decorations; *troupes de forteresse* from the Maginot Line in black berets and wearing badges inscribed '*On ne passe pas*'. There were one or two Poles and a few RAF men, and the dark red-stone streets were full of trucks and cars. A parade was being held near the great yellow cubes of military buildings.

All the cafes were full and it was possible to hear a brass band somewhere in the vicinity. With its green roofs and red walls, and its dark squares full of the statues of ancient warriors, the city was like a disturbed anthill. The streets and waterways were strident with the sound of marching men and revving engines.

Making his number with the local commander, Woodyatt headed for the library. Nicole Maury was almost the first person he saw. She was heading for the stairs as he entered, her arms full of books.

Her mouth widened in a huge grin of delight. 'Jimmee Woodyatt!'

The books dropped in a shower as they embraced.

'Nicole Maury!'

'No, no! Not Nicole Maury now. Nicole Chainat. I am married.'

Woodyatt felt a slight twinge of regret. He had always been a little in love with her. 'And the lucky man?'

'Claude. Claude Chainat. He was studying to be an architect but he was called up like everybody else. They made him a sous-lieutenant because he went to university. What are you doing here? You must come and have a meal.'

'At the farm?'

'No. My parents moved south to Hyères. I'm still here because I work as a librarian. I have an apartment.'

He explained why he was there and, with her assistance, began to search through the street directories. There were several Montrouges, but none seemed to fit the man he was seeking. The telephone directory also gave several but the initials were always wrong, and there appeared to be nothing in the voters' list that seemed to lead to the man he was seeking.

The search took several days and, as they passed, he spent his spare time in the company of Nicole. She was small and neat, with black hair, large eyes, and a good figure. At lunch time they sat opposite each other in pavement cafés drinking beer and eating enormous sandwiches. He had found a room in a hotel opposite the station where the foyer was packed with the families of officers but Nicole would have none of that and insisted on him using her flat. It was very small but there was a room, little bigger than a cupboard, with a single bed. He moved in happily.

The dour Lorrainers, known to the French as 'les Boches d'Est', seemed to hold themselves aloof from the bustle of the army.

'It's just their manner,' Nicole explained. 'They're supposed to be as thick as their own trees, but they're very proud of their province. After the war of 1870 it became German, you know, but we won it back in 1918.'

The next morning was cool following a shower during the night. Little wisps of vapour hung in the low-lying areas among the streams and pools round the Ile de Saulcy. There was a British mess in one of the steep-roofed mansions among the lime trees beyond the Ban St Martin. Producing the papers the Hannah woman had provided, Woodyatt demanded the use of the telephone and began to try every single telephone holder with the name of Montrouge. He had no luck. Trying the library once more, he discovered that Nicole had picked up a clue.

'There was an old man who used to come here,' she said. 'I'd forgotten him because I have not seen him for some time. He liked to sit in the reference room and was always reading the newspapers. I didn't think of him until I was going through the files and found his name. He'd demanded a book and we'd filled in a request form. *His* name was Montrouge.'

He kissed her enthusiastically. 'Where is he now?'

She shrugged.

'What was he like?'

'Tall. Strong-looking. But he was old, you understand. About eighty.'

Woodyatt produced the photograph of the man in Lucerne. 'Would that be him?'

'It might. It's hard to say.'

'Is there any means of finding out where he is now?'

'There was a girl who came to talk to him occasionally. Perhaps you should try to find her.'

'You've been a great help.' Woodyatt smiled. 'Let's celebrate with dinner in the city. We can talk some more about it'.

She studied him with interest. They had always got on well together. He was tall, straight-backed, with good features and fair hair that fell over his forehead in an intriguing way. She grinned her assent.

She was waiting at the library when he arrived. She had been home to change and she seemed to bring a touch of spring to what had become a very dull war, charming, pretty and vivacious as she was. Woodyatt found himself almost forgetting his business there. Her hand went straight out to his and they set off among the dark streets. They ate in a restaurant where there were long tables full of soldiers who fell over themselves to flatter Nicole, teasing her, making sure there was nothing she wanted for.

'I have asked my friend at the library,' she told Woodyatt. 'She has the name of the girl and her address.'

Woodyatt's heart leapt.

'Her name is Dominique Sardier.'

'And she's here in Metz?'

'She was but I haven't seen her for some time. She lives in the Rue Bilot. That's near the Ban St Martin. It's a big house made into flats. It's quite near my apartment. I'll show you later as we go home.'

He kissed her cheek and the soldiers cheered wildly. Their long tables soon grouped together to form a party and everybody started singing. Led by a Frenchman with one arm, they worked their way through *Saint-Cyr, Garde à Vous, La Madelon, Les Artilleurs de Metz* and other French military songs that brought thoughts of clattering hooves, iron-shod artillery wheels and brilliant uniforms.

The young French regulars were full of life and good humour and bore none of the ill-will with which the French reservists all seemed to regard the British. And with Nicole alongside him, there was always the whiff of her perfume in Woodyatt's nostrils, the warmth of her body against his.

It was dark when they left the restaurant and as they walked slowly to her flat through the black-out, the darkness glowed with the firefly pin-pricks of cigarette ends. They stumbled along, arm in arm and she indicated the house where Dominique Sardier lived.

The following morning they ate breakfast at a bakery next door to Nicole's flat then he walked her to the library before heading for the house near the Ban St Martin. As he arrived, he saw several girls run out and head for the bus stop. Like Nicole, they were young with plenty of French chic and he wondered if one of them were the Dominique Sardier he was seeking.

The house seemed empty but a radio was playing a tune. He traced the music to a room down the hall near the stairs where there was a door with its glass upper panels covered by a waxed paper patterned with red, white and blue squares. As he tapped on the glass, it was opened to a gap of no more than six inches. Beyond it he could see the wrinkled face of an old woman. He told her what he was seeking.

'Mademoiselle Sardier,' he said. 'Dominique Sardier.'

'She's not here.'

'Can you tell me where she works?'

'She doesn't work in Metz any more. She left.' His heart sank. 'When did she leave?'

'January. February. About then.'

'Where did she go?'

'Amiens. That way.'

Woodyatt drew a deep breath. Amiens was due north of Paris and around two hundred miles away from Metz.

'Did she go alone?'

'How else would she go? She wasn't married.'

'There was an old man she used to see.'

'Yes, there was. I saw him once.'

'Do you know if he went with her?'

He produced the photograph of Montrouge taken by Pullinger's agent in Switzerland. 'Is that the man?'

The old woman looked up at him. 'I think it is. What's he done? Is he a criminal?'

Woodyatt trotted out the line he had decided on. 'No, Madame,' he said. 'We think he's heir to money in England and, since I'm in the area, I've agreed to try to find him. There might be a reward.'

Her interest increased. Disappearing into her quarters, she returned with a crumpled slip of paper. 'There you are,' she said. 'Dominique Sardier, Rue de Paris, Dreuil. It's about six kilometres outside Amiens. She'll tell you about him.' She grinned. 'But she won't make you very welcome. She doesn't like men.'

four

'Don't go away,' Woodyatt said. 'Don't get a transfer anywhere while I'm gone.'

Nicole laughed and he went on. 'I've got to ask a few questions,' he said. 'That's all.' He hoped it *would* be all and that, after the questions, he could call on the Military Police and the whole thing would be over. 'This girl you turned up did know Montrouge.'

They closed the shutters of the flat. Nicole made coffee and they drank it as they listened to the news. All was still quiet, though there were nervous reports of patrol activity, and east of Metz a German aeroplane had been shot down. But nothing more. All things considered, it seemed a funny war.

The following morning, Woodyatt set off for Amiens, driving across the battlefields of the First War. They bore the scars of that conflict and he saw areas that were still mutilated by trenches and shell holes, and marked with occasional memorials to the fallen. He reached Amiens during the afternoon. It was as full of troops as everywhere else and the feeling of urgency was as clear there as it had been in Metz. Picardy farmers and businessmen mixed with trim-legged shop girls and here and there you could see the red, white and black crest of the province.

Dreuil was a small place, typical of the Somme country, with a row of small houses running along the main street. But, unlike many of the Somme villages, it had some pretensions to attractiveness. There were trees and a glimpse of the river not far from the road. To the East it was possible to see the towering spire of Amiens Cathedral. He found the house without any trouble. It was small and neat, set away by forty metres of meadow from the other houses. There was a small front garden and a white door. His knock went unanswered and he assumed that Dominique Sardier had not yet returned from work. At the next house along, a woman appeared with a child hanging on to her leg. 'She's not here,' she said. 'She's visiting relations. In Paris.'

'What relations?' he asked.

'I don't know. Some uncle, I think. She'll be back on Saturday.'

Woodyatt was back in Metz the following day. When he walked into the library Nicole's face lit up and that night they ate at a little restaurant near her flat. She seemed sad and he probed until he got the reason. She was worried by the war and what it would bring when it came.

'I just want to be married and have children,' she said. 'I just want to grow old in peace.'

The three days before he had to return to Amiens passed in an atmosphere almost of domesticity. Nicole was happy but underlying her happiness there was always an element of worry because the news from Norway had grown worse.

'Perhaps the war won't come after all,' she said. 'Perhaps the politicians are right and if we don't look for it, it will go away.'

When he returned to Amiens, he waited until early evening before calling at the house in the Rue de Paris. This time he found Dominique Sardier at home. He was surprised at her appearance. He had expected someone drab and uninteresting but she seemed brisk and alert. She was tall, in her middle twenties, not pretty in the way Nicole was pretty, but with thick chestnut hair, tremendous green eyes and an excellent figure. She was puzzled by his arrival but she let him into the house. It was neatly furnished with the usual uncomfortable French chairs and an old painting or two that didn't seem worth much. But the curtains were bright and there was a small crucifix over an old roll-top desk against the wall.

'Montrouge?' she said as he framed his question. 'Yes, of course, I know Monsieur Montrouge. Why do you want to know?'

Woodyatt had his answer ready. 'We believe Monsieur Montrouge worked for the allies between 1914 and 1918,' he said. 'We think he might be of help again.'

She shook her head. 'I don't think so,' she said.

'How do you know?'

'He's my uncle.'

'Your uncle?' She seemed to be a real find.

'Well, not exactly. A sort of uncle. My grandfather, Josephe Sardier, from Metz, married a Marie-Adelaide Weil, from Amiens. His sister, Charlotte, married a Georges Picard who came from Alsace, so that their daughter, Jeanne, and my father, also Josephe, were cousins.'

He encouraged her to talk about her family.

'My father was born in 1880,' she explained. 'I was born in 1914 just before he vanished in the great mobilisation. He was killed in 1916 at Verdun. My mother died in 1936.'

'I'm sorry.'

She shrugged. 'It's a long time ago. His cousin, Jeanne, was a little older. She was born in 1870. She married Monsieur Montrouge in 1911. I don't think it was a love match. She spoke German because many people in Alsace and Lorraine speak German and eventually she went to work in Germany. Monsieur Montrouge was also working there. She died last year. I seem now to be his only relative. When you have nobody, even a relative by marriage is worth having.'

She was an unusual young woman. She had a dazzling smile but at times her face became stiff and serious so that he wasn't sure what to make of her.

'Why did they leave Germany?' Woodyatt knew the answer but he wanted to hear this woman's version. She studied him carefully before replying.

'She came some time before him,' she said. 'At the time the Nazis were beating up the Jews and her father was a Jew, so she probably felt it wise. I believe she and my mother were very good friends when they were young and they were always visiting each other.'

'Did they go on visiting after your aunt went to live in Germany?'

She frowned. 'I don't think so. But my aunt was an odd character. Intellectual. Full of strange modern ideas. Perhaps that's why she left him. He told me it was just incompatibility. They lived in Dresden and you had to go to Berlin and then south. It was a long way.'

'What about in 1914?' he asked. 'What happened then? Your father went into the army. What about Monsieur Montrouge?'

She was uncertain. 'I don't think he served in the army at all,' she said. 'He was trapped in Germany by the outbreak of the war, he said, and spent the whole of it in a German camp of some sort.'

'But after the war he remained in Germany.' Woodyatt affected bewilderment. 'I'd have thought he would have wanted to return to France.'

'He got a job with the Occupying Forces.'

'Doing what?'

'He was some sort of teacher of languages. In 1918 in France jobs were hard to get.'

Woodyatt pulled a face. 'They were harder to get in Germany. The Deutsche Mark was devalued until you had to take a barrow-load of banknotes to buy a kilo of butter.'

'He must have been paid from France.' She smiled, confident of her theory. 'Or, perhaps, even in American dollars. Then he would have been well off.' She studied Woodyatt, her eyes steady on his and he noticed again how beautiful they were. 'You seem very interested in my uncle. Why?'

Woodyatt gestured. 'We have a feeling he was a British agent prior to 1914. Perhaps that's why he ended up a prisoner.' It was a good answer and seemed to satisfy her.

'Perhaps so,' she agreed. 'After the war I think he worked for a while as a correspondent for a Paris newspaper. With a special interest in what the Germans were up to. Because they were certainly getting round the Versailles agreement they made in 1919, weren't they? If he were some sort of agent, it would explain a lot.'

'Did you ever meet him at that time?'

'Not until he left Germany. Besides, at that time, life was wonderful.' For a moment her face was transformed by the memory of happiness, and it seemed to glow. 'Though, of course,' she went on, 'always there was the threat of Germany. It put a blight on all those years.'

Woodyatt remembered it only too well, the feeling that sooner or later somebody was going to have to face up to the bullies of Europe and that it might be painful.

'He was in difficulties with money at first,' she went on. 'Later he was able to get money from investments he'd made in Switzerland. He became quite comfortably off. But about that time my aunt died. She went quite quickly.'

'And Monsieur Montrouge? Where is he now?'

She was about to answer but then she stopped dead. 'Why?' she asked again. 'Why are you so very interested?'

Woodyatt gestured. 'There may be rewards for him. I don't know.' The lies came easily. But he wasn't sure they satisfied her. 'All I know is that I was asked to find him. My job's Intelligence.'

'Why would Intelligence be interested?'

'I think they feel that, after his long stay in Germany, he might be able to help. I need to talk to him.'

'Unfortunately, you can't. He decided to go to Paris. He said he'd grown up there and wanted to return.'

Woodyatt paused, his mind working. 'What sort of man is he?' he asked. 'It's important that I know. I have to be certain I have the right man.'

She frowned. 'I don't know really what he's like. I've not known him long and he's – a little secretive.'

She still seemed suspicious of him and he decided a little flattery might help. 'Mademoiselle Sardier,' he said. 'I'm staying at the Hôtel Central near the Place Gambetta. It has an excellent restaurant. I wonder if I can ask you to have dinner with me this evening. We can continue our talk there.'

She seemed startled and he suspected she hadn't been asked out for a long time.

'I have a car,' he persisted. 'May I call for you around seven o'clock?'

She studied him quietly then she smiled. It was dazzling. 'I'll look forward to seeing you,' she said. 'It could be very interesting.'

She had obviously put on her best outfit – a green affair that matched her eyes – and she looked unexpectedly stunning. She had swept her hair above her head so that it showed the long column of her neck and the shape of her shoulders. He was startled at the difference in her.

'Mademoiselle Sardier,' he said. 'You look quite splendid.'

He handed her a bouquet of red roses he had bought near the station a few minutes before. At the time he had thought they were going to be wasted on her. Now he wasn't so sure.

Her eyes sparkled as she took them from him and arranged them in a vase. Against the late sunshine, they were the colour of blood.

They drove to the hotel in the warm evening sunshine. Half of Amiens seemed to be out on the streets, British and French soldiers walking with girls, men strolling with their wives, studying the menus outside the restaurants, taking their apéritifs on the café terraces.

The landlord and the head waiter at the hotel, both of whom obviously knew Dominique Sardier, registered the same surprise that Woodyatt had shown. And he noticed as they entered the dining room that several heads turned. She was impressive: straight, tall, her excellent features topped by the mass of chestnut hair. As Woodyatt held her chair for her, he received a magnificent smile.

'Mademoiselle Sardier,' he said again. 'You really are very beautiful. And I'm not the only man here who's noticed it.'

She was clearly pleased at the compliment and he wondered why no one had remarked on her beauty before tonight.

She seemed to guess his thoughts. 'I am in my Sunday best,' she explained. 'Normally I wear simpler clothes. I am a teacher, and teachers are expected to be anonymous. I soon discovered that a teacher who wears pretty clothes and a pretty hair style attracts attention from the fathers of the children she instructs and that is something the mothers don't like. Teachers are expected to be taken seriously.'

They ate *canard à la Rouennaise* with chablis, followed by coffee and brandy, and Woodyatt found he was enjoying what he had regarded as a duty. It seemed to be time to get down to business.

'Mademoiselle Sardier –' he began.

'I think,' she said, 'that after a meal like that we ought to address each other by our Christian names. What is yours?'

'James.'

She was silent, her head on one side, as if she were trying it for size. 'That is a good name,' she announced. 'Dignified. Strong. You had kings called James.'

Woodyatt smiled. 'Not very good ones.' He paused. 'Dominique, I want to know more about Georges Montrouge.'

She made a slight movement of annoyance. 'Why are you so interested in him? I'm very protective towards him.'

His quarry was very lucky, Woodyatt thought. 'If he was a British agent,' he said, 'he was a brave man and we want to get him to safety. Why are *you* so concerned for him?'

'He's all I have in the world.'

'I'd like his address.'

She smiled. 'Not yet, James Woodyatt. He is my only relative and sometimes in such circumstances one is very much aware there's nobody else who cares whether one lives or dies.'

He studied her for a moment, puzzled. 'Why haven't *you* married?' he asked.

She gave a small wry smile. 'He got away,' she said bluntly.

'There *was* someone?'

'Oh yes.' She spoke lightly but he suspected it was her way of hiding an old wound. 'He was a doctor. I was training to be a nurse. He had a wife in the South somewhere. We became lovers. His name was Maillardrois. Etienne Maillardrois. And I was inexperienced enough in those days to think him wonderful. But he wasn't really. He was not a very skilful lover and often left me frustrated and angry. I called him Monsieur Maladroit.'

She drew a deep breath, surprisingly willing to discuss her life. 'It was a poor sort of affair but it went on and on because I was too immature to know how to end it. Then my mother fell ill and I had to look after her. It changed everything.'

'Did he ask you to marry him?'

'He was always careful not to. Doctors know enough not to take on someone who will be a burden. Perhaps he wanted me – I don't know – but he didn't want my mother, too. I gave up nursing so I could spend more time with her. I became a teacher. Are *you* married?'

'I was. It didn't work out.'

'What happened? You've got my story out of me. I'm entitled to hear yours.'

He laughed. 'When the war came, she decided she preferred navy blue to army khaki.'

'Do you have relations?'

'I have a brother and two sisters. All married. All with children. And plenty of cousins.'

'How lucky you are! Yet you want to take away from me the only relation I've got.'

'No.' Woodyatt knew he was lying. 'But I must find him.' The time seemed to have come to be honest at last. 'I have a confession to make, Dominique,' he said slowly. 'I'm afraid that what I've been telling you hasn't been entirely the truth.'

She studied him coolly. 'Somehow,' she admitted, 'I never thought it was. So what is the truth?'

'I have good reason to believe that this man who's become your uncle by marriage isn't whom you think he is.'

She raised her eyebrows. She didn't seem startled, but he could see she was growing angry. 'So, if he isn't Georges Montrouge, who is he?'

'There is a very strong possibility that he isn't even a Frenchman.'

She gave a twisted smile. 'You're making it very difficult. Let's start by being honest. If he isn't a Frenchman, what is he?'

'A German.'

'No!'

Woodyatt put his hand out but she withdrew hers sharply, her eyes bright with rage.

'Nonsense,' she said. 'Rubbish! It's not possible.'

'It's very possible. I think he went in Germany by the name of Georg von Rothügel. I don't know how good your German is – '

'My German is excellent!'

'Then translate von Rothügel. Compare it with Montrouge.'

Her eyes were glowing with a green fire and her anger gave her an additional unexpected beauty. 'This is ridiculous!'

'Is it? I have also reason to believe that before he became German, he was an Englishman. By the name of Redmond.'

'I don't believe it! Why would an Englishman become a German. And then why should this German become a Frenchman?'

'He was a British soldier,' he went on. 'Sir George Redmond. Think of it, Dominique. George Redmond. Georg von Rothügel. Georges Montrouge. In 1904 he found himself in trouble and chose to disappear. We think the Germans had been watching him for years.'

'It's not possible.'

'It's very possible. The life in Germany you know so little about. The money he put into Swiss banks. He is believed to have given away Allied secrets before the last war and helped to train the Germans for this one.'

'Monsieur Montrouge is an honourable man!'

'Is he? He tricked his English wife into accepting the body of another man as his. He married Jeanne Picard while that first wife was still alive.'

'You have no proof of this.'

'We have all the proof in the world.' Again he tried to lay his hand on hers and again she snatched it away. 'Believe me. I don't give a damn what he's done. I just want to get him to safety, before the Germans find him and liquidate him.'

She gave a soft snort of contempt, her eyes alive with rage. 'It's the most ridiculous story I've ever heard! You brought me here under false pretences!'

'Until a few moments ago I was finding it a most enjoyable experience. I'm sorry it had to go sour. But believe me, I need to find this Georges Montrouge. To get him out of France.'

'You seem to think the Germans are going to fight their way across France as they did in 1914.'

'I hope to God they don't. But, whether they do or not, there are always German agents to take care of him.'

She pushed her chair back and he was aware of heads turning as her voice rose. 'First of all,' she said. 'I think your story is the figment of a wild imagination and, secondly, even if it's true, I think you want to put him in prison. In the Tower of London perhaps.'

'They don't put people in the Tower any more. It's too easy to escape.'

'Captain Woodyatt – '

'I thought it was to be James.'

'I think "Captain Woodyatt" is better under the circumstances. I begin even to believe that *you* aren't who you say you are.' She stood up. 'Thank you for the meal. And for the roses. It was most kind of you. It's a pity I have to suspect it was all for a purpose. Please don't rise. I'll see myself home.'

five

By the time Woodyatt reached the foyer of the hotel there was no sign of Dominique. It was dark outside and silent, but over the silence he heard a peal of laughter and the faint drone of a high-flying aeroplane. For a while he walked about the streets in the centre of the town, wondering what his next move should be. Then, shrugging, he returned to the car. He seemed to have let Pullinger down. It seemed unlikely that he was ever going to meet the man calling himself Montrouge.

The following morning he headed back towards Metz. Perhaps there he could signal Pullinger for advice. Perhaps Pullinger would even take him off what had suddenly become a distasteful job.

Nicole was delighted to see him. Finding him waiting for her outside the library, she ran to him and flung her arms round him.

'You came back! Did you find Montrouge?'

He didn't explain his failure. He drove her home and waited as she changed, then they headed for the dark streets to find a restaurant. She was in a light-hearted mood, and after they had eaten she took him to a dance hall full of soldiers and airmen where they danced together, swaying to the slow time of the music. She was in a romantic mood, her cheek against his.

'It is for my husband Claude,' she explained. 'I miss him very much.'

Woodyatt's mind was far away, still wondering how he could regain Dominique Sardier's confidence. When the dance came to an end, they found a little bar where they drank a nightcap, then walked arm in arm back to the flat. There was still movement about the town, soldiers taking their girls home, a lorry growling past. Then a faint sound came to them and Nicole lifted her head.

'What's that?' she asked.

They stopped dead. It was impossible to hear the noise properly over the cheerful chatter about them in the street. Then suddenly, as if everybody had become aware of the noise, too, the chattering stopped and the sound came again, more distinct but still faint enough for them to be uncertain that they had actually heard anything. For a long time they stood still, then it came again, louder, in a low rumbling like a distant thunderstorm.

'*Les canons*,' Nicole said.

'No,' Woodyatt said. 'It'll be practice bombing. This area's full of practice ranges.'

But it *was* guns. Woodyatt was certain of it. Something was happening further east. Something was moving.

During the night Woodyatt woke to realise that Nicole was moving about the kitchen. A sheet wrapped round her, she was making coffee.

She turned as he entered. 'You will go away now,' she said, studying him with huge eyes. 'Perhaps I shall go away.'

'No.'

'I think so. These last few days have been beautiful and I had forgotten the war. But it won't disappear.'

He had to admit the truth of her, statement.

'If it comes, it will come here,' she added.

'They say tanks can't penetrate the Ardennes.'

'Do you believe it?'

Woodyatt pretended not to know. But he had a feeling the Germans would have thought of something.

They talked for a long time. Back in his bed, Woodyatt opened the shutters so that he could see the sky. It was a perfect night with the stars bright and sharp. There seemed to be a lot of aircraft about and several of them passed overhead. Somewhere in the distance anti-aircraft guns banged away.

It seemed to be noisy all night and when he finally fell asleep, he was restless, his dreams all of war. And something else, too, a vague and haunting worry that depressed him and made him feel afraid. It was as if he were in a nightmare, trying to escape but unable to move.

He woke with a start to see Nicole standing in the doorway. It was already daylight.

'You were dreaming,' she said.

'Yes,' he agreed. 'I was dreaming.'

All the noise seemed to have stopped.

'I've brought your breakfast,' she said, placing a tray on his knees as he struggled to sit up. 'I have to go to work.'

'What time is it?'

'Late. We overslept. You'd better get up. The wireless says the Germans have entered Belgium, Holland and Luxembourg, and begun bombing French cities.'

'What!' He sat up with a jerk that spilled his coffee. 'Are you sure?'

'I can't imagine anyone in France being in doubt about a thing like that.' She sighed. 'It's true enough. I heard it. The army's moving up to the River Dyle and there's heavy fighting.'

'What else?'

'They say everything is under control. Is it, Jimmee?'

Struggling from the bed, Woodyatt began to drink the coffee. 'I'd better get a move on,' he said.

Her expression was bleak. 'What will happen?'

'We shall stop them. They said everything was under control, didn't they?'

She managed a smile. 'French politicians have never been noted for their honesty.'

'This time it's the army. Don't worry.'

'I'll try not to. I'm going to work. If I hear anything I'll telephone you here.'

As she disappeared, he peered out of the window. The sky was empty but he could hear aircraft. Switching on the wireless, he listened as he shaved. A particularly banal sort of music was being played, then, abruptly, it stopped and was interrupted by an announcer. ' – *Les Hollandais combattent très fort et les Boches ont trouvés une résistance très dure.*'

Belgium and Holland had resisted every effort by the British and French to persuade them to allow their borders with Germany to be fortified. Though desperately needing the help of the Allies, they had not dared show any favours in case the Germans had found it an excuse to invade. Now the Nazis had invaded without any excuse at all and desperate attempts were being made to stop them. The British, who had spent the winter continuing the fortifications from the end of the Maginot line to the coast with thousands of tons of concrete and miles of barbed wire, had now left it all behind them to advance in company with the French into open country devoid of any prepared defences. To Woodyatt, it seemed they had allowed themselves to be drawn into a trap.

During the day, he headed for headquarters at Arras to try to find out what was going on. He was surprised to learn he was expected. They had a long message for him from Pullinger.

It reiterated that it was felt in London that Redmond would know who 'X' – or 'Charlie', the man responsible for the leakage of information from England – was, and that Woodyatt should explore this avenue immediately he found Redmond.

The second half of the letter concerned the grave possibility of the Germans using pilotless flying bombs. Woodyatt was inclined to think that Pullinger's vindictiveness and his desire to vindicate his family was becoming out of control. But he had laid it all out carefully, repeating all the details he had given Woodyatt in London so that he would have them at his fingertips.

Headquarters were anxious about the German moves but were by no means lacking in confidence. 'We're all right,' they kept saying. 'But we're not so sure about the French.'

On the way back to Metz, he called at an RAF forward-refuelling field at Longuyon. There was a flight of Hurricanes on the ground and the pilots were standing in a group smoking. They had been up since dawn and had run into a gaggle of German aircraft and shot two of them down.

'We've been expecting it for nine bloody months,' one of them said heavily. 'We shouldn't be surprised now it's come.'

'All the same,' another one added, 'there've been so many alarms and excursions and nothing ever happened, that now it's hard to believe.'

The heat was tremendous and, heading back to Metz, Woodyatt stopped at a small roadside bar where he managed to obtain a meal. When he reached Metz the city seemed like an anthill that had been disturbed. Vehicles and guns were all moving north.

'The Germans are coming through the Ardennes,' a French Transport Officer told him. In complaint he continued, "They won't come through the Ardennes," they told us. "It isn't possible." I could have told them that it was! You can drive a car through the Ardennes so why not a tank?'

'What's happened?'

'We tried to stop them with cavalry. On horses! Name of God, what idiot expected horsed cavalry to stop tanks? So far, their only problem's been the number of their vehicles.

The armée de l'air reports that they stretch back for a hundred miles, packed like sardines.'

The newspapers next day were to carry pictures of French troops moving forward, and of British troops advancing to a rapturous welcome in Belgium. Their vehicles were surrounded by girls showering them with flowers, beer, cigarettes and kisses.

Reaching Nicole's flat, Woodyatt was trying to find out from the wireless what the real position was when the telephone rang. It was Nicole and what she had to say was not entirely unexpected.

'There was another man trying to find Dominique Sardier,' she announced.

'Another? Enquiring about Montrouge?'

'Yes.'

'From you?'

'No. From my friend. I've just heard. She told him the same as she told me. That there was a Dominique Sardier who moved away, who knew where he was.'

'What did he look like, this man?'

'Tall, she said. Very blond. Strong but good-looking. Who was he?'

'I'm making guesses. Did he get Dominique Sardier's address?'

'She sent him to the house where Dominique used to live – where she sent you.'

'Nicole, I'm going round there. I'll call at the library later and tell you what I've found out.'

When he reached the house near the Ban St Martin there was a policeman outside. Near him were two or three girls.

'It's Madame Grune,' they told him. 'The concierge. She's been murdered.'

The door was unguarded and the police showed no surprise when Woodyatt appeared. For safety, he showed the papers Pullinger had provided. They seemed totally uninterested.

'It was robbery,' the police brigadier said. 'It seems she had a little nest egg. The girls who live here say she was always talking about it. Perhaps she talked too much.'

He led Woodyatt down the hall and through the door with the red, white and blue checks. Two heavy black shoes and wrinkled grey lisle stockings showed beyond a small table where a half-eaten meal lay. The shape behind the table was covered with a sheet but unexpectedly the brigadier yanked it back for Woodyatt to see.

Woodyatt had come across death before as a newspaperman but there was something particularly gruesome about Madame Grune's wide eyes staring up at him from a livid face.

'He strangled her,' the brigadier said.

There were what looked like cigarette burns on the cheeks. 'He tortured her,' the policeman said. 'To find out where she kept her money, I suppose. Did you know her?'

Woodyatt explained his interest. 'Was anyone seen?' he asked.

'One of the girls heard her scream. Through the window she saw a man running away.'

'What was he like?'

'Fair-haired. That's all she noticed. You know what people are like. They could pass the President of France in the street and not notice.'

The policeman was eager to discuss the case with Woodyatt, as if he thought he were a British detective. But Woodyatt was eager to be away. It was already late and it was clearly going to be difficult to drive anywhere. Traffic still all seemed to be heading north and the French Transport Officer told him the army was trying to cut off the German advance in the Ardennes.

'All it needed,' he said bitterly, 'was a few bombs. They were packed nose to tail. But all our aeroplanes are up in Belgium trying to stop them there. They've taken the Maastricht bridges and we're trying to smash them. They've got us hopping about like a dog wanting to get out for a leak.'

A colossal traffic jam was building up because the troops trying to move north were running into units of the French Ninth Army who were being forced back and were retreating southwards. There was a great deal of shouting and bad-tempered confusion. To Woodyatt it seemed pointless trying to go anywhere in the dark and he decided to wait until daylight.

Nicole was waiting for him at her flat.

'Nicole,' he said. 'I'm leaving. I have to go back to Amiens.' He explained what he'd learned at the house near the Ban St Martin. 'It wasn't robbery,' he said. 'I think Madame Grune refused to give him the address. She wasn't very keen to give it to me. When *he* turned up soon afterwards, she began to be suspicious. He must have been torturing her to get the information and killed her to stop her talking. The Sardier girl could be in danger.'

She looked bewildered. 'What shall I do without you?' she asked. 'The war's started.'

'The war started last September, Nicole,' he said. 'Unfortunately neither your country nor mine realised it.'

Knowing he was leaving the following morning and that, with things as they were, it might be difficult to return, they decided to eat in town. They found the restaurant where the soldiers had sung and flirted with Nicole, but now they were all gone. The place was quiet and the mood depressed. They ate in silence.

When they returned to the flat, Woodyatt followed Nicole inside where she moved about silently, attending to the blackout. Eventually, a small light went on and she stood near him, facing him, her face blank and expressionless. Putting his arms round her, he kissed her gently.

'You have been here some time,' she said. 'You have never mentioned your wife.'

He shrugged.

'It is all over?'

'It didn't last long.'

'Are you very bitter?'

'I'm getting over it.'

'It changes things,' she said.

'What does?'

'The fact that it didn't last long. Are you comfortable in your room?'

'Yes.'

'I think the bed is very small.'

'It is a bit.'

'I think you would have slept better in my bed. It is bigger and softer.' She gave a nervous little giggle. 'And I am very warm and cosy. I think also I would sleep better close to you. But I am a good wife and I miss my Claude. It would have been easy but it has all been so proper. So English. So fair play.'

Sometime during the night Woodyatt woke to find the guns going again and Nicole sitting in her little salon. She was crying. As he sat alongside her and put his arms round her, she leaned limply against him.

'Why?' he asked. 'Why are you crying?'

'I don't know. You. Me. Claude. It was so lovely. But it's all going to end soon. We know the Germans are coming.'

'Perhaps it'll be us who will go into Germany.'

She shook her head. 'French soldiers don't have the spirit to advance. All they'll do is wait for the Germans. I'm afraid.' She clung to him. 'Are you in love with me, Jimmee?'

He wasn't sure how to answer. She was a delightful companion, full of fun, intelligent and pretty, and he had always been a little in love with her. She saved him the embarrassment of having to work out a reply.

'I am not in love with you. I was once. But then I met Claude. And I got married. Things never work out the way you expect, do they? Because there *was* a time when I thought you and I might marry.'

'There was a time when I *hoped* we would. My mother certainly did.'

'But I still love you – because I have known you since I was a little girl and one does love people who are familiar. But I am not "in love" with you.' She gave a little shrug. 'Though after your stay here, I could easily be again.' She sighed. 'One must love for today. There may not be any tomorrow. A woman needs to be loved,' she went on. 'And I am so afraid it might never happen now. Especially since the guns started. They *are* guns, aren't they?'

'Yes. They're guns.'

'Perhaps I shall join my parents.' She smiled. 'I have written to Claude. He will know what to do and how to get in touch with me. Surely the Germans will never reach Hyères.' She blinked away the tears. 'It's so bewildering, so sudden, and it would be sad to die in a war without love.'

He kissed her and she clung fiercely to him, her mouth seeking his. As the guns died, she became quiet in his arms and eventually fell asleep, still clutching him tightly. Long after he heard her breathing steady, he stared into the darkness, wide-eyed.

It was a nightmare journey to Amiens. The traffic made the going slow and he was held up again and again at cross roads to allow a column of military vehicles to pass. Several times his papers were demanded and there seemed to be a great deal of panic. A British military policeman explained. 'They reckon Jerry's dropping parachutists everywhere,' he said.

'Dressed in British and French uniforms. Disguised as women.'

He grinned. 'If you see a nun wearing hob-nailed boots, sir, you'll know to be careful.'

The rumours multiplied and several times Woodyatt saw people stuffing cars with suitcases and packages as if they didn't intend to take chances. Probably they'd been refugees in the last war and thought it wiser to be on the safe side.

Despite everything, however, the countryside looked remarkably peaceful and there was little sign of air activity. Then he heard the sound of engines and looked up. Aeroplanes had appeared from nowhere and a German machine he recognised as a Dornier 215 was being harassed by two British Hurricanes. The Dornier was low down and zigzagging wildly and the traffic came to a stop to watch. Suddenly the Dornier's speed dropped abruptly, so that the Hurricanes overshot, and it made a slow half-circuit round a field until it hit a ridge, bounced, came down again and slithered along the ground – panels and pieces of engine cowling flying into the air before it came to rest with a rocking motion.

A few French soldiers moved cautiously towards it. As they approached, the roof of the Dornier's cockpit opened and the pilot appeared, waving his arms, and clambered down to the ground. The Frenchmen ignored him and fished down into the fuselage to drag out the rear gunner who was either badly wounded or dead. People stood up in their vehicles and clapped, and one of the French soldiers bowed and pointed to the circling Hurricanes as if acknowledging that the applause was really theirs. Everybody looked up and clapped again.

It was oppressively hot as the traffic started once more. As the French soldiers hoisted the unwounded German to his feet, nearby an old man was tilling his land with a horse-drawn harrow. A boy followed in the newly cut farrow. Both of them were totally indifferent to what had happened. Then explosions were heard and the drone of more aircraft. Woodyatt had seen a group of Heinkels turning over the eastern horizon but they had all vanished except one, and as it approached he decided it might be a good idea to leave the car and be ready to take shelter in the ditch alongside the road. Other people followed him.

The Heinkel had vanished behind a low hill then without warning it reappeared, roaring over the rise at tremendous speed. There was a whisper, a whistle, then an unearthly shriek that split the heavens. Everybody flung themselves flat and clawed at the earth. There was a series of ear-splitting crashes and Woodyatt saw the Morris and a big lorry just ahead of it bounce on their tyres as the bombs went off. Then the scream of engines was gone and the French soldiers were loosing off their rifles in a broken crackle of firing in the hope of hitting something.

Nobody appeared to have been hurt but all at once they saw the boy who had been helping the old farmer running towards them. He was pointing towards a heap on the skyline and they made out the horses lying together, with the old man who had been guiding them just behind.

Woodyatt went with the soldiers and one or two civilians to see what could be done. The old man was dead but the horses were still alive – just. One of the French soldiers shot them.

It went on like that throughout the journey. Long periods of quiet when the traffic moved on, forcing its way through unexpected jams at crossroads; military vehicles moving north and east across the route; panic-stricken civilians; rumours; an occasional aircraft. The violence was twice as shocking after the tranquillity of the past weeks. The Phoney

War had ended with a vengeance and in its place had come a hurricane sweeping across France's eastern flank.

The spire of Amiens cathedral came up against the sky and soon afterwards a weary Woodyatt was driving into the square past the hotel where Dominique Sardier had walked out on him. The city was silent under the black-out and no traffic was moving. He glanced at his watch. It was approaching midnight and he wondered how, even with a warning of danger, you got inside an unmarried lady's house at that hour.

When he reached Dreuil, the sky was clear and full of stars and he could see the river reflecting its light in little glints like diamonds. He stopped near Dominique's house. It was in darkness. Parking the car off the road under the trees, he switched off the lights and approached on foot, keeping to the grass verge to deaden the sound of his footsteps. He had no wish to alarm her.

There was no sign of life and he hoped to God she hadn't already headed for Paris to warn Montrouge that he was on his track. She hadn't believed his story, that was clear, and her desire to protect the old man was equally clear. It was even quite possible that she had decided he should move from wherever he was hiding at the moment. Woodyatt had no doubt he *was* hiding, no doubt at all by now that Montrouge had once been von Rothügel who had once been Redmond.

Since the house stood on its own, it was possible to move round the back along the fence. There was still no sign of life, and he thought it was deserted. Then he saw a chink of light in one of the ground floor windows and realised that she had not left after all, even that she was still awake and downstairs. He moved nearer, starting as he knocked over a stake from among a pile leaning against a corrugated iron shed that was being used as a garage. Fortunately, the stake fell on to a patch of grass without a sound.

As he approached the house he heard a faint mewing noise he couldn't understand. The shutters were closed but one of them was a bad fit and he suddenly wondered if she had Montrouge in there with her. It would have fitted in with what he had learned of her character. Creeping close, he realised he could see into the room he remembered as her living room. As he put his face to the glass, the first thing he found himself looking at was a man – a young man.

My God, he thought at once, she's a dark horse! She had a secret lover...she'd replaced Monsieur Maladroit with someone else! He could see her beyond him, partially obscured by the man's shape, and she appeared to be naked. He was looking at her bare shoulders and arms.

The man was wearing a short coat despite the heat. He was talking and as he stepped to one side, Woodyatt suddenly realised what was happening. Dominique Sardier was sitting in a chair her hands tied behind its back, her ankles lashed to the legs with what looked like a clothes-line. There was a gag in her mouth, held in place by a silk scarf secured tightly enough round her head to make her cheeks bulge. The mewing noises he had heard were her cries of pain and terror through the gag. Chestnut hair fell in strands over terrified eyes. The man had wrenched open her dress – that same green dress that matched her eyes, the same dress she had worn to have dinner with Woodyatt – and dragged it down so that she was naked to the waist.

Dominique's visitor was smoking and Woodyatt now saw that on her breast there was a bright pink spot and that tears were streaming down her cheeks. She was shaking her head with a desperate firmness and Woodyatt realised that the man must be an associate of the blond character who had tortured the old woman in Metz. He was doing the same here and for the same reason.

Wondering how to deal with the situation, Woodyatt tried the door gently, but it was locked or bolted. He had his revolver strapped to his waist but inside there was a gun on the table and there was obviously not the slightest chance of bursting into the house without being shot. And the surrounding houses were too distant to take any notice of any strange sounds – especially now that the odd echoes of war could be heard.

The man in the house took a deep drag at his cigarette, blew out the smoke then, leaning forward, he pressed the glowing end against the girl's breast. Tears streamed down her cheeks and she shook her head in agony, unable to scream because of the gag.

Woodyatt heard Dominique's assailant speak. '*L'adresse*,' he said. '*L'adresse. L'adresse.* If you are prepared to give it to me, nod and I will let you go.'

Desperate to do something, Woodyatt remembered the stakes he had disturbed. Grabbing one of them, he dragged it across the corrugated iron of the shed. When he looked through the window again he saw the man inside was standing with his head cocked at the terrified girl on the chair. Eventually he glanced at the door, picked up the gun and moved out of Woodyatt's vision. Standing with his back to the wall close to the door, Woodyatt waited with the stake in his hands, his breath stilled in his throat. After a few moments, the door clicked and he heard the sound of a bolt being drawn. Woodyatt flattened himself against the wall. First of all the gun appeared through the opened door, the barrel just visible in the light from the stars. Then slowly, after what seemed an interminable wait, the man's arm. Woodyatt swung the stake with all his strength.

six

Coming unseen out of the darkness, the heavy stake smashed down across the stranger's forearm and the gun went flying. Bringing the stake up again, Woodyatt sent the gunman himself staggering back inside the house, where he sprawled against the wall, face covered with blood, nose and mouth pulped by the heavy piece of wood. Woodyatt grabbed him by the collar, kicked the door shut and dragged him face-down into the living room. All the while Dominique stared at him with horrified eyes as if this were some new terror she had to endure.

Her tormentor was unconscious and looked as if he wouldn't cause trouble for a while. Woodyatt quickly untied the knots that held her to the chair and unfastened the scarf holding the gag in her mouth. When she tried to rise to her feet, almost collapsing against him, he put his arm round her, letting her lean, half-fainting, against him. Eventually she managed to struggle upright, then sat down on the chair again, her head hanging, her arms covering her scarred breasts.

Using the ropes that had lashed Dominique to the chair, Woodyatt tied the intruder's hands behind his back. In doing so he probably broke the man's arm, but he was quite indifferent and even surprised at his own ruthlessness.

'He was going to burn me again,' Dominique whispered through the tangle of hair that fell over her face. Her hands moved feebly, trying to hold the ruins of the dress in place.

'He wanted Montrouge's address?'

'Yes.'

She lay back in the chair, staring up at him. He took off his trench coat and laid it over her and she gave him a weak look of thanks.

'Take your time,' he said. 'He can't harm you now. Was he alone?'

'I think so.' Her head was wobbling a little. 'But he mentioned another man.'

Woodyatt went to the door and, locking it, checked the front door and the windows.

'Have you any brandy?'

Her head moved to indicate a small cupboard. On top he noticed the vase containing the red roses he had bought her. Inside was a half-full bottle of Courvoisier. He found a glass. It was thick and far from being a brandy balloon but he sloshed the spirit into it and handed it to her. She swallowed too much, coughed, and hiccoughed as the raw spirit burned her stomach.

'All of it.'

She did as she was told and he refilled the glass – generously.

'How did he get in?'

'He came to the door as it grew dark. He looked perfectly all right.'

Woodyatt glanced at the man on the floor. His face was a mask of blood. 'He doesn't now.'

She looked up at him, her eyes appealing for understanding. 'I thought *you* had sent him.'

'I think you'd better put something on those burns,' Woodyatt advised.

She rose to her feet and went unsteadily to the kitchen where she opened a cupboard and took out a tube of ointment.

'I bought it when I burned my hand on the stove. I'll find something else to wear.'

He watched her go up the stairs, then bent over the man on the floor. He was stirring now. The best thing to do with him would be to hand him over to the police and get out of Dreuil before his partner turned up.

After a while Dominique reappeared. She had dressed in a skirt and a loose blouse and had done her hair and put on a little make-up. He made her sit down and poured himself a brandy. 'Another?' he asked.

She didn't take much persuading and he decided that it might make her more willing to answer the questions she had earlier refused.

'Do you accept now that what I told you is true?' he asked.

Her head inclined slowly. 'Yes.'

'You understand how important it is that I find Montrouge?' Woodyatt indicated the man on the floor. 'Is he German?'

'He spoke French. I thought he was Alsatian.'

'He's a German agent, whatever nationality he is. And the Germans are after Montrouge because he can give us information and they're desperate to prevent that.'

'I understand.'

'Where is Montrouge now?'

'In Paris.'

'You have the address?'

She nodded.

'Will you take me to him?'

She nodded again, tiredly, and he straightened up briskly.

'Right, I'm going to take this filth to the police. Lock the doors after me. I'll be back –'

'No!' The cry was almost a scream. 'No! Don't leave me here! Please! Let me come with you.'

He paused. 'Very well. Collect anything you're likely to need. We may not come back.'

He was surprised to see it was growing light as they pushed the injured man into the car. There had been a brief inquisition in the living room before they had helped him outside. He had said his name was Wiart, Alois Wiart, but refused to admit he worked for the Germans.

'Who sent you here?' Woodyatt demanded.

'Nobody.'

Woodyatt hit him hard across the face. He made no sound so Woodyatt grabbed at his injured arm. This time he screamed. 'No!'

'I'll break the other. Who sent you?'

'Zamerski.'

'Full name?'

His eyes wild, his face damp with sweat from the pain, Wiart moaned. 'Hanno Zamerski.'

'What's he want?'

'I don't know. I was told to get an address, that's all.'

'Why?'

Wiart explained between sobs and gasps that Montrouge had been described as a wealthy man. With things as they were along the frontier, he had been persuaded it was a good time in the confusion to put pressure on him for money.

'I don't believe a word of it. Who's Zamerski? Is he a German agent?'

'I don't know.'

'Why does he want Montrouge's address?'

'I don't know. He didn't tell me.'

'What's he look like?'

'Tall, fair.'

'Was he in Metz?'

'Yes. Yes.'

Dominique strapped the injured limb to Wiart's chest. She showed no emotion, not even when he moaned in anguish. As they helped him into the car he cried out again. But Woodyatt had no time to waste. He gave Wiart's gun to Dominique and told her to watch him. 'If he tries anything,' he said, 'shoot him. Could you?'

'Yes.'

As they passed the cathedral on the way to the police station, she asked him to stop. 'I want to say a little prayer. I wish to thank God for my deliverance.'

It seemed to Woodyatt that God had had far less to do with her deliverance than James Woodyatt but he didn't argue.

He waited in the car in a fury of impatience, listening to the moans of Wiart from the rear seat. When she returned she asked if he never went to church.

'No,' he said.

The police station was busy when they entered.

'Look after this,' Woodyatt said, indicating Wiart. 'He's a spy.'

The police brigadier seemed to think he was panicking. 'Everybody's telling us about spies,' he said. 'What's he done?'

'He burned me,' Dominique said.

'Why?'

'For information.'

'You're Dominique Sardier. I know you. You're a teacher. What information can you have? And how do we know he burned you?'

'Do you want me to strip and show you the marks?'

The policeman looked startled but Dominique's expression didn't alter. Woodyatt had a feeling that her loathing for Wiart was such that she would have done just that if asked. But they got nowhere and in the end Woodyatt pushed Wiart back in the car.

'That man's injured,' the brigadier said.

'I know,' Woodyatt agreed, 'I injured him.'

'He should go to hospital.'

'He's going to prison first. And if you won't accept him I'll find someone who will.'

As they took the Paris road, they passed an RAF airfield. It was small and the machines were all on the ground. The men sprawled round them looked exhausted, as if they'd been flying for days. They weren't interested in Wiart.

'Sorry old boy,' one of them said. 'We've got quite enough with Jerry. We're expecting to be off again at any moment. They've bombed Joinville, St Dizier and Châlons.'

Even as he spoke a telephone bell went. Someone shouted and they all started running for the aircraft.

Woodyatt watched the planes leave the ground, then he buttonholed a sergeant who was passing on a bicycle. 'Where's your guardroom?' he asked.

'We haven't got one,' the sergeant said. 'We've only just arrived here and we haven't had time to arrange one.'

'What do you do with your prisoners?'

'We haven't got any.'

Woodyatt was growing angry. 'Suppose you shot down a Dornier and the crew survived? What would you do with them?'

'Send them to headquarters.'

'Suppose you hadn't time? Surely to Christ you'd lock 'em up!'

'Well, there's a shed over there. We could stick 'em in there. There's a key in the door.'

Woodyatt drove to the shed, the sergeant following because he was curious to know what was going on.

As Wiart was dragged from the car, he yelled out – making the sergeant even more curious. 'That feller's hurt,' he said. 'He ought to see the MO.'

'Save the MO for your own casualties.' Woodyatt shoved Wiart into the shed and slammed the door. 'Do what you like with him,' he said. 'But don't let him go.' Taking the heavy key from the lock, he threw it as far as he could into the next field.

'You can't do that!' the sergeant was indignant. 'Suppose we have to leave in a hurry? We shan't be able to get him out.'

'You could always set fire to the shed,' Woodyatt suggested heading for the car.

As Woodyatt headed for Paris with Dominique, they began to hear news of what was happening in the East. After making their first strike round the northern end of the Maginot line through Belgium, the Germans had directed a second blow through the Ardennes that had caught the French army completely off-balance.

Already the situation shown on the maps in the newspapers was beginning to look disquieting. The campaign in Holland had almost ended and the fate of Belgium seemed to be all but sealed. Glider-borne troops had captured modern fortresses and bridges over the Albert Canal. The Belgian air force, with its outdated planes, was helpless. The RAF had taken over the attempt to destroy the Maastricht bridges and its bomber force had shrunk to almost nothing. The front already seemed to be crumbling in a welter of indecision.

News sheets were announcing parachutists everywhere and everybody was expecting Mussolini to join in with an attack in the South.

Queen Wilhelmina of Holland had had to bolt for Britain and whenever Woodyatt stopped the car, they found people asking what would happen if the French Army turned out to be as useless against the German panzers as the vaunted Polish cavalry, the flooding of Holland and the Albert Canal had proved to be.

'I shall shoot myself rather than live under the Germans,' they heard one old man say. 'I had to suffer them from 1914 to 1918. But not again.'

The British front seemed to be holding but the BEF was being ordered to withdraw to the River Escaut because the French front on their right had been broken. Woodyatt, who had been brought up to believe that the French generals were the best strategists in the world, began to wonder if somebody had got it wrong. It was also beginning to look as if the Chamberlain government in England had been totally incompetent. The soldiers he spoke to were hoping that Churchill, who had taken Chamberlain's place, would stuff his cabinet with a lot of crooks.

'The honest men don't seem to have done much good,' a tired-looking RASC officer said. He was angry because something had gone wrong with the communications system. 'Either that,' he guessed, 'or the bloody Germans have got into it. Troop carriers aren't turning up and lorries are going astray. We're going to have to retreat and it looks as if we're going to have to do it on our own two feet.'

Dominique was bewildered by what was happening around them. She was still unable to appreciate Montrouge's involvement.

'But what did he do?' she asked.

'He went over to the Germans. He gave them military secrets.'

She seemed unable to believe him. 'But why?'

The need to explain was interrupted by a halt to identify themselves to a group of young British soldiers manning a barricade. The tommies had received reports of parachutists seen coming down with unexplained streaks of light. The streaks had turned out to be tracer bullets and no parachutes had been found but the alarm had affected everybody and they were all on edge. During the halt, a flood of refugees arrived. They came in cars and buses and on bicycles, carrying blankets tied with string.

The confusion was unbelievable and there were enormous crowds of Belgian soldiers evacuating with far greater purposefulness than the civilians. By this time, the quiet skies of the first days of May had vanished and aircraft were constantly heard overhead. Several times Woodyatt's car was showered by spent cartridges fired by the fighters.

The full extent of the catastrophe was not yet known, however, because the newspapers were vague. When the wireless worked it seemed only able to repeat ad nauseam the prepared reports that indicated that all was going well, when quite obviously it wasn't. One thing that was certain was that the Germans were across the Meuse at Sedan and running wild behind the French lines. No one knew exactly where they were, only that the French Ninth Army had been routed.

'For Christ's sake, keep your eyes peeled, sir,' a British sergeant told Woodyatt. 'The bastards could turn up any time.'

There seemed to be French deserters everywhere, dirty in their ill-fitting greatcoats and crested blue steel helmets. Most of them were without rifles, just the long ugly, sword-bayonets hanging from their belts. They were reservists, middle-aged men out of condition, overweight and pallid under their grime. Some had even removed their boots. Among them were Algerian or Senegalese colonial troops, including a whole crowd of them who watched a white NCO, unshaven and with bloodshot eyes, trying to drag a horse to its feet. As Woodyatt and his passenger passed, the horse lifted its head and let it fall back with a thump that seemed to shake the earth.

Occasionally they saw groups of senior French officers. They seemed bewildered and demoralised and there were wild rumours of subalterns and NCOs, who had tried to stop the rot, being shot by their own men. The deserters had stories of thousands of German tanks and paratroopers everywhere behind them.

The few British they met seemed to have lost all confidence in their French allies. There were no flowers to be seen now, and the sullen populace were too engrossed in their own problems to be interested in the BEF. While whole villages were deserted by all but cats and dogs and frightening in their stillness, the roads leading to the coast grew more choked with every hour. At a village called Marchain, they stopped at a café because Dominique craved a coffee but the waitress was just wheeling out a bicycle. 'No service,' she said. She looked at Woodyatt's uniform. 'In case you don't know, the Boches are due here at any moment.'

Despite the fact that Amiens was so close to Paris, they were on the road for two days. They managed by bribery to obtain a room for Dominique the first night, while Woodyatt slept in the car. The following day they were just passing as a bomber crashed among nearby trees and two French Bloc fighters came in to land in a field alongside. The traffic had come to a stop and one of the fighters halted close to the boundary fence. They watched as the soldiers lifted the pilot out, his head like a mop of blood.

By this time they were among British line-of-communication troops who, having collected every comfort they could to make the bitter winter easy, had been told to pull back and who could be seen carrying radios, football boots and tennis rackets.

When they bumped into British officers of any seniority, however, Woodyatt was pleased to see how efficient they seemed to be.

'It's no longer "*On ne passe pas*," ' one of them observed dryly. 'It's now a case of "*Mon Dieu,* already?" '

At this Dominique gave an angry look, but said nothing. She was tougher than she looked and seemed to have recovered from the shock of what Wiart had done to her. She was calm and willing to be helpful, though Woodyatt had a feeling she still didn't trust *him*.

Near a village called Wassigne-en-Bois, Woodyatt was driving almost automatically. He seemed to have been driving forever and he was just looking forward to a halt when Dominique snatched at his arm. 'Stop!'

He was about to ask why when just ahead he saw a tank. Instinctively he knew it was German because he had never seen a British tank of that size. Looking round desperately, he saw a side road on his left and swung the car into it. It led to another small village and they stopped at the end of the street to investigate.

There was no sign of life but there were bicycles parked outside a bar. Peering through the window, Woodyatt was horrified to find himself staring at Germans. They wore helmets and tunics with their sleeves rolled up, and the tables were piled with their weapons. Behind the bar, the owner, his eyes like saucers, was placing bottles on the counter.

Creeping away, Woodyatt found Dominique nervously waiting by the car. 'Get in,' he snapped.

Turning the vehicle round, he headed out of the village only to run into a group of French cavalrymen who blocked the road with their horses. To pass them, Woodyatt drove the car with its near wheels on a steep bank so that it leaned over at an incredible angle. Dominique stood up in her seat.

'*Les Allemands*' she screamed, pointing.

As they drove free of the bank, they became aware of the cavalrymen swinging their horses round in confusion and the clattering of hooves as they smashed their way through the hedge into the neighbouring field. As the car neared the main road again, Dominique shrieked.

'There's another!' she yelled and Woodyatt saw the turret and gun of what could only be a second German tank.

'In here!' she panicked.

111

They were passing the open gate to a farmyard and, without arguing, Woodyatt swung the car through it. The farm was deserted and the house was burned down and still smoking. A line of craters stretched into the field beyond, where the cavalrymen had disappeared, and the dusty surface of the yard was scattered with dead chickens, feathers and a dead dog. There was an open barn at the other side and, still moving at speed, Woodyatt swung the car into it – past the craters with their charred, pulverised earth. Without either of them questioning what they were doing, they leapt from the car and dragged the barn doors shut. The one on Woodyatt's side had sagged on its hinges and it took all his strength. Dominique appeared alongside him, adding her weight, her breath coming in pants. As the door finally slammed shut, they dived behind the hay stacked at the end of the barn and lay silent, clutched in each other's arms.

They listened as the tank drew nearer. It appeared to stop outside the farmyard and they heard German voices.

'They must be right across our path,' Woodyatt said, awed at the speed with which the Germans had advanced.

'Sssh!' She signed him to silence. 'They're saying they must move north.'

They then heard the clatter and screech of the tank's tracks and the rumble of its powerful engine, but eventually the noise died away. Cautiously, they approached the barn door and peered through the gaps in the planks. Blue exhaust smoke still hung in the air.

'I think they've gone,' Woodyatt said. 'Stay here.'

'No!' Dominique snatched at his sleeve. 'You stay here. I'll go. You're in uniform.' And she walked slowly across the yard to the road, peered along it and returned to announce, 'They've gone!'

Together they studied the map and decided to head south. The Germans appeared to be swinging towards the coast to cut off the BEF. Reversing the car out of the barn, Woodyatt headed warily down the road. There was no sign of any more danger. 'I think we've lost them,' he said, jamming his foot hard on the accelerator.

After a while they came across a British unit sheltering in a little copse and Woodyatt drove in among the foliage and stopped the car. An officer told him he couldn't stay but Woodyatt produced Pullinger's famous papers – the papers he had sworn would produce help from anybody. The officer stared at them, frowning. 'It's a lot of bloody cock,' he said angrily. 'How do I know they're genuine?'

He had a point and even when Woodyatt pointed out that the signatures were not faked he was still not believed. However, the officer withdrew his objections and they stayed where they were. They also passed on the information about the German tanks and troops at Wassigne, and the officer noted them on his map.

'The buggers pop up like mushrooms,' he agreed.

They managed to beg a loaf, a few slices of meat and a bottle of wine and were about to settle down to eat and drink when Woodyatt happened to look up and saw a small Storch reconnaissance machine circling just to the East. Glancing round at the soldiers, he saw fires lit and smoke rising. Immediately, he swept up the food and wine and bustled Dominique to the car.

'Why?' she said. 'We're safe among the trees.'

'The safest place to be,' he pointed out, 'is in the middle of an open field. This wood's marked on the map and I'll bet that Storch is pinpointing it already.'

Shouting to the officer, he indicated the aeroplane. Where upon the sergeants started yelling and the soldiers began to run to their vehicles. As they did so, there was a whirr and a tremendous crack as a shrapnel shell burst overhead. Woodyatt grabbed the girl and pushed her to the car.

'Underneath!' he snapped.

More shells began to rattle and bang above the trees. Branches and twigs, snipped off by the red-hot steel shrapnel balls, came down in a shower – followed by fluttering leaves. The soldiers, mostly inexperienced conscripts, were dashing about frantically looking for shelter. Mugs of tea and dixies of food were scattered in the panic.

Cowering half under the car with Woodyatt, Dominique had her eyes screwed shut, hands over her ears against the noise. Every now and then splinters clattered like football rattles against the vehicles.

'Spread out! Spread out!' the officer was shouting, then there was another flash and a crack like a giant whip and his voice stopped abruptly. A lorry went up in a blossom of flame and black greasy smoke. The soldiers were disappearing over a fold of ground at the edge of the wood to shelter in a ditch by the side of the road. Then, as suddenly as it had started, the racket stopped. By now several vehicles were burning and Woodyatt could hear moaning. He found Dominique bent over a man on the ground, sponging his face with a handkerchief that was rapidly becoming soggy from the blood that dripped into the pulped earth.

'Come along!' he said harshly. 'We should be away from here.'

'I can't leave him.'

He disregarded her appeal and grabbed her arm. One of the soldiers jeered at him, thinking he was only interested in bolting, but Woodyatt ignored it and dragged her to the car. Miraculously, apart from a few marks, it seemed undamaged but his suitcase had been ripped open by a shell fragment.

'That man I left will die,' she accused.

'So will a lot of others,' he said. 'Perhaps if we can find Montrouge before the Germans do, a few might not.'

He pushed her into the car and started the engine with a roar. As he moved off, other vehicles began to follow almost immediately.

Dominique sat mutely, hating her companion with her silence. They had not progressed very far south. There seemed to be hundreds of French soldiers around them and Woodyatt had unfastened the flap of his revolver holster. The men about them were the ruins of an army. Their officers had thrown in their hands and they had become a horde of drab, dusty figures lacking any morale. Here and there one or two of them tramped by with heads up, weapons still in their hands, unshaven like all the French army, which had never set a lot of store by smartness, but with something about them that showed they were not defeated. On the road junctions and in the villages women watched them pass, their eyes sad. But for the others they had nothing but contempt. Some were staring towards the east as if they expected the conquering Germans at any minute.

Ahead of them the countryside was a vast plain with shallow valleys and low hills, and along the road in front of them stretched a vast column of people. There were cars roofed with mattresses; horses and carts; wagons covered with nets carrying pigs and calves; people with bicycles or barrows; people leading donkeys, pushing prams, dragging wailing children. A few British army vehicles were trying to move in the opposite direction but were unable to make progress against the flood. After a while it all came to a halt, and a British military policeman appeared from nowhere.

'Going the wrong way, aren't you? – sir,' he said. The contempt in his look as he stared at Dominique was obvious.

Woodyatt shoved Pullinger's papers at him and, red-faced, he saluted and stepped back.

Ahead was a small town, a cluster of ugly red-brick houses with front gardens facing shabby fields. It was there that Woodyatt began to realise for the first time that France was facing defeat. A row of anti-aircraft guns which had been blown up by artificers, their split barrels like vast metal flowers, stood in the roadway. In a square a herd of cavalry horses were quite unattended, the monogram of the Republic on their saddle cloths, the air around them full of the smell of sweat and stained leather. A group of Panhard armoured cars ground up, pouring out exhaust smoke, tricolour roundels on their sides. They carried pet names – 'Minou', 'Pascal', 'Riri'. Nearby, beyond the veil of dust that hung everywhere, girls were still piling stooks of corn in a field.

It was impossible to push through and Woodyatt stopped the car. Alongside was a church, its door wide open. Heading towards it were women wearing shawls on their heads and carrying rosaries. Dominique announced that she was going inside.

'To light a candle,' she said.

Woodyatt stared after her angrily. Before the war he had been inclined to regard soldiering as a low undignified business in which chilly tubes of metal known as guns had to be handled. Nevertheless, when war had broken out he had felt it his duty to join up at once. Now he had discovered that his part in the war was not at all what he had expected.

'Speak French?' he had been asked by the interviewing officer.

'Yes, sir.'

'Good. Just the chap we need.'

'What for, sir?'

'Intelligence, man. Intelligence.'

From there Pullinger had snatched him up and now here he was, struggling through the wreckage of a defeat with an unwilling and unsympathetic French girl, as he tried to get to Paris to unravel an ancient puzzle that everyone else in the world had forgotten.

The traffic started to move and he began to curse his missing companion. She turned up just in time for him to ease the car into a gap in the stream of vehicles.

'How was the weather in Heaven?'

She gave him a furious look. 'I said a prayer,' she snapped. 'Who was it for this time?'

'You.'

The traffic moved steadily until it came to the centre of the town, where it halted once more. Across their path, passing over a crossroads just ahead, was another heart-rending tide of refugees – a vast black-clad column of people like the flood from a broken dam. They were Belgians and French from the border areas and they had swamped the place. They were carrying all their worldly possessions, their mattresses and bedding on the tops of cars. Some even had beds in their carts. Others had their belongings wrapped in blankets and tied to their backs. Fashionable women tottered along in high-heeled shoes, still wearing smart hats and coats. They were all short of sleep but afraid to halt and rest. An old man wheeled his wife in a barrow; others pushed perambulators. One youth lay sprawled in the gutter, exhausted.

There seemed to be thousands of them: weary-faced women, stolid-featured men, bewildered children. One over-loaded cart had come to a stop and the ancient horse between the shafts hadn't the strength to move it again. As he watched, Woodyatt became aware of the thin hum of an aeroplane engine that could be detected above the murmur of the refugees and the susurration of their movement past the car.

'Oh, Christ!' he said.

Dominique gave him a contemptuous look, but before she could say anything he had grabbed her arm and dragged her from the vehicle. She reacted by swinging her other arm, and hitting his head with the flat of her hand with some force. He almost flung her into the ditch.

Stukas had arrived above them and, as Woodyatt watched, the first one did a half-roll and swooped down at tremendous speed, a scream wailing from the sirens attached to the wheels. It seemed to come directly for them.

As they crouched in the ditch, Dominique clung to Woodyatt burying her face in his chest, her fingers digging into his arms. The ground seemed to heave in a cloud of yellow and grey smoke, like sea rolling on to a shore. More planes came down, one after another, and she gave little yelps of terror with every explosion. A house collapsed with a roar. Even through the din the thin screaming of children could be heard.

Then suddenly the world was silent again in a way that seemed uncanny after all the noise. Woodyatt lifted his head warily. Dominique still clung to him and he realised he had one hand behind her shoulders, pressing her to him. As their fingers unlocked, she gave him a shamefaced look.

'I am sorry I struck you,' she said stiffly. 'I was angry with you.'

'Still – ' there was an infuriating satisfaction in her words ' – if I hadn't gone into the church we'd have been further forward and would probably have been blown up. Will it be like this all the time?'

'God forbid.'

The centre of the little town was nothing but rubble. The air was filled with a high ululation of misery and terror, and with the shouts of stretcher-bearers struggling to drag people from the wreckage. Dominique rose and, drawing a deep breath, headed for the nearest spread-eagled figure. Stooping over it, she lifted an eyelid, felt the pulse, shook her head and turned away to bend over the next – a soldier whose uniform was saturated with blood. He was covered with dust and crying for water. As Woodyatt reached for his bottle, she smacked his hand away.

'No water!' she snapped. 'He's got a stomach wound.' And she looked squarely at him. 'Please don't try to stop me this time,' she said. 'These people need me and Monsieur Montrouge will not go away.'

The bombing had effectively closed the road to the military traffic carrying reinforcements to the regiments reeling back from the frontier. Men and women were desperately working at a pile of rubble, tossing bricks aside to get at a woman trapped beneath it. Only her head and shoulders were visible, her hair was coated with plaster dust, and beside her lay an injured child. Nearby a young man was flat on his back, staring at the sky, his beret over one eye in a drunken fashion.

As he knelt alongside Dominique, Woodyatt became aware that the movement west had started again. Indifferent to the needs of the injured, the survivors had gathered their belongings. Brushing off the dust, they began to trudge on again, numbly, silently, interested only in safety. An old priest was trying to stop them, begging them to help.

It was some time before Woodyatt himself moved on again. Dominique had insisted on doing what she could until the doctors and army orderlies arrived. Woodyatt tried to help but he had no intention of moving far from the little Morris. Given half a chance, someone would steal it, he knew.

Eventually she joined him and, as the road cleared, they left the village. Beyond the houses Woodyatt stopped and dug out his maps.

'Do you know this part of the world?' he asked.

'No,' she said coldly. 'Why?'

'It seems damned silly to go on trying to press ahead with all these people. They're taking the shortest route. *We* don't have to.'

He opened the map and spread it over their knees as the crowd continued to shuffle past.

'We're on the direct Amiens–Beauvais–Paris road,' he said. 'I suggest we leave it. Amiens–Abbeville to the coast is going to be important soon because the Allies are bound to try to launch a counter-attack. That's why the roads are being bombed. I suggest we try a different route.' His finger jabbed. 'This one, for instance, via Poix, Marseille-en-Beauvaisis, Gisors and Pontoise. Then we'd come into Paris from the other side. It's a long way round but it will probably be clearer.'

'Unless,' she said sharply, 'all the English, who lived in Paris because they thought it was more fun than their own cold country, are taking that route for Calais and the Channel coast to go home.'

He was startled at her cynicism. 'You have a point,' he admitted. 'But I think we'll chance it. We have a full tank because I filled it before I left, and two eight-litre tins in the back.'

'You have thought of everything.'

'You know what Napoleon said. Because a nail was lost, a horse shoe was lost, because a horse shoe was lost, a horse was lost – 'It wasn't Napoleon. It was Benjamin Franklin.' He shrugged. 'I'm sure Napoleon thought it a good idea, too.'

He was beginning to wish he had never clapped eyes on her. Yet she looked attractive with her hair tumbled, her face flushed, her clothes stained with dirt, all her dignity gone.

She was silent for a long time. 'What will happen to France?' she asked. 'Is she defeated?'

'Nobody's defeated until they think they're defeated.'

'I think France was defeated before it started,' she said bitterly. 'I suppose now there will be a reshuffle of the government. They will form a new cabinet and present themselves for inspection. The same old gang as before with some stuffed dummy in front to talk to the Germans.' She turned and looked straight at Woodyatt. 'I don't know what you want from my uncle,' she ended, 'but if it will help to destroy that monster in Berlin, then I am willing to help.'

eight

The journey round Paris wasn't as easy as Woodyatt had hoped. Dominique had been right. Dozens of cars were heading north for the coast but the latest rumour was that the Germans were heading for Calais and Boulogne, and the only way to get to England was via Dieppe. The traffic was turning west at Beauvais and across their route. In addition, Pontoise had been bombed and they had to make a detour to Meulan and St Germain-en-Laye.

Woodyatt was worried. They had taken longer than expected on the short drive from Amiens. He was terrified the Germans or a German agent, directed by Zamerski, would have arrived ahead of them. The streets of St Germain were almost empty, with only a few pedestrians and few cars and taxis. Many of the cars bore Belgian registration and there was a feeling of uncertainty about the place. Nancy, Lille, Lyon and Colmar had been bombed and everybody was aware that danger was drawing nearer. Yet the invasion – though its advent ought to have been obvious – seemed to have evoked intense surprise.

All the government appeared to have done was to have replaced the Commander-in-Chief, cancelled the Whitsun holiday and brought out decree after decree curtailing civil liberties. Places of entertainment were closed, newspapers were cut to a single folded sheet and music was forbidden on the radio. All that was left were unconvincing news bulletins with '*On les aura*' repeated ad nauseam.

It was noticeable that the identity of the Germans had changed. When they had bombed Poland, they had been referred to as 'Les Allemands'. Now that they were bombing France they had become 'Les Boches' again. It was noticeable, also, that the china dogs Woodyatt had seen in the gift shops – cocking their legs against copies of Mein Kampf – had all suddenly disappeared.

There had still been no air raid on Paris, however, and Woodyatt could only assume it was because the German bombers were busy elsewhere. Nobody was admitting anything, though, and the wireless repeatedly announced, 'La situation est sérieuse; mais elle n'est ni critique ni désespérée.' Which, Woodyatt thought, was a hell of a thing to say after only three or four days of attack.

As they stopped for coffee, an RAF man, wearing a muffler of cotton wool and a bandage over a wound in his neck, told them the Parisians were expecting the railway stations to be bombed that night.

'I should find somewhere to stay with a good cellar,' he said. 'The French are bolting from their forward airfields. So are we, come to that. But they're doing it faster. Jerry's not bombing them though, because he's expecting to be needing them himself, I reckon.'

Because of the traffic, they decided to stay the night in St Germain. It wasn't difficult to find a bed because, although refugees were pouring into Paris from the east, more were pouring out at the other side for Brittany and the south. They had to share the room but Dominique didn't argue, sleeping fully dressed on the bed while Woodyatt dozed in a chair. She had accepted the strange ménage-a-deux and said little. But she had come to life, too, as though for years she had lived a life of unbelievable dullness and was finding the situation exciting.

Once, when he asked her how her burns were, she answered unemotionally, 'I shall survive.'

Despite the amount of traffic, there were no buses. They were being used to bring in refugees from Reims and transport troops towards the front. But they were having problems because the Luftwaffe was bombing and machine-gunning the roads. What they had thought was lack of skill on the part of individual pilots was, in fact, policy – to clutter the roads with terrified refugees to stop reinforcements moving forward.

There were no French anti-aircraft guns, but a lot of nonsense was being offered on the wireless about the French 75s being good for destroying tanks. There was also a lot of talk about the French genius for improvisation. Woodyatt listened cynically. Though everybody seemed to know what should be done, nobody seemed to be doing it.

Dominique looked tired and Woodyatt decided they should eat breakfast before they searched for Montrouge. As they drained their coffee he asked where he was.

'I don't know,' she said.

Woodyatt was aware of his face growing red with anger.

'Well, I do and I don't,' she explained.

'What in the name of God does that mean?'

She flashed him an angry glance. 'When I last saw him, he was about to move his rooms. He said he preferred to keep it quiet.'

'Why?'

'That was his affair.'

'It might be mine.'

'He said he'd leave a message for me at a bar.'

'What's it's name?'

'*Au Petit Alsacien.*'

'Where is it?'

'Montparnasse. Rue de la Gaieté.'

He bundled her out of the restaurant without speaking.

Their route led them by the War Office. As they passed, a policeman stepped into the road and held up his hand.

Something was happening because there were a lot of large black cars drawn up by the pavement. Then they saw General Weygand appear. He had just replaced Gamelin as Commander-in-Chief of the French army. He looked dapper, alert and full of vitality and good humour. For a moment, Woodyatt's hopes rose because he looked like a man in command of the situation. But, then, behind him came Marshal Pétain, the victor of Verdun. He looked solemn and resembled a doddering old woman with his stooped shoulders and white moustache. Woodyatt's hopes sank again.

The cars moved off and they were allowed to proceed. The *Petit Alsacien* was a shabby little bar that was part of a hotel which looked as if it let its rooms for one night stands. Woodyatt followed Dominique inside. She seemed nervous but, to his surprise, the message was waiting. It was in an envelope and it consisted of one line. 'Furnished apartment. 81, Rue de Vanves, Arrondissement 14.'

'What happens when we get there?' Woodyatt asked sarcastically. 'Will there be a man with one eye and a parrot on his shoulder?'

'Yes,' she snapped. 'He will be wearing a striped jersey and we will match two halves of a coin.'

Woodyatt glared. 'Why all this elaborate hide and seek?'

'He felt he needed protection. He's an old man.'

'Ordinary old men don't need protection.'

She jerked her hand at the newspaper they had bought. It indicated that German soldiers in the Ardennes were gorging themselves on French butter and wine. 'They do now,' she snapped.

They found the Rue de Vanves on the map. It was near the Boulevard Pasteur and in the shabbier part of the district. It wasn't easy getting there because there were a lot of cars heading for the Porte de Versailles and the West. Many of them were laden with luggage and looked top-heavy. In one of them were children with their faces pressed to the window, and a woman weeping.

They found themselves in a drab area and number 81 was an old building where great chunks of plaster had fallen from the walls, revealing ancient red bricks and timbers. The old man who acted as concierge was sitting in the courtyard in the sunshine reading a newspaper as if it were a normal peaceful summer day. When Dominique asked for Montrouge, he jerked a thumb.

'Top floor. Four flights of stairs. Take a deep breath.'

The top landing was as drab as the rest of the building and, as they knocked on the door, they heard something drop inside the apartment. There was a long silence then they heard bolts being drawn.

As the door opened, Woodyatt found himself finally facing his quarry.

Part Three

o n e

The apartment beyond the door had the look of all furnished apartments, unloved and colourless with old and shabby furniture and no personal touches whatsoever. The man in the doorway had broad shoulders and was still very upright. His suit was smart and well-pressed. Everything about him said old soldier, though the deep-set eyes were faded and now less deep-set than sunken. He wore a white moustache but, despite the hollow cheeks and temples, Woodyatt felt he could see the man in the pictures he carried – Major General Sir George Redmond, General Georg von Rothügel, Georges Montrouge.

The old man reached out to Dominique and kissed her on both cheeks. 'My dear,' he said. 'You found me.'

He looked at Woodyatt who wondered for a second, as the old man saw his uniform, if there were the minutest flash of fear.

'And who is this?' he asked. 'Don't tell me you have fallen in love with a British officer. It's something I would advise against.'

'I'm too wise to fall in love,' Dominique said sharply.

'Nonsense. Who is he?'

'This is Captain Woodyatt. He's been trying to contact you.'

'Why?' The question came sharply.

Woodyatt drew a deep breath and trotted out the story he had prepared. 'I understand you were once a French agent,

Monsieur.' It would do for the time being until he could get the old man away from Dominique's protective influence. 'It was felt you needed to be got to safety.'

The old man looked at him shrewdly. 'Why is Britain interested in me? Why not France?'

'Britain and France are allies. And we have details in Britain, Monsieur, that France doesn't have.'

Once more there was a flash of concern, then the old man studied him and seemed to dismiss him from his mind. 'Have you come far?' he asked Dominique.

'From Amiens. We were bombed twice and we ran into German tanks.'

The old man clicked his tongue. 'I can't imagine what the army's doing to allow it. You must be tired. You must stay here. There's a spare bed. Your young man will doubtless be able to sleep on the floor. I've slept on the floor many times.'

'When?' Woodyatt asked casually. 'As a soldier?'

If it had been a slip, Montrouge was immediately in command of the situation. 'All Frenchmen are subject to military service,' he said. 'Unlike England which, for some reason, has always been terrified of conscription, France calls up *all* her young men. Apart from the halt, the blind and the maimed, they are all soldiers at some time in their lives.'

He had spoken in English. It was idiomatic confident English but it was French-accented. He was smiling at Woodyatt almost as though enjoying taunting him. As he turned to Dominique, he switched back to French. This accent, Woodyatt noticed, was harsh. His French was perfect, but was there something behind it? A different root, a British background? Somehow he sounded like a man who was speaking French because he had *learned* French, not because it was his native tongue.

'Perhaps you would like a drink?'

He produced a bottle of whisky. As he moved about, his step was an old man's careful tread and it was impossible to tell whether he were limping or not, and, if so, which leg he favoured. As he handed them their drinks, Woodyatt noticed he hadn't poured one for himself.

'Aren't you having one?' he asked.

The old man paused. Woodyatt could see a brandy bottle on the sideboard and he waited for him to pour one and reach for the soda. But he shook his head. 'A little early for me,' he said. 'At my age, one learns to be careful.'

'The Germans seem to be everywhere,' he went on. 'They're rounding up our people like cattle.'

In these surroundings it was hard to think of him as Redmond or von Rothügel. 'During the last war,' Woodyatt said, 'I believe *you* were a prisoner in Germany.'

Montrouge turned towards him. 'Yes. I was unlucky.'

'Where were you?'

'As far as you can get from the French frontier. I was in Dresden.'

'Why Dresden?'

Montrouge looked steadily at him and answered as if the question were stupid. 'Because I was living in Dresden.'

He turned again to Dominique. 'Do you wish to tidy yourself up? Travelling is very wearing in the heat.' He gestured. 'Through there. There are clean towels. I'm very particular.'

He glanced at Woodyatt with narrowed eyes. They were blue, Woodyatt noticed – the right colour. His face, his jaw, his eyes, his ears, all seemed to fit the pictures he carried.

'You'd better tell me what you want, young man,' Montrouge said slowly as the door closed behind the girl. 'Wars always throw up dubious characters who are after something for themselves. Safe jobs. Decorations. Money. Women. Are you pursuing my niece?'

'No,' Woodyatt said.

'She only needs a little encouragement and she would be beautiful. Badly let down some years ago, I believe. It made her a little wary. But, of course, love is all that women think about. It colours the whole of their lives. But she's intelligent, has a splendid shape and – '

Woodyatt ignored the line of conversation which, he felt sure, was deliberately pursued to distract him. 'You lived in Germany a long time, Monsieur?'

'Yes I did.'

'You speak German?'

'Excellent German. I also speak excellent English.'

'What about when you were made a prisoner? Did they interrogate you?'

'Why should they? I wasn't important. But, yes, I suppose they did.' The old man's eyes glinted. 'But I told them nothing.'

Was he implying that he had every intention of telling Woodyatt nothing too?

'You must have met some very interesting people,' Woodyatt went on. It was like a game of cat and mouse. 'Germany in those days was very military in inclination.'

'Oh, yes. Everybody wore a uniform. Even stationmasters. Even students. Germany was a madhouse before 1914.' The old man laughed. 'The Kaiser was breathing fire against everybody, especially his uncle, Edward VII. *Preussen über alles.* They did nothing but talk of war and they had nothing but contempt for every other nation. Yet Prussianism was such a ridiculous system. Everything depended on the Kaiser's caprices. He liked to boast he could rely on his troops being where he wanted them when he wanted them and in good order – at any time. Foreign diplomats laughed. They knew commanding officers were always tipped off by the staff so they could set off for their destination before the orders were officially issued.'

'You saw it all?'

'I lived with it. The German Empire was vulgar and the Kaiser was silly. With that ridiculous moustache, he looked like a ferret peering over a hedge. Poor Wilhelm. Anywhere else he might have had his leg pulled a little. It would have done him good.'

'You met him?'

'A number of times. He was always with the army and often I was, too. I was always with one officer or another. At the Metropole, the Wintergarten. At concerts at the Zoologische Garten. In the Romanische Café on the Kürfurstendamm. Berlin was a very social place and the German officers weren't half so terrifying as wartime propaganda would have you believe. And they did have a wider education than their British counterparts.'

'You knew British generals?'

'For a year or two I ran a language crammer in England for men hoping to get into the military academy.'

The talk was boastful, as though the old man was proud of the people he had known, of his entrée into select circles.

'But the British were a poor lot in those days,' he went on. 'It was considered that you didn't need brains to be a soldier, just a good family and a figure that looked well in uniform. There were a lot of grey-headed nincompoops about. Haig – very unimaginative. Sir John French – as stupid as one of his horses.'

The old man was still smiling. It irritated Woodyatt and his next question came out more sharply than he'd intended. 'How did the German staff know the British generals were so unskilled? Did you run a crammer for them, too?'

Woodyatt had allowed himself to be sarcastic but the old man didn't seem in the slightest perturbed. The smile returned. 'My language school wasn't just a backroom affair.'

'Did you ever meet Alfred Redl, the Chief of Austrian Intelligence? You must have heard of him. He was exposed as a spy for Russia. They blackmailed him into it.'

'Yes. I heard of him.'

'Ever meet a man called Redmond?'

Montrouge paused, then his mouth twisted. 'Yes. I remember him, too.'

'What was he like?'

'Brighter than the rest.'

'He was accused of homosexual acts.'

'I heard that, too.'

Woodyatt paused. 'Have you noticed that your name, Montrouge, could be a loose translation of Redmond?'

'So it could.'

'There was a German general. Georg von Rothügel. That's Redmond, too, isn't it?'

'I suppose it is.' Montrouge gave Woodyatt a long cool stare. 'Are you trying to suggest something, young man?'

'There's a strong belief in England that von Rothügel was Redmond, that Redmond faked a suicide in Paris and joined the Germans, who welcomed him with open arms.'

This time the old man laughed outright. 'Well, they would, wouldn't they?'

Woodyatt tried another approach. 'There was one other who committed suicide. Hector MacDonald. He was a major-general, too.'

'He was a contemporary of Redmond's.'

'You know the British army list well.'

'It's not very difficult to obtain a copy – even in Germany.'

'You got to know an awful lot. Surely the German officer hierarchy was one of the most exclusive clubs in society. How did you get into it?'

The old man's smile came again. 'I am a remarkable character.'

I bet you are, Woodyatt said to himself. I'll just bet you are. It was like a fencing bout, with Woodyatt doing all the thrusting and the old man all the parrying.

'I was always in the centre of things,' he explained.

'In Dresden? Dresden's a long way from Berlin.'

'There was a good train service.'

'Why did you come back to France?'

'I was growing old. I wanted to return to my native country. Why do you ask?'

'Because,' Woodyatt said slowly, 'it's thought that you were once Georg von Rothügel. And before that Sir George Redmond.'

The old man was silent for a while.

'That's a strange thing to say, young man,' he observed at last. 'Redmond must have died years ago.'

'Have you seen an obituary?'

'Since you ask, no. Why are you so interested in him?'

'We want him.'

'We?'

'British Intelligence.'

'To put him in the Tower of London?'

'To protect him. The Germans want him, too. He once told them how British generals thought. Perhaps now he could tell us how the Germans are thinking.'

'Where did you get the impression I am Redmond?'

'If you're not, why are German agents trying to find your address?'

There was a long silence. The news seemed genuinely to have startled the old man. His eyes flickered over Woodyatt's face as if he were uncertain what to say.

'If you're eager to make headway with my niece,' he said at last, 'this won't help.'

He began to laugh at Woodyatt. It seemed artificial and Woodyatt responded angrily. 'If it's any interest to you,' he snapped, 'your niece doesn't believe any longer that you're who you say you are.'

'You've been changing her mind?'

'Her mind was changed by a man who tortured her to find your address.'

135

Montrouge clearly didn't believe him. 'I don't see any signs of torture.'

'That's because they're in a place she's unlikely to show you.'

'But *you* saw them?'

His flippant attitude made Woodyatt see red. 'I saw them because I happened to rescue her,' he exploded. 'She'd been tied to a chair, stripped to the waist and burned with cigarettes.'

'Why didn't she tell me?'

'Because she's suffering a great deal from the fact that she can no longer believe all that you've told her.'

Did he see a momentary flicker of concern? Or was it alarm, even fear? 'It was a man called Wiart. He worked for someone called Zamerski. Do you know anyone of that name?'

'Of course not. Why should I?' But there was a hesitation. 'Are you here to interrogate me?'

'No. I'm what might be called a brute-force Intelligence officer. There are much cleverer people than I am to take you apart. My job's simply to deliver you into their hands.'

There was a pause while Montrouge stared coldly at Woodyatt, then he changed the subject abruptly. 'This Redmond you seek. Surely he's long since been forgotten. People surely couldn't care less after forty years. It's nothing more than an epitaph on an old tomb. Especially when you're my age.'

'I'm not your age. Neither are my superiors. For that matter, neither is Hitler.'

Montrouge was again silent for a moment, as if digesting what Woodyatt had said. 'Do you think this man, this Redmond, will have a *crise de conscience*?' he asked eventually. 'And give himself up to retrieve his honour? Honour is an out-of-date concept. Suppose you find him? What would you do with him?'

Was the old bastard bargaining, Woodyatt wondered. 'We'd get him out of France,' he said.

The old man sniffed. 'With the situation what it is in France, young man,' he said briskly, 'I suspect the task might make great demands on you. And then? Is he to be charged under the Official Secrets Act?'

'I understand everything will be waived, providing he's prepared to help. A pardon of sorts would be available.'

'Would it indeed?'

'It's believed he knows things that would be of immense value to us.'

'By whom is it believed?'

'My superior officer for a start. Man called Pullinger.' Montrouge seemed to be staring into the past. 'There was a man called Pullinger running British Intelligence at the time of the Redmond affair,' he said. 'In 1904.'

'His father. How do you know about him?'

'The Germans knew exactly who was running what. He wasn't considered very good.' The sarcastic smile reappeared. 'This is all very interesting, but I always thought it wasn't considered fair play in the British army to deal with spies – that it wasn't quite *cricket*.'

'The Nazis don't play cricket.'

The old man was again silent for a moment and Woodyatt felt he was weighing up pros and cons. 'This pardon,' he said. 'It would be in return for what *exactly*?'

'That doesn't concern me.'

'Suppose he didn't wish to go?'

'He'd be well advised to.'

'You're not suggesting he'd be kept safe in England and given a pension?'

'Why not?'

'It would still be imprisonment. Not in a jail, perhaps. He would perhaps even have a house. With chintzes and a photograph of Mother on the sideboard.' There was a sneer in the voice now. 'But there would always be a guard in the kitchen.' He had described Pullinger's ideas exactly.

The old man switched the conversation again. 'I've heard that General Gamelin has shot himself,' he said. 'I'm surprised he managed it. The Germans had a list of British and German generals they could forget as being not very dangerous. Gamelin was one.'

'You saw the list, I suppose?'

'Oh, yes. I had many friends on the staff. Had you heard that the government here has issued a decree that all male civilians except the aged and the infirm – which includes me, I assume – must leave Paris at once? They're taking care there shall be no munition workers for the Germans to recruit when they arrive. Perhaps they're considering carrying the war to England. Will England resist?'

'I haven't the slightest doubt she will.'

'How the French government expects all males to leave the city I can't imagine. All cars are being commandeered by the army, the buses are being used to carry refugees and troops, and the trains have stopped running. I asked at the Gare de Lyon.'

'Why?'

Montrouge smiled. 'Why?' he said. 'Because, like everybody else, I want to leave Paris before the Germans come.'

t w o

In London the newspapers indicated fighting was continuing and that the situation in France was serious. But there was no suggestion of an imminent catastrophe. People were still going about their business normally, their faces grave as they studied the headlines. But they were far from disturbed because only a few were aware of the proportions of the disaster.

Slamming the door of his Whitehall office behind him, Pullinger tossed his hat at the coat stand, missed and watched it fall to the floor. He made no attempt to pick it up, knowing that Almira Hannah would be in within seconds. When she appeared she picked up the hat without comment and hung it on the appropriate peg.

'Anything happening?' Pullinger asked.

'Only if you call the Germans wiping the floor with the BEF anything.'

He studied her. She was a very attractive woman in a crisp blouse and skirt. She always looked cool and was never panicked into rushing anything. He wondered if he should ask her to marry him. They had been enjoying weekends together for months and it was about time he made her an honest woman. After all it was wartime and wartime was when you did that sort of thing.

'We seem to be getting them out by sea,' he commented.

'Without their guns.'

'Unfortunately.'

'There's one other thing. A message from Woodyatt. He seems to have found our man.'

Pullinger sat down, lit a cigarette and looked up. 'Where?'

'Where we thought. In Metz. But he's gone to Paris and Woodyatt's after him. It's just a "stand-by" message. It came from headquarters.'

'Better send him one back then.'

'I've also turned up someone who knew Redmond. As recently as 1936. He was a near neighbour in Dresden – a Jew who fled to England and started up a small business in Gateshead. Part of that scheme to build factories and let them at peppercorn rents. The idea originally was simply to help depressed areas but it's coming in very useful now. Some of them are doing very well, and in view of the fact that the BEF's coming back without its weapons, perhaps we're going to be glad of people like him. His name's Joachim Ketscher. Calls himself John Kess. He says he'll be glad to help us.'

Pullinger sat very still for a moment, his face expressionless then he came to life abruptly.

'Instruct Woodyatt to bring Redmond home at once.'

Because they had left Dreuil in a hurry, Dominique needed to do some essential shopping. But the street outside kept filling up with men from the broken regiments to the East. They appeared in ones and twos and small groups, gritty dust in the lines on their faces, dirty and unshaven and for the most part without rifles. They were hungry and begging for food; some were even trying to bully the nearby bars to give them wine. Some of them had removed their boots to show their blisters and among them were some wounded men who sat on the edge of the pavement, feet in the gutter, complaining bitterly that their officers had deserted them. One of them had had his sleeve slit open to allow his arm to be bandaged.

Dominique insisted on removing the filthy rags. Underneath was a dreadful gash.

'Shell splinter,' the wounded soldier said.

Sending Woodyatt to the nearest pharmacy, Dominique began to recruit the women who had appeared from neighbouring houses and apartments. Hot water arrived and sheets were torn up. Nobody questioned Dominique's right to order them about. She knew what to do and they did what she told them without question. Eventually, someone contacted the police and soon afterwards lorries appeared and the men were collected and driven away. Dominique watched them go with tears in her eyes.

She decided to put off her shopping until the afternoon and they ate a light snack of ham, salad, bread and wine; then, in a determined, no-nonsense fashion, she collected her things for her shopping expedition. Afraid Montrouge might slip away in their absence, Woodyatt decided not to accompany her.

As the old man dozed in a chair, Woodyatt sat opposite him, studying him. Could this really be the infamous George Surtees Redmond? Was it possible? So far he'd given nothing away and Woodyatt had been unable to detect any of the things Darby had warned him about. Several times he had seemed to be on the point of disclosing something from his past but on every occasion he had recovered himself and Woodyatt had faced a blank wall again.

In the end, it was Woodyatt who dozed off in the heat and when he woke the old man was wide awake and staring at him over the top of a newspaper.

'You are not much of a guard, young man,' he said with a grim smile. 'I could have plunged a carving knife into your heart while you slept.'

'It wouldn't have been a very good idea,' Woodyatt said. 'Dominique's the sort of busybody who would have reported it at once.'

'I suppose you're right. But she's a very attractive young woman, don't you think? Are you interested in her?'

'No.'

'Frenchwomen make much better wives than those stuffy Englishwomen with their dogs and their pearls.'

'You knew a few?'

'One or two.'

'You also know a lot about Redmond.'

'A book came out in Germany at the time of his defection. It sold very well. The Germans liked to read things that proved what they had already decided – that England was decadent.'

'Your Germans weren't exactly models of purity themselves.'

The old man shrugged. 'I suppose it was that East Prussian landscape. It made them a bit odd. Unbelievably flat and cold. Tatty towns teeming with Poles and Jews. Bored garrisons. The women became restless and the officers were ripe for mischief.' Montrouge's eye had a wary glint in it. 'Berlin and Potsdam were very different, of course. There was a hothouse atmosphere in Berlin and hints about unsavoury practices in the group round the Kaiser. The entire cavalry was supposed to be riddled with it – even the horses. Important men were accused of pederasty.'

Montrouge smiled disconcertingly. 'It all came out in a magazine article. There was a feeling that pacifists with strange morals were running the country's affairs and it was high time to get rid of them. The military commandant of Berlin, a general at court, and the colonel of the Garde de Corps were dismissed from the service. There was even a big court case because one of them was stupid enough to bring a libel action. He lost it and the Kaiser used it as an excuse to purge the military of what he called "moral impurities". It was quite farcical. You could see men shrinking before your very eyes. Especially when rankers were brought in to give evidence. Wilhelm replaced one man with another who dropped dead while dancing *Swan Lake* dressed in tights and tutu at a house party he was attending.'

'Were you there?'

'Half the Kaiser's entourage was there. Wilhelm was terrified. He bolted so suddenly his train caused disruption on the railways for days.'

'Why are you telling me all this?'

'So you'll know I was there. You seem to need convincing.' Was the old man inviting him to believe he *was* Redmond or exactly the opposite? Woodyatt offered his cigarette case. Montrouge accepted graciously and Woodyatt couldn't help feeling a touch of admiration for the way he remained so cool.

'Wilhelm should have put a stop to it long before he did,' Montrouge went on. 'But he was insecure. Always unsure of himself, in spite of all that bombast. He was always imagining plots against him. So much so, people thought he suffered from hallucinations. He was known as William the Witless.'

'Didn't Redmond ever wonder why he'd bothered to change sides?'

Montrouge was silent for a while, as though staring back into the past and not much liking what he saw. 'Perhaps he did wonder,' he agreed. 'Perhaps he did. It was a very disturbed period. It was perfect for diplomacy or for the operations of an astute Intelligence Service. The British could have detached Germany's allies. But they were abysmal. They preferred to behave like gentlemen and look the other way.'

The old man seemed unable to stop talking. Was it because he had spent too many years containing his opinions or was it in the way of a diversion to head off dangerous questions?

'Your opinion of the British in 1914 seems to agree with Redmond's. What about their allies? The Russians, for instance.'

'In those days everybody thought them mere sheep.'

'What about the French? Do you dislike them, too?'

Montrouge gestured. 'Look about you. What is there to make *anyone* like them?'

'Is there *anybody* you believe in?'

'I believe in myself,' Montrouge snapped.

Woodyatt decided he hadn't a scrap of charity in him anywhere. 'I met Gerrit,' he said abruptly, trying the name for size. 'Field Marshal Gerrit.'

Montrouge's interest was caught at once. 'Is he still alive?'

'Very much so. Did you know him?'

'Of him.'

'Ever meet him?'

'Once or twice. I was a translator at a Franco-British staff conference. Nice man.'

'He knew you well.'

'I wouldn't have thought he'd have noticed me – an unknown translator.'

'I mean, when you were Redmond.'

'I never was Redmond.' The words were snapped out irritably. Woodyatt paused. 'I also saw Varah,' he said quietly.

The old man's head jerked up. 'Sir Horace Varah?'

'You knew *him*, too? Were you in Burma?'

'I never met him,' Montrouge said coldly. 'I knew of his part in the affair, of course. A stupid man. It all appeared in the French and German papers of the period. It caused as much fuss as the Dreyfus affair.' Woodyatt felt that at last he had the old bastard uncomfortable and wriggling.

'I also talked to Witkins,' he said.

Montrouge eyed him warily. 'Witkins? Who's he?'

'Medical officer. The man who caught Redmond in flagrante.'

Montrouge raised his eyebrows. 'Was he? And the other man? Nicolson?'

'You knew Nicolson, too?'

'I never met any of them. I supposed all these people to be dead now.'

'*You're* not dead,' Woodyatt countered.

'No. I suppose they must have been about my age.'

'Witkins is a brigadier now.'

'He talked about the case to you?'

'Quite a lot.'

'I'm surprised any of them remember.'

'*You* remember. Witkins knew all the facts. And not just the facts – the appearance, the habits, of Redmond.'

'After all these years?'

Just as the interrogation seemed to be going well it was interrupted by the click of the door. As Dominique appeared, Woodyatt could almost feel the relief in the old man's manner. He pulled himself out of the chair at once and, taking her parcels, laid them on the table, taking a long time to arrange them carefully.

'Did you get everything you wanted?'

She nodded. She had also bought a newspaper which indicated the French were now hoping to organise a continuous front from the Somme to the Vosges.

'*Continuous front?*' Montrouge's lip curled. 'Do they think they can fight this war as they did in 1916?'

He picked up the newspaper. 'The United States Ambassador,' he observed, 'claims they've taken General Giraud prisoner.' He shrugged. 'They always take Giraud prisoner. They did last time. Nothing changes.'

Woodyatt suggested they eat out and Montrouge smiled his approval.

'There is a good restaurant on the corner,' he said cheerfully. 'I can recommend their veal in sherry. I don't often get out to eat these days. I'm a prisoner up here, you see.'

They took their aperitifs at a little bar along the road, sitting on the pavement in the heat of the evening. Paris was still not panicking, though a lot of people had left. But spring had come like a green mist in the trees, and the public gardens were full of primroses, primulas and violets. Women wore bright dresses and chic hats. People were drinking champagne as if they felt there wouldn't be many more opportunities, and all the bars and cafés seemed to have music. Outside one of them, Woodyatt ran into a Blenheim pilot and his observer who had been shot down and had slipped into Paris to try to find where their squadron had moved to. They weren't talking, just staring into the middle distance and gnawing match-sticks. The pilot told Woodyatt that Blenheims were flying coffins and that his squadron had lost twenty-four complete crews since the fighting had started.

He had somehow acquired a *London Evening News* and when he left he handed it to Woodyatt. From it, England seemed strangely normal and at peace. The British troops in the North were now being pushed up to the coast and it looked as though they were about to face another difficult period of Anglo-French relations. The chief bone of contention was Churchill's unwillingness to send more RAF fighters to France to save a situation that seemed to be already lost. The ill feeling had grown sharper as the BEF had begun to escape. The French had always been contemptuous of the British army. In Britain, people had been led to believe the BEF was a separate force and the British commander-in-chief a power in his own right. The French were only too well aware it was only a small portion of the whole and that the British commander didn't even answer directly to the French leader.

The newspaper seemed to have little to offer beyond cricket scores and scandals, but it was a relief to read something other than French cynicism. The French papers had been claiming bitterly for days that they had been let down. But while they were claiming the British were saying

'England first', they were only too obviously echoing them with '*La France d'abord*'. Calais appeared to be lost and the corridor between the northern and southern armies was now a hundred miles wide. With the best will in the world, Woodyatt couldn't see anyone plugging that gap.

The waiter was hovering nearby and Dominique settled for a sweet vermouth; Woodyatt for a whisky and water. He turned to Montrouge.

'I'll have a brandy,' he said.

It seemed a strange drink to start a meal, but then the old man touched the waiter's arm. 'With Perrier water,' he said. He looked at Woodyatt almost as if teasing him. 'Brandy and soda. *C'est bon pour les intestines.*'

The talk around them concerned the new Prime Minister. Reynaud was being derided for wanting to continue the war, and the King of the Belgians was considered pro-Hitler. 'It's his German blood,' a woman at a nearby table commented loudly.

'Perhaps he thinks France will quit, too,' her partner said. 'Well, won't we?'

The question brought silence. There were now two and a half million Belgian refugees and soldiers in France, and nobody knew how reliable they were. But a tremendous fight was being put up near Dunkirk, with the British and French navies working wonders. Woodyatt guessed his brother would be there and he listened for the answer.

It came slowly, doubtfully. 'We will if we feel we must. That's French democracy.'

The comment left Woodyatt in no mood to be friendly with either of his companions and it was Montrouge who kept the talk stuttering along.

'I hear the government's leaving Paris and going to Tours,' he said. He seemed to be enjoying the alarm and confusion around him. 'I shall go south.'

'What will you do for money?' Dominique asked.

'I shall be all right. I have money in Switzerland. I also have money in France. Come to that, in England, too.'

'Under what name?' Woodyatt asked sarcastically.

'That's my business.'

'And why England?'

The old man looked at him calmly. 'In case you've not noticed, England is cut off from Europe by the Channel. I saw how things were shaping. I saw it long before the politicians grasped it.'

'Perhaps in Germany you were well-placed to see what was coming,' Woodyatt suggested.

'Indeed.' Montrouge's smile was confident. 'It could be said to have been an advantage.'

The restaurant owner's wife, who had a son with the French army, was red-eyed with weeping and the woman at the next table was now talking of storing tinned meat, rusks and bottled fruit.

'Good God,' her companion said, 'you don't think there's going to be a siege?'

When they returned to the flat, Montrouge announced he was going to bed. 'I always retire early,' he said and disappeared without saying goodnight. But they could hear him moving about in his room for a long time afterwards and Woodyatt wondered what the hell he was up to.

There were a few minutes silence. Alone together, Woodyatt and the girl were both uncomfortable.

'I don't think he's the man you say he is,' Dominique said.

'Then why are you prepared to help me get him out of France?'

'He needs help,' she snapped. It seemed to worry her. 'Must we go?' she asked.

'Unless you want to be here to welcome the Germans.'

'*He'll* never go.'

'He might when he sees there's no alternative.'

'What will they do to him in England? Won't he be punished?'

'The police don't close their files on murders. If he *is* Redmond and Redmond is von Rothügel – and I intend to find out – then he could have been involved with the loss of thousands of lives in the last war. British *and* French.'

'But you have no proof.'

'I'm hoping he'll provide it.'

'He's always been kind to me.'

'Nothing more? Your aunt: she left him, didn't she? Have you ever wondered why? He claims it was incompatibility. What did *she* say?'

'She said there were others in his life.'

'What do you think she meant?'

'Other women, I suppose.'

'Did he ever make a pass at you.'

'Don't be silly. He's an old man.'

'You're a beautiful woman.' She blushed as he spoke. 'If he made passes at other women, did you never wonder why he didn't try it on with you?'

'No.'

'Did it never occur to you that the "others" your aunt referred to weren't women?'

'What else would they be?'

'Men. Young men.'

three

The arguing continued for the next few days: Woodyatt doggedly pursuing his theme; the old man dodging the answers; Dominique bitterly hostile again but still uncertain what to believe. Her common sense told her Woodyatt's guess was probably right but her loyalty was still to Montrouge. She simply didn't want to believe Woodyatt.

All the time, Woodyatt was trying to trick the old man into some sort of slip that would lead to a possible identification and eventually to a confession. But Montrouge was quick-witted and as slippery as an eel. He never gave the impression of deliberately avoiding questions but he always had answers and Woodyatt could only assume he'd been thinking about them for years. He kept him under continuous scrutiny, hoping something would identify him once and for all. He had seen him drink brandy and soda, but it seemed the only clue he was going to get. He had seen him touch his nose but the gesture could hardly have been described as the habit Sir Martin Gerrit had suggested. At times he seemed to limp. Perhaps it was nothing more than arthritis in an old man's joints. There was no sign of the scar on his jaw but after all this time it would have been very faint. And according to Brigadier Witkins, it had never been very big anyway, while any scar on his hand seemed to have faded into the folds and creases of old age.

By this time there were rumours that a new British army was gathering on the Somme and the eastern suburbs of Paris were enduring air raids. More and more people were leaving the city. There was talk of the government moving to Tours and the Paris banks were being evacuated. At the British Embassy Woodyatt was told the Banque de France had got rid of all its gold – a third to the United States, another third to London, and the rest to Bordeaux.

'At least,' Montrouge said, 'England will now have enough money to continue the war. The Dutch and the Belgians have also sent their gold to London.'

The news agencies had already gone to Tours and the Paris papers were predicting the arrival of the Germans within the week. The evacuation of the British and French forces in the North was going well, despite the loss in ships, but it was clearly now beginning to grow difficult. Marseilles had been bombed and an aircraft which had been shot down had landed on the gasworks and caused a tremendous explosion.

'Typical of the Marseillais to overdo things,' Montrouge said with grim sarcasm.

By this time everybody was wondering why Paris wasn't being systematically bombed. Was it because the Germans wanted the city intact for a victory march through its streets?

'They did it in 1871,' Dominique said bitterly. 'They're obviously going to do it again.'

The waitress at the restaurant where they ate said leaflets had been picked up indicating that the Germans intended to dance in the streets on Bastille Day. Meanwhile the politicians continued to squabble, blaming each other and getting nowhere. The latest joke was that, in addition to storing tinned food, you should store chewing gum because, if you were shot up while fleeing the city, you could plug the holes in the petrol tank with it and also use it to stop your teeth chattering.

As the ships vanished from Dunkirk and the North fell silent, everybody expected the Germans to push for Rouen and Reims to isolate Paris. To Woodyatt it didn't seem to matter which way they did it. They were quite clearly expecting the capital to drop into their laps like a ripe plum.

He was growing worried about his attempts to persuade Montrouge to leave. He couldn't drag him, tied hand and foot, to the car. And he still hadn't enough definite proof to demand the help Pullinger had offered. He would look a fool arriving in London with some angry old man who turned out to be someone else entirely. Yet he dare not leave him in Paris. Having found him, he daren't leave him anywhere.

The newspapers were now reporting that the Germans were advancing up the Seine. Shops and restaurants were boarded up and the streets were deserted except for an occasional overladen motor car. The air was always full of the smell of burning and the city seemed to tremble to the rumble of the gunfire.

'We must leave soon,' Woodyatt told Dominique. 'Can you get him to pack something? Tell him we're just looking for a safer area.'

He decided to try the Embassy for news. More soldiers had arrived in trains from the North and the East and it was hard to get past. Outside the Embassy were a few British soldiers and airmen who had been cut off from their units and were trying to get information on where to go. The entrance hall was full of shouting, arguing people, many of them British civilian residents of Paris who were demanding safe passages home.

Woodyatt spent a good quarter of an hour moving among them, trying to find someone who could give him a sound appreciation of the situation. Eventually, someone remembered having heard his name and it appeared there was a message for him from Pullinger. It was a long letter. It had been addressed to army headquarters and forwarded to the Embassy. It informed him that a German refugee called

Ketscher had been found who could confirm Redmond's identity.

'General Dornberger, head of German rocket plans,' it continued, 'was a friend at one time of von Rothügel. Dornberger is the leading German authority on long range ballistic missiles. We have also learned that Hermann Oberth, who proposed liquid fuel for rocket propulsion, is a Saxon and is believed to come from Meissen – which is no more than ten miles from Dresden where Rothügel is known to have lived. They also might well have known each other.'

The letter also indicated that Pullinger was still worried by the presence of a German agent in the top echelons of the civil service. 'We discover now it's been going on since 1925,' he wrote. 'It's almost certain he was in contact with your man, because von Rothegel was running the British section of German Intelligence up to 1927. We *must* have him. When do you want us to lay on an escort?'

It was possible to telephone. 'No more than two minutes,' Woodyatt was told. 'After that you'll have to use the telegraph. We've been ordered to keep the line open for diplomatic sources.'

Pullinger sounded excited. 'Look,' he said. 'Camorgis has it on reliable authority that "Charlie", whoever he is, will be one of the people the Germans will use if it comes to peace talks.'

'Do you think peace talks are likely?'

'After what's happened, Hitler's doubtless got contingency plans.'

'Then you'd better check all those civil-service types who're likely to be put forward to handle the business.'

'We can hardly do that if peace talks don't take place.' Pullinger sounded irritated. 'Churchill won't even listen to the idea. So we must know this bloody "Charlie's" real name. *Now*. It could take us weeks to find him and he could do a lot of damage in that time. The situation's very delicate.'

'Do you imagine I don't know?'

'Where's Redmond now?'

'Here in Paris.'

'Have you talked to him?'

'Of course. But he isn't exactly talking to me.'

'See that he does and – '

The line was cut off in the middle of Pullinger's sentence. Woodyatt smiled grimly, guessing that Pullinger would be seething.

The Embassy had little time to spare for what seemed a wild-goose chase. They were busy evacuating documents and staff. Woodyatt tried to dispatch a telegram to Pullinger giving a few details but every wire, every radio, every telephone was red-hot with messages to and from London. In the end, he sent a message by ordinary telegram via Malta. It cost him a fortune.

He finally managed to get an interview with the ambassador. He looked worn out and desperate, but treated Woodyatt politely, and money was advanced when Woodyatt produced the letters he had been given. Pullinger had been right. Though some of the men who had signed the papers were no longer part of the British government, their names still carried weight.

'I don't suppose,' the ambassador said, 'that you'll get any reply to your message. I can't see how it'll reach you. We're leaving. This city's gone mad and nobody's doing their job.'

He introduced Woodyatt to one of the under-secretaries, a man about his own age called Lord, and informed him that anything he needed would be supplied.

'Provided,' the ambassador said with a tired smile, 'that it's still possible to supply it.'

By this time the Germans had smashed all semblance of a French line and had fanned out behind on either side. Tanks roamed freely around the countryside and the huge French armies were crumbling into chaos.

As Woodyatt left the Embassy, Paris looked lovelier than ever. The evening sky was pale green and orange over St Germain des Prés and the place was calm and still. The streets were shadowed and empty-looking, though there were cars parked near doorways and people kept appearing with packages and suitcases.

A few policemen lurked at alley ends, alert for fifth columnists spreading defeatism. There had been a lot of bold talk from the French government and an announcement: '*Pas de rupture de front, nous avons tenu, malgré l'infiltration entre les points d'appui.*' There had been no break in the front. They had held on, despite the infiltration between strong points. They were still fantasising about a new offensive, believing the line Weygand was said to have formed would hold. Woodyatt didn't swallow a word of it and it was obvious nobody else did either. Why was there to be a big prayer meeting at the Sacré Coeur if people weren't hoping for a miracle?

The old man had gone to bed when he returned to 81, Rue de Vanves.

'He insists he won't leave,' Dominique said. 'He says that when he goes, he'll go on his own and in his own good time.'

She was on the verge of tears. As Woodyatt touched her shoulder, she looked up at him with such despair he automatically put his arms round her and she leaned wearily against him.

'He's the only person I have.' The words came out in a sort of sigh.

Then, as though ashamed of her show of weakness, she snapped upright again and pushed him away. 'I'll try again tomorrow,' she said.

Montrouge stayed in bed late the following morning. Woodyatt thought it was a deliberate ploy to avoid questions. Dominique took him coffee and through the closed door Woodyatt could hear her talking to him.

During the afternoon, she said she had managed to prevail on the old man to allow her to pack a few clothes for him.

'He put other things in, too,' she said. 'And he locked the case. I think they were chiefly papers.'

Woodyatt had just crammed the cases into the back of the car and locked it in one of the garages which occupied the ground floor round the courtyard when the sirens went.

'*Casques et masques!*' The concierge scuttled out, wearing a helmet and yelling for everyone to have their gasmasks ready.

They struggled to get Montrouge to the air-raid shelter. It was only at the end of the street but he was slow and insisted on putting on a long overcoat that came down to his ankles.

'Shelters are cold,' he insisted. 'Besides, what does it matter? I'm too old to worry what happens to me.'

There was a sustained burst of anti-aircraft fire and they could hear the shell fragments tinkling to the road. When the 'All Clear' sounded they saw smoke rising near the Pont Mirabeau and someone said the Germans had hit the Citroën works and a block of flats near the bridge. On his way to the Embassy to find out if there had been any answer to his message, Woodyatt saw a bombed house – its outer wall gone, it was just a mountain of debris in the street with curtains and bedclothes flapping. It looked like a giant doll's house with the front open.

He had decided to give Montrouge another two days then drag him to the car and leave whether he liked it or not. Though the Channel ports were all closed by this time, ships were still leaving for England from St Nazaire and Bordeaux.

The French were clearly giving up. Despite the big talk from the politicians and generals, morale had disintegrated.

There was even outrage among the working class of Paris who had been told that if they abandoned the city they could be regarded as deserters. Having watched the wealthy leaving in droves, it was something they weren't prepared to accept.

There was a tremendous battle going on in the North. Weygand had announced that two thousand tanks had been thrown forward to defeat the Germans.

'It will come to nothing,' Montrouge said flatly and for once Woodyatt believed him.

The local restaurant was crowded, as if those who remained in the neighbourhood were determined to get the last out of the dying city. They had reached their sweet course when the air-raid siren went again and the proprietor appeared, waving his arms.

'The cellar,' he said, indicating a door behind the bar. 'We have wine. We shall not be unhappy.'

They pushed down the stairs to a dusty vaulted room which contained dozens of bottles and there they sat in silence, feeling the earth shake as the bombs exploded. The proprietor offered free wine but it was of poor quality, and he noticeably didn't forget to collect the price of the meals that had been eaten upstairs. Sitting in the gloom, Woodyatt wondered what had happened to Nicole. By this time she was probably in Hyères. Poor Nicole! Her husband was probably fleeing for his life. Or captured. Or dead even.

It was nearly midnight when the 'All Clear' went. Montrouge had fallen asleep and for a moment Woodyatt envied him. Age had its advantages.

As the siren died away, there was one last explosion. It was big and it sounded close. Somebody laughed and suggested that the Germans knew where they were. Pushing Montrouge up the stairs, they headed into the street. In the darkness the smell of smoke was strong and the *sapeurs-pompiers* were rushing past with their fire engines.

The Rue de Vanves was barricaded against the public and Woodyatt was horrified to see that Number 81 had cascaded into a pile of bricks, timbers, slates and glass. The front of the building had collapsed and curtains were flapping in the breeze. A piano rested among the rubble, and the rescue workers were just carrying a body away on a stretcher.

'Holy Mother of God,' Dominique whispered, crossing herself.

Montrouge stared at the wreckage almost as if it didn't concern him. Woodyatt edged forward. The garages had the whole weight of the building on top of them. The doors had burst outwards in splintered planks and he could just see their car under tons of rubble.

'Was this the last?' he asked one of the fireman.

'Sure.' The fireman was heaving at a piece of timber. 'Delayed action. Must have been half an hour after they'd gone.'

'Was it definitely a bomb?'

'It wasn't a firework.'

'An aerial bomb?'

'What other kind would it be?'

'If the Germans can drop parachutists dressed as nuns, they can plant bombs. To make people clear out.'

A school down the street had been opened as a shelter and they led the old man there. He sat in silence, clutching his stick, staring ahead, deep in thought.

As daylight came, they heard over the wireless that the battle in the North had reached a critical stage. The enemy was near the Marne and pushing towards Pontoise. Gunfire could be heard already.

Paris remained strangely calm, although hundreds of luggage-laden cars left for the South during the day and, in the evening, the streets were deserted except for the armed guards on government buildings and metro stations. The scent of resin and the smell of burning trees filled the air as if the woods to the North were on fire.

Wondering if it would be possible to leave by rail, Woodyatt tried the Gare de Lyon but it was surrounded by a yelling mob of people all fighting to get in. The interior was packed, the crowds outside sitting on the pavement. The smell was disgusting. Babies screamed and old people sat with their heads bowed wearily. Among the seething mass the police were growing desperate. There was no food and no milk, and the people who had been there all night were demanding that the neighbouring shops should be forced to open. The sick were stretched on luggage trolleys with a few Sisters of Charity trying to help them, their faces moist in the humid air.

The Gare d'Austerlitz was the same and more families were still arriving. One woman appeared with five trunks, three suitcases, two hatboxes and a pug dog, and immediately became stuck. Dumped down by a taxi, she couldn't get on a train, but she couldn't move her luggage on her own, and dared not leave it because the Paris underworld was taking full advantage of the confusion.

Even as Woodyatt watched, a ferret of a man in a muffler snatched one of her cases. She screamed and in a moment the whole area was involved in a noisy scuffle. Police whistles screeched and two men in uniform appeared, swinging lead-lined capes to clear a path. For no good reason fists began to fly and the shouting increased as the mob of people surged backwards and forwards. Struggling to get clear, Woodyatt found himself face to face with the man who had started it all. He was carrying the case he had stolen.

'That's the man,' Woodyatt said, closing in on him. A knife appeared and, without thinking, Woodyatt swung his fist and the man went down.

As the police came up, full of congratulations, Woodyatt could only feel surprise. He had never considered himself a man of action.

The police were pleased and escorted him with the thief to an office in the forecourt of the station. He was questioned and then allowed to go. Free from the crowd, he managed to get inside the station by climbing a gate. A harassed official told him the lines were constantly being bombed. As a result there was no timetable and, anyway, there wasn't an inch of room on the trains. With escape by rail clearly out of the question, Woodyatt began to try garages in the hope of hiring or even buying a car. But nothing that would move was available.

In desperation, he headed back to the Embassy, where he found the staff on the point of leaving. He dragged Lord, the man who had been directed to help him, from a huddle of minor officials who were burning documents and told him he had to find him a car.

Lord gave a shrill laugh. 'There isn't a car in Paris that hasn't been commandeered or reserved!'

Woodyatt flourished Pullinger's papers. 'I need a car and a tank full of petrol.'

'Good God, man, what do you take me for?'

Woodyatt ignored the bleat of protest. 'I'll be back for it tomorrow,' he said.

Heading for the shelter, he passed the wreckage of 81, Rue de Vanves. The flames had been put out and the firemen were clambering about the ruins. They had cleared the garage sufficiently for him to reclaim the battered suitcases and as he did so, the fireman he had spoken to the day before grinned at him.

'You were right,' he said. 'This bomb didn't come from up there.' He jerked his thumb at the sky. 'It was left in a suitcase in the hall. We found a battery. The *salauds*. Who were they after? You?'

four

The knowledge that they were still being followed made up Woodyatt's mind. He had hoped they would be able to lose themselves in Paris with its thousands of inhabitants and crowds of refugees. Even the hordes of defeated soldiery pouring into the capital ought to have been a screen and it came as a shock that somehow Zamerski had managed to find them. This and the nearness of the Germans meant it was time to move on. And quickly.

'We leave tomorrow,' Woodyatt announced. 'Whether he likes it or not.'

Dominique managed a twisted smile. 'There'll be no trouble,' she said. 'He'll come.'

'What changed his mind?'

She shrugged, 'He wouldn't say.'

They spent a restless night in the shelter. The old man's explanation of his change of heart was brisk and uninformative. 'I've seen war before,' he said. 'It includes lice, socks rotting on your feet, the stink of your own body.'

Woodyatt smiled. 'And where did *you* experience these discomforts?' he asked. 'You weren't in the last war.'

Montrouge didn't answer and sat back in his chair, his head down, his hat over his eyes, clutching his walking stick. Woodyatt lay on the bare floor. Dominique slept beside him on a thin mattress that had been found for her. During the night Woodyatt woke to find her staring at him, and he put out his hand and touched her fingers.

161

'We'll be all right,' he said.

She showed no sign of having heard.

When it was daylight, they rose, sharing the shelter's meagre facilities to clean themselves up, then Woodyatt set off for the Embassy.

On the way he saw diplomatic cars leaving with armed militia on their running boards. One or two cafés were operating and he saw a bar left unlocked, its till wide open and ransacked.

The ambassador had already left for the South and Lord was about to follow. 'No point in staying any longer,' he said.

He fished in his pocket and produced a bunch of keys and the rotor arm from a car's distributor. 'There you are,' he said. 'It's outside. You can't mistake it. It's red with a Dijon number. Belonged to one of the secretaries who's gone to England.'

'What about petrol?'

'Full. Two full cans in the boot.'

'Thank you. Is there any news?'

'Nothing much. I'm off soon. I don't fancy clerking for a set of bloody Nazis. I didn't fancy clerking anyway. I think I'll join the army.'

Parking the car outside the shelter, Woodyatt went in search of Dominique. The old man still sat with his hat over his eyes, hiding his face, and she was bent over him, talking softly to him.

'I've got a car,' Woodyatt said.

'I think we should get him into it,' she whispered back.

'And go at once. A man came, enquiring for him. He was tall and thin. He had a mean face.'

'Go on.'

'I said nothing. I noticed also that my uncle – my –' she hesitated ' – that Monsieur Montrouge said nothing. Why should he do that? The man was asking for a Monsieur

Montrouge and if he is Monsieur Montrouge, why didn't he say so?'

'What did he tell you?'

'He tells me nothing. He just accepts that someone's out to destroy him. That's all he'll say.'

'Tell him we're going somewhere safe.'

'How long will it take?'

'We'll go in easy stages. I have to get him back in one piece, not kill him with exhaustion. To St Nazaire – two days. We could stop one night. If that's no good, we could try Bordeaux. That might take more. Three.'

It was stiflingly hot as she slipped across the road to the church opposite. Woodyatt didn't bother to protest. She didn't take so long this time and they pushed the old man into the car and tucked him down in the front seat, his hat still jammed down on his head. The boot could take only the two suitcases and they had to put Woodyatt's hold-all on the rear seat with Dominique. People were wandering about the streets as they left, as if they didn't know what to do. They even passed a cinema with a small queue outside. What sort of people were these, Woodyatt wondered, who could go and watch a film when the world was falling apart about their ears?

In the Boulevard Montparnasse near to the station they ran into a fresh mass of troops. They had just arrived. Ragged, tired and dirty, they were the demoralised remnants of a routed army, drifting into Paris and wandering about aimlessly.

This time they weren't in ones and twos and small groups. They were a great mass, as if half a dozen fully loaded trains had arrived and disgorged their shabby passengers on to the Paris streets. In their ill-fitting uniforms, packs slung anyhow on their shoulders, unarmed except for the long ugly bayonets at their hips, they spilled over into bars, noisy, argumentative and aggressive. They didn't know where to go and there was no one to tell them. The pavement was littered with wine bottles, cigarette ends and discarded steel helmets. Some of them were staggering about drunkenly, shouting anti-war slogans.

For a long time the three occupants of the car sat watching them stream past. It was as though the whole French army had suddenly been flung down around them. Then Dominique spoke, 'Why doesn't someone tell them what to do?' she asked.

Up ahead, the infuriated and defeated men found a car containing three officers. They started rocking it from side to side on its springs. As it went over there was a huge shout like the baying of hounds after a quarry and the officers could be seen running away, hatless and with blood on their faces. The car was set on fire and the whole area was filled with the stink of burning rubber amid clouds of black smoke and smuts.

Eventually men of the Paris garrison arrived, fully armed and properly led, and the defeated men, still arguing, singing and shouting slogans, were formed up and marched off. One of them had made a banner out of a sheet and it was held up at the head of the column. '*A bas la guerre!*' it announced, and there were cheers, jeers, and cries of disgust and hatred for the politicians, the generals and the wealthy Parisians they seemed to consider the cause of their wretchedness.

Dusk was falling as the street was finally cleared and Woodyatt's party was able to continue. They drove along the Boulevard Lefebvre. At every petrol pump there were queues of cars trying to fill up. At one they were obliged to stop because of the jam caused by drivers trying to get in. An argument was going on between one of them and the owner who wore his arm in a sling and was yelling a protest. 'I can't do any more,' he was insisting. 'I've been pumping for three days solid and my arm's buggered.'

The sky was blood-red with the sunset but a black fog draped the city. Someone said it was the smoke screen the Germans had put up for the crossing of the Seine. Someone else claimed it was from the oil dumps that had been set on fire. Smuts drifted everywhere, blackening clothes and faces.

'Where are we going now?' Montrouge demanded as they set off again.

'Never mind,' Dominique soothed. 'We're only finding shelter. The Germans will be here soon.'

There had been an accident at the Porte de Versailles and traffic was being diverted via St Cloud. It was pitch-dark by the time they were back on the Versailles road and they could still hear the guns behind them. As they turned a corner, there was a panicky shout to extinguish the head lights.

At Versailles, the traffic jam was unbelievable, the stream of vehicles heading west and south was held up by military police near the statue of Louis XIV outside the great chateau. They could only sit in the car and wait. All they could see were a few lights but they could hear shouts and the rumbling of engines. The word was passed down eventually that an endless column of army vehicles was crossing their path. They had already discovered that when two convoys met, the one that took precedence was the one commanded by the officer with the loudest voice and the biggest selection of expletives. Woodyatt began to see that his estimate of the time it would take to reach safety was wildly inaccurate.

Even when the military vehicles had gone, they managed to move only in jolts and jerks a yard or two at a time. In front of them was a car loaded with a mattress that had two bicycles lashed on top. There had been some bombing near Auffargis and a crater in the road was being repaired, so that they all had to sit and wait, listening to the croaking of frogs in the marshy land to the right.

Eventually they started off again and, finding a side road he knew, Woodyatt turned into it. It was empty and they made good time. But they were all tired. Indeed Montrouge had been dozing gently ever since they'd left, head down, as silent and still as if he were dead. They decided to pull off the tarmac and try to sleep for a while. The old man was sprawled against the door in the front seat, huddled deep in his overcoat. Woodyatt climbed out and he and Dominique sat at opposite ends of the rear seat, trying to make themselves comfortable in the corners.

When Woodyatt woke he was surprised to find Dominique's head on his shoulder and his arm round her. He couldn't remember moving during the night and could only assume they had moved nearer to each other for warmth.

What had been a deserted road when they arrived had filled up during the night. The area under the trees was full of cars. Nearby a policeman was moving along, waking the drivers.

'Move on,' he was saying. 'We don't want cars bunched together. The German planes will spot them.'

At the car behind he stopped. 'Montrouge?' he was saying. 'Is your name Montrouge?'

Woodyatt's eyes met Dominique's and, as the policeman appeared alongside, they sat up. 'There's a type back there looking for his father,' the policeman said. 'He's old and wandered off during the night. Name of Montrouge.' He studied the still figure of the old man slumped in the front seat. 'How about him?'

'We'd hardly be likely to have someone else's father sleeping in our car, would we?' Dominique said spiritedly. 'That's my uncle. His name's Vassin.'

The policeman shrugged. 'Sorry to trouble you, Madame, but some funny things are happening at the moment. All sorts of people are travelling in other people's cars.'

The threat was still there. Woodyatt had thought they'd thrown off their pursuers but clearly not. Moreover they were obviously ruthless and would stop at nothing. He needed to put as much distance between themselves and Paris as he could.

As Woodyatt put the car in gear, Montrouge lifted his hat from his eyes. 'I am nobody's father,' he muttered. 'So it can't be me he's seeking.'

Although the red Renault looked dashing, it was under-powered and old, and they made poor time. The road was seething with vehicles, tearing past them, at times two abreast.

An empty train rattled by on the line to Paris, watched by people wheeling bicycles and trying to balance them with the heavy bundles of their possessions. Occasionally they came across a sad procession of villagers from the area around: children driving goats; a grandfather leading a horse dragging a wagon filled with chairs, tables, wardrobes, mattresses; women and babies, some grim-faced, some weeping.

Reaching a small town where they heard the station restaurant was open, they decided to eat breakfast there. But the station was filled with people, most of them country dwellers in their best black suits and Sunday dresses. Little girls with ribbons in their hair as though they were going to a festival sat on piles of luggage which cluttered the entrance. Many of the would-be passengers were on the wrong platform, oblivious to the fact that any train they boarded would take them north towards the front. The station-master was at his wits' end.

'The Germans are nowhere near,' he said. 'The panic's being caused by fifth columnists.'

The restaurant had been closed because of the crowds and as they returned to the car they passed an engine hissing and puffing quietly in a siding. The station-master was tramping up and down the platform. 'There are to be no more trains today,' he was yelling. 'It's not my fault. I've got my orders. Military expediencies demand – '

His voice was drowned as a train howled past. Through the windows they caught glimpses of uniforms and crested steel helmets. At the end were flat cars loaded with the massive bulk of tanks.

They had to walk some distance and cross the track by scrambling down an embankment, Woodyatt and Dominique helping Montrouge. The crowd outside had grown enormously and were baying like animals. In the middle of them, by the wall of the Maine, was a man whose face was covered with blood. They could see fists and sticks rising and falling.

'The bastard was posting a notice advising people to leave because the Germans are about to arrive,' someone yelled. 'It's untrue! They're nowhere about!'

But the damage was done and the exodus had already started. Vehicles were on the move, adding to the confusion caused by the stream of traffic heading west and south. Among them, pedestrians who had walked miles to reach safety pushed past, indicating their bleeding feet and trying to beg lifts.

Woodyatt and his passengers managed to edge their way from the town centre only to be halted at the next crossroads. An NCO of the armée de l'air, clean and alert-looking, was sitting astride a motor cycle waiting for a chance to join the traffic. As they watched, a fat and self-important policeman strode up to him.

'Vos papiers,' he demanded.

The airman looked up. 'I'm on duty.'

'Vos papiers. How otherwise do I know you're not a deserter?'

'I'm on duty, I tell you!'

The airman was indignant but his indignation only made the policeman more stubborn. 'You could be a German parachutist in disguise. How do I know you're not?'

The shouting brought several other policemen to the scene and the airman was surrounded. The motor cycle went over with a crash, the rider under it. He was dragged out, spitting with fury, but the policemen were impervious to his yells of protest and he was hauled off, limping heavily. Woodyatt saw him struck in the face and, as he vanished, a soldier with an unshaven chin and dirty uniform, who might well have been a real deserter, hoisted the motor cycle to its wheels, sat astride it and started the engine. Giving a quick look around, he let in the clutch and disappeared at speed. The policemen dragging away their suspected parachutist didn't even notice.

The incident was symptomatic of the general panic, suspicion and confusion. France had gone mad, and, glancing at Dominique, Woodyatt saw she had tears in her eyes.

Both sides of the street out of the town were crammed with parked cars and vans. Restive horses snorted and stamped in the shafts of carts and traps which the owners were trying to load. The through-traffic slowed to a crawl and Woodyatt decided they had better lay down emergency supplies of food.

They were able to buy three gristly steaks, one or two tins and a bottle of wine but there was no bread. But then they heard word of a baker down a side street and decided to give him a try.

'Non!' the baker yelled furiously, waving his arms at Woodyatt. 'It's all for the army!' He indicated soldiers in a lorry waiting outside. Even as he spoke, a big Citroën carrying a Red Cross flag drew up and two men climbed out.

They were British residents in France who, because they were above military age, had volunteered to work for the

Red Cross. They wore regulation French uniforms and the Citroën they drove had been presented by Persil, Ltd, and was fitted to take stretchers.

As Woodyatt argued his case the air-raid siren sounded and the lorry containing the soldiers vanished abruptly. The baker was immediately behind it.

When the wail of the siren died there was a tremendous bang that shook the building and brought bottles down from a shelf behind the counter. The sound of tinkling glass and running from outside was followed by the appearance of a huge cloud of black smoke mushrooming into the sky beyond the nearby buildings.

The two ambulance drivers looked at Woodyatt. 'I think we should serve ourselves, don't you?' one of them said and began to pull loaves from the oven.

As he was doing so, an old woman appeared in the doorway. She had obviously been on her way to collect bread and she was white with plaster dust, as if a ceiling had collapsed on her.

'There you are, Madame,' the ambulance driver said, handing her a loaf. 'With the compliments of the management. Take care. It's hot.'

She stared at him, bewildered, then she shoved the loaf into her bag and vanished at speed.

Flinging a loaf to Woodyatt, the ambulance men threw down a few francs as payment, and vanished, their arms full of bread. Woodyatt did the same and shot after them, tossing the hot loaf from hand to hand as he ran.

The explosion could not have been a bomb because by the time he came in sight of the car the 'All Clear' had gone. The air was full of whirling dust, and a worried Dominique was waiting on a corner where she could see both the bakery and the car.

She indicated the loaf he carried. 'I bet that was expensive under the circumstances,' she said.

'On the contrary. It was very cheap. I stole it.'

Grabbing her hand, he swung her round. The old woman, still white with plaster dust, passed them and she turned and grinned conspiratorially at them. They grinned back at her then started to run, hand in hand like children.

With the food they had managed to buy, they decided to eat a solid breakfast by the roadside and, finding a convenient place, stopped beneath the trees.

The old man looked with amusement at the three miserable steaks Woodyatt had managed to obtain. 'How do you propose to cook them, young man?' he asked.

For once, Woodyatt was ahead of him and had thought of that. With the tools from the car, he removed the grille from the front of the bonnet and, propping it up on stones, proceeded to build a fire under it with twigs which they collected. Despite the toughness, in the fresh air the meat tasted wonderful.

'Bravo, young man!' Montrouge enthused. 'What initiative. What knowledge of woodcraft. You would have learned this, I suppose, in Baden-Powell's Boy Scouts.' He pronounced it as *Bwa Scoo* in the French fashion. 'No doubt you were in his little army, training for soldiering as a boy. The man was an ass.'

'Did you know him?'

'Never met him in my life,' Montrouge said jauntily.

As they set off again, the traffic consisted mostly of small cars hung with pots, pans, even birdcages. If a car broke down the owners set up a temporary home in a field. Since they were all in second gear most of the time, petrol consumption was high. When the fuel ran out the cars were pushed into a ditch, their mattresses dangling from them like dead men hanging on barbed wire, and the occupants set off on foot. Occasionally they saw children and old people sitting in patient groups, waiting for families who had left them in search of food. In every village there were queues at the shops and at all the pumps and wells. But there was never any fuss, as if the people were already accepting the reality of France's defeat.

Many of the refugees had tried to save too much, even cumbersome bedsteads and grandfather clocks. There were dozens of overloaded vehicles which had capsized with smashed axles. Some had been pushed well aside to clear the road but nobody was willing to wait. As soon as the car stopped, the people from the vehicles behind climbed out, pushed it out of the way, climbed back to their seats and drove on. An old woman wearing sabots was dragging along a treadle sewing machine on wheels, with an ancient dog on top. Every car that passed had a head sticking out, yelling at her to get out of the way. She plodded on, deaf to the world.

One village was full of more gaping reservists in uniform. It was clear that the disciplined machinery of the army had broken down. The road was littered with discarded packs, greatcoats, mess tins, rifles, bandoliers. Abandoned military vehicles were stuck in the hedgerows, their tyres punctured, their radiators blackened. One was on fire and the branches around it were ablaze, too, and crackling like machine-gun fire.

'*Une sale guerre*,' the men were saying. '*Une saloperie de guerre!*'

Lost and bewildered, the soldiers watched their superiors abandoning them. As a car containing a handsome army officer and a smart woman approached, one pale young lad scooped up a handful of mud and flung it. It struck the officer on the cheek. He pretended it hadn't happened and drove on like a man in a trance. It seemed to set the soldiers going.

'Look at that!' the young soldier yelled. 'Off with his tart! They're all the same!'

There was the sound of breaking glass as a lunatic rampage was launched. Shop windows were broken and bottles were looted from the bars. The constant appearance of the wretched men involved was depressing. The children of a joyless era, victims of unemployment and the cynicism of ambitious politicians, they were creating havoc all over France.

At Rambouillet there was another traffic jam. Taxis were honking and a bus ahead was stuck, the driver shouting abuse at an army lorry with a high canvas canopy. A British military-police section was on duty, trying to sort out the vehicles and looking for British-owned cars. As Woodyatt drew to a stop, a Bren carrier driven by a bony red-faced man with a ginger moustache drew up alongside. He was displaying a Grenadier Guards badge on his cap, which he wore in the usual Guards' style over his nose.

'You!' One of the military policemen pointed at him. 'Get outa the fucking way!'

The Guardsman regarded him with a cold eye. 'I'll get outa the way when I feel like it,' he retorted. 'And I'll thank you not to swear at the fucking Brigade of Guards.'

The policeman grinned and there was a bark of laughter from Montrouge. Woodyatt looked quickly at him. It wasn't the sort of retort a civilian, or a Frenchman, or a German would appreciate, though a British serviceman of any rank or any age, certainly would.

Entering the town, they decided here was a chance to take a coffee to finish off their meal. The shops had all opened by this time but people were still standing at their doors and windows in their night clothes, bewildered by the endless procession of vehicles. There was an air of despairing irritation everywhere. This encompassed the waiters in the bars as well as the customers, and they had to wait for their coffee.

The roads were hot by the time they got away again and still jammed with traffic. The stink around them was of human sweat, petrol fumes and dust. People were sitting at the side of the road looking as if they would never get to their feet again. Montrouge said he needed to stretch his legs.

'I'm an old man,' he said briskly. 'Old men can't sit in the same position for long periods!'

As they stopped to let him get out, a lorry-load of girls who looked like factory workers went past, some of them singing, some weeping. Resuming their journey once again, they passed an aerodrome which had been flattened by bombers. The wooden hangars were still smouldering in a pall of blue smoke, and a Morane stood on its nose among the line of bomb craters. All they could see was a tangled mass of metal and there didn't seem to be an unbroken pane of glass for miles. Officers of the armée de l'air, often with their wives, were driving away: their aeroplanes following on enormous floats with petrol bowsers and lorry-loads of men. Woodyatt wondered why they weren't in the air.

After a while it started to rain and they put the hood up. In the next town awnings erected for market day were being used as shelters by exhausted refugees and a noisy war of words was going on between them and the stall-holders who were trying to get their goods on display.

Most of the shops were closed and long queues had formed outside any that were open. The interiors were packed with shouting, gesticulating people and by the time customers fought their way to the counter of their choice, there was often nothing left but tins of sardines. The shelves had been stripped bare. Down the street another crowd was hammering on the door of a baker's. The glass broke and a great whoop of triumph went up as the mob surged inside. The baker had not been working but the locals emerged with stale rolls and baguettes, cakes and tarts, and left the shop a wreck.

As Woodyatt restarted the car, babies seemed to be crying everywhere, but in the bars he could hear music and people laughing because they had been drinking on empty stomachs.

As they left, the route became easier, though here and there it was blocked by piles of stone as if they'd been dumped as barriers against tanks. As they approached Chartres, they passed a car parked at the side of the road. A tall, thin man leaning against it was watching the passing vehicles, examining each one closely, bending and peering inside as they passed.

'Is that the bastard who was working for Zamerski?' Woodyatt yelled.

It was too late. Dominique hadn't seen him. But she had noticed another man behind the wheel of the stationary car. He had been wiping the perspiration from his face and as his hat was in his hand, she had been able to notice that he was fair-haired – and pink-faced.

The bastards were right behind them, Woodyatt decided. He had little doubt that they had been spotted. He reacted in the only way possible: he crouched over the wheel and thrust his foot down on the accelerator.

They didn't stop for some time and ate a late lunch at a small hotel at a village just south of Chartres. The place stank of spilled beer, wine, dry rot and stale urine from a lavatory down the hall with a door that didn't close properly. Montrouge pushed his plate away.

'What dreadful chefs they have these days,' he said fretfully. 'Fit only to cook for Tartars.'

He appeared to be falling asleep at the table and Woodyatt was in a dilemma. Sleeping upright in a car was no way for a man of eighty to rest. He had to get him back to England but it wasn't in the plan to kill him in the process. They had to get a room for the night and, because of the crowds, early afternoon seemed a good time to start trying.

The hotel was full of people. At one table there were two men in city suits and stiff collars, even spats, sitting with a blonde woman loaded down with jewellery as if she were wearing all she possessed. There was something about them that indicated they were Paris gangsters with their moll, flushed out by the approach of the Germans and seeking their pickings in safer surroundings.

By the use of a large denomination note, Woodyatt managed to secure a room. It contained one bed and an armchair and they pushed the old man up the stairs. He still clutched his suitcase. Only once had Woodyatt seen it open and then, apart from a few clothes, he had noticed it seemed largely full of papers.

They had barely got Montrouge settled when the proprietor of the hotel appeared. 'I must ask you to move,' he said.

'We've only just arrived,' Dominique snapped.

'I must insist, nevertheless. The room was booked. My wife didn't realise. There is a room in the annexe you can have. This is for a sick man, so the doctor can come and go easily. He is a very important man. He's also a very old man.'

'So is our man,' Woodyatt said.

'This one is eighty.'

'So is ours.'

'If I may say so, Monsieur, my old man is a very old eighty. Yours is not.'

Montrouge had been listening with interest. Without help, he swung his legs off the bed. 'I will move,' he said. 'What does it matter whether I sleep here or down the garden? At my age it makes little difference.'

With promises from the proprietor to reduce the price, even to throw in a free meal, they trudged down the stairs again and down the length of a neglected garden. At the end was a building which looked as though it had once been a barn. Inside, it had been newly converted into a set of rooms and bathrooms.

Once again they got the old man established on the bed. He offered no thanks. The other room contained a narrow bed and Dominique looked enquiringly at Woodyatt.

'I'll sleep in the car,' he growled.

It was a lovely evening. There was a jade-green sky with a brush-stroke of pink across it, and for a while after dinner, they sat at a table outside and took Cognac with their coffee. Montrouge, Woodyatt noticed, drank the brandy with soda water. Inside the bar, the two men he had identified as Parisian gangsters were playing cards with the blonde woman and making a lot of noise.

Eventually, Montrouge said he was tired and they escorted him to his room in the annexe. There was a separate entrance to the garden at the back of the hotel and a patch of gravel where cars were parked.

Two or three white-painted iron tables and chairs were placed outside where people could eat their breakfast in summer, and Woodyatt sat drinking with Dominique until it grew dark. Every now and then they heard a rumble in the distance. At first they thought it was guns but decided in the end it was approaching thunder. It added an air of menace.

For a while they remained silent, then Woodyatt drew a deep breath. 'Have you made up your mind yet?' he asked.

'What about?'

'Our friend, Montrouge.'

'I think you are right. I don't know why but I think so. I have no proof, of course.'

'Neither,' Woodyatt said gloomily, 'have I. However, we're going via Angouleme to see someone who knows him better than I do. Someone who knew him in 1904 when it all happened. He was assistant military attaché at the Paris Embassy at the time.'

Dominique was silent for a while. 'Will he be able to identify him?'

'He says he will.'

'After all these years?'

'He says he'd be able to identify him even after a lifetime.'

'He sounds as though he doesn't like him.'

JOHN HARRIS

'I don't think he does. The affair did him a lot of harm.'

Dominique was already dressed when Woodyatt knocked on her door the following morning.

Next door, Montrouge was at the wash basin. 'I'm not ready,' he said. 'I like to be clean.'

'So did Gorgeous George.'

The old man's head came up quickly. 'Who did?'

'Gorgeous George. That's what they called Redmond. It was a joke when he was in South Africa.'

The old man laughed and went on with his ablutions. 'Still on about that, young man? You never give up, do you? You seem to have collected a great deal of frivolous information.' He studied the two of them cynically. 'Did you have a good night?'

'I slept in the car,' Woodyatt snapped.

The old man looked at Dominique. 'How very unenterprising,' he said. 'By the way, I left my razor in that room we quitted last night. I need it. You'd better get it for me.'

He was speaking to Woodyatt as if he were a batman. For a moment Woodyatt ignored the request then he decided he didn't want any delay and went in search of the razor.

When he reached the hotel the staff were busy with breakfast, for the most part hovering round the blonde woman and her companions. There was no sign of the proprietor or his wife and Woodyatt decided to take a chance. Mounting the stairs to the room they had briefly occupied, he knocked on the door.

There was no sound from inside and no answer to his knock and he decided the occupants were probably at breakfast. Cautiously he opened the door, ready to close it again if the occupant was asleep. What he saw sent him staggering back.

On the bed was the figure of an old man, smaller than Montrouge, shrivelled and thin. He was in pyjamas and his mouth was open, his eyes were staring, his face ghastly. He seemed to be red from the waist up, his features smeared, his white hair standing on end with dried blood. The whole bed seemed to be soaked with it and it had splashed on to the walls, the floor, even on to the ceiling. The clawing hands were crimson and there was a smeared hand print near the door. On the pale lino on the floor was the print of a shoe in crimson.

five

The traffic was still hurrying by on the road past the hotel as the police cars bumped on to the grass verge. The policemen immediately suspected Woodyatt.

'You were the one who found him?' they asked.

'Yes.'

'What were you doing there?'

He explained about the razor.

'He was killed with a razor. It's still there. Why didn't you call the proprietor?'

'He was nowhere to be seen.'

'Did *you* do it?'

Woodyatt was recovering a little by this time. 'If you looked, you'd see the blood's dry.'

'You could have done it last night. Are you a British officer?'

'Yes.'

'Why aren't you with your army, running away in the North?'

'I'm here because my duty brings me here.'

'Are you alone?'

'I'm travelling with two others.'

'Bring them here.'

Still shaken, Woodyatt explained to Dominique what had happened.

She looked shocked. 'Did they think it was Monsieur Montrouge they were killing?' she asked.

180

Woodyatt had no doubt of it.

When they reached the main building, the police were still busy and the owner was frantic with panic at the savagery of the murder. His wife was wailing and alongside her a girl with a maid's apron was weeping. The proprietor looked at Woodyatt reproachfully. 'It wasn't my fault,' he whimpered. 'There was no need for this.'

The police were surprised to find that Woodyatt's companions were civilians. 'Who are they?' they demanded.

Woodyatt explained that it was his job to get Montrouge to England and that Dominique was a nurse accompanying them.

'Why do they want him in England?'

'Because he's important.'

'There are too many important English to be got to safety while France is allowed to suffer. How do we know you're not a German agent?'

As they turned away, Woodyatt heard Montrouge's voice just behind him. 'I think, young man,' he observed quietly, 'that you are in a great deal of trouble.'

Woodyatt had little doubt that he was right but he was far less concerned by the policemen's attitude than by the knowledge that they had had a very narrow escape. Their pursuers were more than willing to murder and only by chance had Montrouge been saved. The one thing in his mind was that Zamerski, unaware of the mistaken identity, might feel his task had been accomplished and that from now on he would leave them alone. They needed to put a lot of distance behind them.

In the end, despite their early antagonism, the police soon realised that the smudged red footprint on the floor of the bedroom bore no relation to Woodyatt's shoe and they dropped their suspicions – even becoming friendly enough through their stiff officialdom to allow themselves to be questioned.

'They were after his money,' they said. 'It seems he owned a store in Paris and was on his way to Biarritz. He had a lot with him.'

Woodyatt and his companions were warned they would be questioned again but were allowed to have breakfast. He noticed that the blonde woman and the two men in the city suits and spats had disappeared.

Afterwards, like everybody else in the hotel, they were interrogated once more. This meant being herded into the bar with the proprietor, his family and staff, but the policemen didn't seem as concerned as they should have been and kept stopping to listen to the radio. France was falling to pieces about their ears and every few minutes some new disaster was announced. A thousand tragedies were being enacted round them. Frenchmen were still being killed in the North. The Germans were sweeping across the country. Among the hundreds moving along the roads, every minute brought some crisis or personal loss. It was impossible to stop the flood of refugees and any attempt to do so would have caused a riot. Without doubt the policemen's minds were on their own families.

As they sat waiting, Montrouge leaned towards Woodyatt. 'I think it would be wiser to leave,' he said quietly.

Woodyatt agreed with him.

'They have far weightier things on their minds. The murder of an old man in a hotel bedroom isn't of much moment just now.'

The number waiting for interrogation had dwindled considerably and it was obvious some people were slipping off quietly. As Woodyatt looked round for an unguarded exit, Montrouge's voice came again.

'There's a way out near the kitchen,' he murmured.

'How do you know?'

'My plumbing is not as young as it was. It leads me regularly to the lavatory. There's a door alongside that leads into the yard. From the yard you can get to the car.'

'Do you usually look for alternative exits to hotels?'

Montrouge smiled. 'Oh, always. When I was young there were women and the women had husbands.'

They slipped out while the policemen were drinking coffee offered by the proprietor. Pushing Montrouge into the car, Woodyatt set off in a hurry. Nobody tried to stop them.

It had been Woodyatt's intention to head for St Nazaire because he had heard that ships had appeared there to lift the British troops. But the owner of the petrol station where they stopped had placed a radio on the step of his office. He had it going at full blast so that people could know what was happening, and they learnt that the Germans had occupied Paris, and the wings of their army were now sweeping past on either side of the city – heading towards South Brittany.

There was no sign of military activity west of Chartres. The countryside looked normal: the only obtrusive note was struck by the abandoned cars stuck in the hedgerows, with the families who had been riding in them sitting hopelessly, devoid of energy, among their luggage.

The roads were still a tangle of vehicles. There were lorry loads of soldiers among them, who all seemed to have food while the civilians were going hungry. One or two of them showed compassion, and some loaves were given away with oil-stained hands. A big black car ahead of Woodyatt's was commandeered by military police and immediately filled with officers and driven south, leaving the owners standing by the roadside. It seemed a funny way to defend *La Patrie*.

As they halted to allow Montrouge to stretch his legs, a lorry-load of wounded appeared, their faces blank, their eyes dead. It was followed by another lorry full of young, untouched men which, as it edged past, was watched by people with bicycles, cars and horses.

One of the soldiers shouted from his perch on the side of the vehicle. 'Don't worry,' he yelled. ' The war's ending!'

'*Cochons!*' an old woman screamed back at him. '*Lâches!* You're a set of cowards. A bit of Nazi discipline would do you good.'

Eventually, they came up against a group of British soldiers brewing tea by the roadside. Approaching the officer, a young lieutenant who looked about sixteen, Woodyatt showed his papers and indicated Montrouge. 'I have to get him to England,' he said.

'Why?' The question was inevitable.

'He's a British agent.'

'He must be a hundred years old.'

Woodyatt agreed. 'Getting on that way. He has to be taken to England before the Germans come.'

The young lieutenant offered them tins of bully beef and meat and vegetables, and a paper bag full of tea and sugar. 'You'll have to milk a cow,' he pointed out. 'We did.' He also allowed Woodyatt a glance at his map. 'We're heading for Bordeaux,' he said. 'I've heard there are ships there to take people back to Blighty.'

'What about St Nazaire?'

'Nothing doing. Jerry's flattening it. They got the liner, *Lancastria*. Full of our people. Hell of a casualty list.'

Woodyatt drew a deep breath. 'I think I'll try Bordeaux, too,' he said.

Like every other town they had seen, Tours was full of people. They were sitting on the café terraces or standing in the bars as though they didn't know what to do. All the time more cars and lorries kept arriving, moving hopelessly among the little blue trams and the parked vehicles which were filled with sleeping people who had arrived ahead of them.

As the sleepers began to wake, they developed into the usual howling mob of desperate people ready to believe anything. When a *garde mobile* started shouting at a scruffy-looking soldier who was obviously a deserter trying to go home, the excited crowd joined in until the soldier took to his heels.

Woodyatt's party found a bar where, though meals were not served, it was possible for anyone who bought wine to sit at a long table in the garden to eat their own food. Montrouge was tired and said he hadn't slept at all the night before. Having heard him snoring, Woodyatt knew he had.

They decided to stop for the night but every hotel, every room, was full and, since it was too late to go any further, they agreed to sleep in the car.

Dominique was looking weary but the old man seemed to be taking everything remarkably well. Perhaps, Woodyatt decided, everything that happened to him simply went over his head, cushioned by his age.

Next day there suddenly seemed to be plenty of food and they found a restaurant where they ate good soup and *boeuf à la mode* with strawberries and cream to follow. It seemed weird that there should be so much available at a time when France was in a state of collapse.

Since the departure of the government from Paris, Tours had become the provisional capital and many of the people in the restaurants seemed to be politicians. With them were the inevitable squads of political journalists and, somehow, with their smart suits, they made it seem like a congress. The only discordant note was provided by the blonde woman and the city-suited, spatted pair they had seen at the hotel where the murder had taken place, and who were filling a table in the corner.

The food and wine seemed to have brought everyone back to life but then a shout rang out, '*Les canons!*' Over the buzz of conversation they heard the rumble of guns and all the lights went out. It didn't seem to damp the party spirit. The proprietor brought candles in bottles with a promptitude that suggested he had done it many times before.

The talk seemed entirely to concern what was happening in the North – '*Les Boches, sont-ils à Paris?*' – and there were gruesome stories of women and children trampled to death at the stations. The feeling was pessimistic, with curses for General Gamelin and the former premier, Daladier, and complaints about the '*massacre de la jeunesse française*'. Then someone said the Germans weren't wild beasts after all. It quietened the gloom and seemed to calm the fears, as if preparing them to sit back comfortably to accept the debacle.

Finding a side street, Woodyatt parked the car and, settling Montrouge in the rear seat, he and Dominique arranged themselves to sleep in the front. They talked for a while about the fighting, for once without stiffness or hostility. For the first time, Woodyatt was feeling safe from pursuers but he was still worried about what to do next in the situation that was developing. It was one which neither he nor Pullinger had envisaged. The new French Premier, Reynaud, had promised that whatever happened in France the fight would continue from the French colonies in North Africa. This could only mean that the Germans would push harder and deeper into France to prevent the escape of the French armies. Woodyatt could not afford to waste time and the burden of responsibility was heavy.

'Will England negotiate?' Dominique asked.

'Never.'

She was silent for a while and they could hear Montrouge's steady deep breathing. 'Will they follow us?' she said eventually.

'Probably not now they think they've removed our friend from the scene.'

She shuddered, sighed and, leaning against the side of the car, began to settle herself for sleep.

'You couldn't be much further away if you were sitting in the road,' Woodyatt commented.

'Would you like me nearer?' she asked.

'There'd be no harm in it.'

She gave him one of her unexpected smiles. 'I think you would like to seduce me.'

He laughed. 'It's an idea that commends itself. But not in the front seat of a car, with an old man snoring in the back.'

'Perhaps you are not going to seduce me after all,' she said. They struggled to make themselves comfortable. All Woodyatt could do was sit bolt upright and try to sleep with his head on his chest. The street was dark and still and when the air-raid alarm went neither of them showed any inclination to move.

'Do you want to find a shelter?' Woodyatt asked.

'No.' The answer was brisk and unequivocal.

'Good. Neither do I.'

The 'All Clear' went soon afterwards. At the other end of the seat, Woodyatt heard Dominique fidgeting to find comfort and became aware that the night was surprisingly chilly now the sun had gone.

'I'm cold,' he said.

There was no reply.

'Are you cold?'

'Yes.'

He reached out and pulled her to him. 'You'll be more comfortable and we shall both be warmer.'

Woodyatt awoke stiff and cold and with his arm numb. He had slept badly, his mind still filled with thoughts of the murder and the crimson memory of the old man at the hotel. For a moment he remained still, angrily wishing he had Pullinger alongside him to handle some of the responsibility and face some of the horror. Resentfully, unwillingly, he stirred. As he did so, Dominique sat up.

Her exhausted sleep had been blissful but it hadn't lasted long and she had wakened to find herself worried. About France. About the old man. Worried, too, at the back of her mind that, with his questions, Woodyatt had destroyed the warm feeling she had had for Montrouge. She had welcomed him into her life, delighted to have a family if only by marriage, but she was concerned now that her warmth had existed only because of her loneliness. She was worried, too, because she had begun to realise that Montrouge was selfish, sarcastic and by no means grateful. Woodyatt had tried hard to provide a degree of comfort, had never treated him as a prisoner, but had received nothing by way of thanks in return. For that matter, she realised with a feeling of guilt, he had received very little from herself.

Woodyatt studied her face. 'You've been crying.'

She shrugged. 'A little.' She gestured about her at the parked cars, the unshaven men and the unmade-up women stretching their limbs on the pavement. 'Wouldn't you? If this were *your* country.'

Woodyatt managed to buy a newspaper. The Germans were approaching Burgundy now and had reached Normandy and Brittany, and there was no longer any attempt to fight back.

They took breakfast at an open-air bar alongside what had become an office of the Ministry of Information. It had once been a post office and was situated in a shabby street which contained a square centred by a 1918 war memorial consisting of a naked girl wearing a helmet and carrying a sword. Next to it was a *pissoir*. It seemed somehow to reflect what had happened to France. The square was crowded with cars bearing Paris number plates.

Dominique found a tap in the yard of the bar where they could wash, and they joined a little queue of people trying to get at the water. As Woodyatt waited his turn, he was approached by a woman wearing a fur coat despite the heat.

'Can you drive, Monsieur?'

'Yes, Madame.'

'I can offer you a car if you would be prepared to drive me south.'

Woodyatt shrugged. 'I regret, Madame, I am already driving a car full of people.'

She seemed on the verge of tears. 'I have plenty of money,' she said. 'I would even pay you. I have a daughter in Marseilles. But I can't drive and my chauffeur has vanished.'

As she turned away, a French officer, young, smart and good-looking, stepped from the back of the queue. 'I can drive, Madame,' he said.

'You're an officer. Why are you not fighting?'

'I'm on sick leave, Madame. I'll help you.'

During this exchange Woodyatt saw a big black Ford go past; it contained two men in city suits and an unmistakable blonde. Then, as he returned to the Renault, a smart red Peugeot pulled out of one of the gateways down the street. It passed him, heading for the main road, and he saw the young officer at the wheel, the woman at his side. The officer looked as fit as a fiddle and it seemed to Woodyatt like a simple case of *sauve qui peut*. He wanted to weep.

Woodyatt had decided to try to avoid Poitiers, considering that the most direct route would be the one that everybody would use and that it would therefore not be the fastest. Now he decided, instead of using the main roads, to try to stick to side roads all the way. They left the town in a rabble of vehicles, trying to push past lorries, tanks and gun limbers which for a change seemed to be heading for the front. Red Cross vans passed them carrying not wounded, but men with rifles.

After a while they were forced back towards the main road by a diversion caused by bombing ahead of them. Passing through a village with a store, they stopped to buy cigarettes for the old man but the air-raid siren went and they were sent to a shelter. Woodyatt was worried the car would be stolen, but the air raid came nowhere near them and soon afterwards they were allowed to continue. They had only been moving again for half an hour when they passed through a small town that was totally deserted.

Nothing moved. The silence and the stillness were eerie. It was as if a sudden plague had removed every living soul. All doors were closed except for one or two which moved in the growing wind. Through them it was possible to see the undisturbed interiors, tables set, tablecloths rippling in the breeze, newspapers on chairs, their sheets flapping. It was as if some dreadful warning had arrived and the owners had dropped everything to run. It could only have been caused by fifth-columnist alarms because there didn't appear to be a German vehicle within miles.

Then they saw a hungry-looking dog slinking away and a cat sitting on a wall blinking in the sunshine. Their solitariness made the silence seem worse.

'Let's get away from here,' Dominique begged. 'It's frightening.'

As they turned away, they heard the grind of an engine and a British Bedford lorry appeared. It stopped alongside their car, bringing the dead village suddenly and frighteningly alive. The canvas cover was rolled back and they saw that the rear of the lorry was filled with the shining thin-skinned tins of petrol the British had been using. The bright idea of some economy-minded idiot in London, they were a cheap substitute for a solid petrol can and easily punctured, so that troops desperate for spare petrol had all too often found they had only half what they thought they had.

The lorry also contained half a dozen French soldiers. They were unshaven, pasty-looking, dirty and flabby, but they were all armed to the teeth – not only with rifles but also with revolvers.

'Hello, English,' one of them called across to Woodyatt. 'How do you like our lorry?'

It was a jeer and Woodyatt realised he would have to be careful with his reply or he would find himself on the wrong end of one of the rifles.

'That looks like British petrol,' he said.

'It is, English. But the British ran away and left it so we helped ourselves. It should be worth a bit on the black market, don't you think? Are you going to fight us for it?'

Woodyatt felt Dominique's fingers curl round his free hand and squeeze it tightly.

'Please,' she whispered. 'Let us go.'

'No,' he called to the Frenchman. 'Finders keepers. It's yours. I hope you enjoy it.'

'That's the reply we like, English,' the Frenchman said. 'After all, the English started the war, didn't they? I'm glad you don't want to start another.'

Woodyatt let in the clutch and the little Renault moved away, followed by laughter and jeers.

'They'd have shot us all if we'd stayed,' Dominique said.

'And –' the old man's voice came from the rear seat, full of amusement ' – doesn't he who runs away live to fight another day?'

They drove out of the village quickly. In the rear mirror Woodyatt saw the French soldiers had climbed down from the lorry and were kicking in the door of one of the houses.

As they reached the busy main road, above the hum of the traffic they heard the sound of aircraft. The shout went up at once – 'Les avions!' Immediately, the column of vehicles came to a stop, so suddenly Woodyatt almost ran into the car in front. A big pantechnicon behind stopped within an inch of the Renault's rear.

There were two minute specks in the sky then the noise of engines grew louder. People vanished from the road as if they had melted away, abandoning their vehicles to scatter into the fields, leaving the doors open and their possessions unguarded. Dominique began to bundle the old man out and, snatching the keys of the car, Woodyatt hurried to help her.

It wasn't easy to get an unwilling old man of eighty with nothing to lose to crouch down with them. As the aeroplanes appeared, a few vehicles were still moving and machine guns among the army lorries opened up. The planes were Me109s and they were flying along the column of vehicles, low down, just skimming the trees.

There was a crescendo of noise, a scream, then a crash and the sound of stones and dirt pattering down to echo the clatter of machine guns. The aeroplanes vanished as suddenly as they had come, leaving a cloud of smoke and the road littered with debris, earth, asphalt, a crumpled mattress, a charred pram. There was even a horse lying in the shafts of a cart, legs moving feebly, its stomach ripped open, its entrails steaming in the road. Woodyatt rose to a drifting grey fog of smoke, still with the feel of stones against his chest, his tongue on the grit in his mouth. Numbed and sickened, he and Dominique pushed Montrouge in front of them and installed him in his seat again as the column of traffic began to move off. Ahead, smoke was rising in the air and they could hear a high thin sound, like a dog howling, quite clearly over the noise of engines. Soon they had to skirt a crater in the road. Alongside it several cars were lying on their sides full of holes, but the moving column didn't attempt to stop. Among the wrecked vehicles was a red Peugeot. It was burning and standing nearby was a woman with blood on her face. She was staring at her red-stained hands and screaming in a harsh dry way that made the veins stand out on her neck.

It was the woman in the fur coat who had been trying to find a driver. The man lying dead in the driver's seat was the one she had found – the young officer – and his clothes were already on fire.

six

As they set off again, still shocked and weary of the mounting horror, the powerful limousines began to vanish. All that were left were the small cars, and at the side of the road, the broken-down and those out of petrol.

By this time people were growing used to the nomadic existence and were even greeting others they had seen on the road the day before. Woodyatt noticed the two evil-looking men in city suits and spats again, a family whose children pulled faces at him through the rear window of their car and an elderly lady, with a chauffeur, who offered a genteel wave. The same cyclists passed them again and again, nodding a greeting as they went by.

As they drove through the lovely Touraine countryside they were offered wine by farmers and shopkeepers at almost every village shop they entered.

'Help yourselves,' they were told. 'If you don't, the Germans will.'

Just ahead of them was another red Renault like their own whose driver gestured as if they belonged to a club established for wanderers. Now that they were away from the crowded roads round Paris, the shops were full of food. There were mountains of it: strawberries; cherries; peaches; tinned delicacies; sausages; chickens.

The news was as grey as the hazy clouds that covered the sun. A local newspaper informed them that the Cabinet had fallen and Daladier was back in office. As they stopped to stretch their limbs during the afternoon, Montrouge began to question where they were going.

'Are you attempting to take me to England, young man?' he said. 'I'm tired and if that's what you're up to, I can't resist you. I'm too old. But you are wasting your time. I have no secrets.'

Despite his protests, he remained remarkably alert. This, Woodyatt decided, was no frail old pensioner but a tough and resilient man with his wits about him.

'Is it your intention to go to Bordeaux?' Montrouge asked.

'Yes.' Woodyatt's reply was short and harsh.

'Then you're going the wrong way. This road leads towards Niort.'

'We're going to Niort. I have a friend near there and I want to make sure he's safe.'

Montrouge eyed Woodyatt warily, and Woodyatt caught a hint of concern in his face.

'I don't believe you,' he said. 'What a clever fellow you are and how well you manage to conceal the fact! I suspect you have a surprise up your sleeve.'

Again there was that amused glint in his eye, as if he believed he had Woodyatt's measure and was more than a match for him. The wish to catch him out was growing in Woodyatt into an obsession as powerful as Pullinger's.

The old man was studying him in that diverted way of his, as though they were all taking part in an entertaining game. 'You are wasting so much time, young man. Always you talk of pursuers. Where are these pursuers? I see no pursuers. I think we've lost them.'

During the afternoon, they were forced on to another diversion. The Germans were bombing the road ahead and the roundabout route took them over a long, narrow wooden bridge across a river. There was trepidation in every face as the column of traffic crawled along. The bridge had been bombed and looked none too safe and everybody was visualising a disaster.

Just in front of them was the lorry filled with British petrol and driven by deserters. The police were struggling to halt the flow of traffic and allowing no more than one car on to the bridge at a time. As a lorry passed across, the bridge could be heard creaking in the growing wind that came down the river. The drivers were obeying the police instructions minutely, keeping carefully to the left-hand side of the bridge away from the damage. Then as the air filled with the sound of aeroplanes in the distance the panic started again. More cars moved forward, their drivers ignoring the police.

From where they waited, Woodyatt saw a whole line of vehicles pushing on to the bridge. Then they heard a groan and a wail that was like a sob of despair as they saw the bridge lean slowly over to one side. Screaming women began to leap from their cars and run but the bridge leaned further and further until it finally collapsed into the river, carrying all its cargo into the water.

Dominique was first out of the Renault. Woodyatt was just behind her. Some of the lost vehicles were already submerged but a few people had managed to scramble clear and struggle to the bank. Rescuers were climbing down the steep slope to the river's edge and pulling the swimmers, and anything that floated, ashore.

Some of the dead were laid out on the steep muddy bank of the river in a row. There were two children among them and an old man shook a fist at the sky.

There wasn't much they could do but comfort the injured and the shocked. Someone had managed to find a telephone and ambulances began to arrive. As they screamed to a stop, Dominique dragged herself up the bank, her feet slipping on the mud the water from the rescuers' feet had created.

'It wasn't the Germans,' she said in a flat voice. 'It was simple panic.'

Returning to the car they found two men loading their luggage into it and about to drive away. As Woodyatt dragged them out, they turned on him, fists swinging. As it developed into a rough-house, Woodyatt was afraid that his uniform might cause him to be singled out and that other French people might join in against him. The nightmarish journey was producing a single-minded aggression all round: the need to survive. He was depressed by the continuing situation and angry at the French acceptance of things, and laid in with a will. He was eager to work off some of his animosity and floored one of the men with ease. As he looked round for the other, he saw him staggering away under a blow from one of his own dropped suitcases, snatched up by the handle and swung with all her strength by Dominique.

As the men stumbled to their feet and disappeared, Woodyatt put his arm round her shoulders and gave her a brief hug.

'Thank you,' he said.

Montrouge beamed benignly at them from the back of the car. He seemed quite unmoved by the disturbance. 'How touching,' he said. 'France to the rescue of Britain as usual.'

Woodyatt turned on him angrily. 'They'd have taken you with them,' he snapped.

'I doubt it.'

'They'd have dumped you round the first corner.'

Montrouge's smile didn't slip. 'They wouldn't have got that far,' he said.

'I suppose you'd have stopped them.'

'Oh, yes.'

'At your age? How?'

'I'm a surprising man. One up to Britain, though. We must be grateful for her small contribution in the common confusion.'

'We owe Britain nothing,' Dominique said sharply.

'And, of course – ' the old man's voice became sonorous with sarcasm as he repeated a comment Woodyatt had heard a dozen times before ' – Britain forced us into the war.'

'If you believe that,' Woodyatt snarled, 'you'll believe anything.'

It was obvious the thefts of and from cars were increasing and several people were yelling with fury at finding items of luggage gone. Not far away a man and a woman were screaming that their vehicle had vanished while they had been helping the injured.

There was no point in hanging around. Tragedies such as they had just witnessed were happening over the whole of Northern France and the ambulance-men and the police were now in charge.

'Get in the car,' Woodyatt snapped at Dominique.

For a moment she looked as though she were about to respond to his brusque command with spirit but she changed her mind and climbed in without a word.

There was another bridge further downstream and, as order began to re-emerge, Woodyatt backed the car away and swung it about to head along the bank of the river. Just ahead of them was the lorry containing the British petrol. Woodyatt held well back, aware that the petrol cans it carried were notoriously fragile and liable to leak easily, and aware also that the French soldiers in the lorry all seemed to be smoking.

As they reached safety among the trees at the other side of the river, they again heard aircraft and three Messerschmitts howled overhead low enough for them to see the pilots looking down and the numbers on the fuselages. As they vanished, they heard their guns going. The sound of anti-aircraft fire followed and they saw the machines lifting away into the sky and a column of black smoke rising ahead of them.

The traffic came to a stop once more and they took the opportunity to get Montrouge out to stretch his legs. He seemed to be completely unmoved by all that was happening around him, quite calm, never ruffled, and always with that infuriating amused look on his face. He was slow getting back into the car as the traffic finally began to move again, and everybody behind started shouting. It was typical of him that he paused and regarded them with a look that ought to have shrivelled them.

Ahead several cars were burning. The Messerschmitts had caught the refugees at the junction of two roads and people were trying to clear a passage. Bodies were stretched out on the grass and several men were struggling to attach a rope to a smashed cart and drag it away with a lorry. A woman was kneeling in the grass by a halted car and wailing over a screaming small boy with blood on his face. Watched by a despairing man, she was begging for help and Dominique went towards her. For a long time she bent over the child, while the woman wept with gratitude.

'How I hate the Germans!' Dominique said. She was tearing up a shirt the woman had given her. Signing to Woodyatt to hold the squirming child, she applied the bandages she had made. The boy was hysterical with pain but somehow she managed to calm him and between them they were able to staunch the blood. In her gratitude the woman kissed Dominique and the man insisted on pumping Woodyatt's hand. As they rose, the road was being cleared and traffic began to move. When the cars opened out, they saw that several vehicles had been hit. Among them was the red Renault whose owner had given them a friendly wave. His car was full of holes, and the tyres were punctured, and he was staring at it with a baffled look.

As the car containing the wounded child began to pull away, Woodyatt returned to their own car with a grim face. The sight of the red Renault had set his mind working. Did it have some meaning? It was the second red car that had been strafed by Messerschmitts. Were they still being followed? He had thought after the murder in the hotel outside Chartres that their pursuers would have been satisfied they had caught their quarry.

When he passed on his suspicions to Dominique, she gave him a sick nervous look. 'Is it possible?' she said.

'I don't know,' he replied. 'But I think we should get rid of this car as soon as possible.'

seven

As Woodyatt and his passengers reached the end of the diversion, they came to a large village called Marville. It had a single main street with lanes leading off round the backs of the houses which were a mixture of brick and wood. Garages and stables were interspersed between them.

The place was full of cars and tramping refugees. Among them were groups of grubby-looking soldiers heading south, grinning and shouting lewd comments at the women and girls who stood at their doors. The villagers had all turned out to watch the traffic, although it must already have been going on for days.

Among the cars was the big Ford containing the two dark-jowled Parisians who looked like gangsters, and their blonde girlfriend. They were outside a garage arguing with the attendant in an attempt to get petrol. Also there was the Bedford lorry with its load of stolen British petrol. One of the soldiers had his head in the bonnet with the garage proprietor. The others stood around, grinning and watching the sky, cigarettes hanging from their lips.

'Your lorries are no good, English,' the driver yelled as he saw Woodyatt. 'They won't go.'

The lorry had clearly been over-driven and it seemed a good idea to give it a wide berth. Quite apart from the problem of the drunken and quixotic French soldiers who were revelling in their power, Woodyatt didn't trust their cigarettes because the floor of the lorry was probably swimming with leaked petrol by now.

The traffic continued to move slowly past, cars honking and jostling, their occupants shouting insults at each other in their anxiety to keep well ahead of the Germans. The argument about petrol between the Parisian gangsters and the garage attendant ended abruptly.

'No!' the garage attendant roared. 'We haven't *any* petrol left!'

'Well – ' one of the Parisians pointed to the lorry ' – how about some of that?'

One of the soldiers moved round the lorry and stuck the muzzle of his rifle in the Parisian's stomach. 'Move!' he said. 'You heard what he said.'

Muttering to himself, the Parisian climbed into his car and they moved away, the blonde staring back balefully through the rear window.

It was necessary to check the Renault's oil and water. It was an old vehicle and used a lot. The engine seemed to be running hot and steam was coming from under the bonnet. As Woodyatt stopped the car and surveyed it, an old man popped up beside him. He was short, thickset and wore an enormous grey beard. 'There's water down here,' he said, gesturing. 'And I have a workshop with petrol and oil.'

He climbed on to the running board and directed them off the main street into one of the lanes that looped round the houses and back to the main road. It dipped down to a stream and was lined by the wooden huts, garages and barns that stood at the back of the houses in the main street.

'You can fill your radiator from that,' the old man said, indicating the stream.

They parked in the shade among a clump of trees and the old Frenchman directed them to a large wooden garage whose doors stood wide open. 'I have spare petrol,' he announced. 'I will sell you some. My name is George Hugo.

That is a splendid name, though Victor Hugo is no relation. You'll have heard of Victor Hugo, of course. A great man, don't you agree?'

Woodyatt wouldn't have dreamed of disagreeing with their helper.

'And I am an old soldier of the 179th Regiment,' Hugo continued. 'I fought at Verdun. I can't think what today's soldiers are doing to allow this chaos. *Où est l'esprit de Quatorze?* Where is the spirit of 1914?' With that, he opened the Renault's bonnet and released the radiator cap. A cloud of steam leapt into the air.

'I think it has a leak,' Woodyatt said.

'You need a can of water with you,' Hugo agreed. 'I can let you have one.'

They refilled the car with petrol and checked the oil and water, and Hugo let them have a can of petrol as a spare. Woodyatt paid him more than he asked.

'It's a pleasure,' Hugo said. 'I am an old soldier, aren't I? We shall still win. It might take time as in 1918 but we shall win, Monsieur. I'll go and find a can for the water.' As he disappeared into the depths of his garage, he beamed at them. 'Times are strange,' he said. 'I keep a shotgun in the garage. People try to steal what I've got.'

'How well you manage, young man,' Montrouge smiled as they waited by the car. 'Quite the diplomat. Personally, I've always thought anyone called Hugo a crashing bore.'

Woodyatt ignored him. 'Get in the car,' he advised Dominique. 'We'll need to make a quick getaway.'

As they waited for Hugo to return, a car turned into the lane from the other end. Two men began to climb out and Woodyatt wondered for a fraction of a second if they, too, were having trouble. Then, with a shock, he realised that one of the men was tall and thin and that the other had thick blond hair showing beneath his hat. They were looking about them, puzzled. His heart thumped as he recognised them. There was no doubt but that they had long since identified Woodyatt's red car and had probably been following it for some time. He looked about him. The lane was deserted because the whole village was watching the enormous spectacle of the traffic in the main street. Even Hugo had vanished. They could hear him clattering about in the depths of his garage. The roar of the traffic was audible but the deserted lane itself seemed curiously silent.

Woodyatt drew a deep breath. There was no sign or possibility of help. For days – years almost, it seemed he had been aware of the threat behind them, a dark shadow over his shoulder. Now, here, with the first physical contact a contact from which it was clear he was not going to be able to escape – the threat was about to explode into a harsh and bloody reality.

He looked at Dominique. 'Can you drive?' he asked.

'Yes.'

'Well our blond friend and his sidekick have arrived. They've discovered they made a mistake and they've picked us up again.'

As her head jerked round, the old man in the back of the car looked up with interest.

'What are you up to, young man?' he asked.

'Our friends from the hotel have arrived,' Woodyatt said. 'Keep your head down. They haven't spotted you yet.'

The Renault was facing the wrong way. The other car had entered the lane from the opposite end and they would have to pass it to escape.

'What are you going to do?' Dominique asked.

'God knows.' Woodyatt carefully closed the bonnet of the car and secured it. 'I'll have to face them. Be ready to go. Fast. Wait round the corner near the main road. They won't dare anything there. I'll join you if I can. If I don't make it, take the old man to Bray-en-Basse. Its near Niort in the Charente. Ask for Colonel Darby. He's British and well-known. He's expecting us. He'll take care of everything. If he's vanished, head south. Save yourself. You'll have to do without the can of water.'

'What about you?'

'I'll manage.'

She looked distressed but he gestured her to be ready.

The two men had spotted them now and began to walk towards Woodyatt, who eased his revolver in its holster. He felt like the hero of a Western heading for the final shoot-out.

The thin man had a gun in his hand and they seemed about to walk straight past Woodyatt to the car where they had seen the old man. It was obvious who their target was. The thin character raised the gun and Woodyatt realised it was now or never. Shades of Gary Cooper and a host of Western heroes flashed through his mind.

Despite the silence of the immediate surroundings, the crash of the shot was lost in the rumbling roar of the traffic beyond the houses. Woodyatt's aim was poor and the bullet clanged against the iron roof of a garage further along the lane so that the corrugated sheets leapt and clattered. The thin man looked startled, as though he hadn't expected to be interrupted in his work. His blond partner, Zamerski, dodged behind their car. Turning, the one with the gun fired at Woodyatt and the bullet whined past his ear. To Woodyatt's surprise, his own second shot hit the man full in the chest. It lifted him off his feet and dropped him on his back. At this, Zamerski's head came up and Woodyatt fired again but his target swung away.

Help arrived from an unexpected quarter as Hugo appeared in the doorway of his garage. He was carrying a can and an old battered-looking rifle. As Zamerski lifted his head again, Hugo dropped the can and fired wildly.

Zamerski seemed to realise, like Woodyatt, that he was missing his chance. Ducking his head down, he charged, firing as he ran. Woodyatt seemed to be immune. None of

Zamerski's shots hit him. He got off one single shot himself, then they were clutching each other on the edge of the stream, each struggling to fire. Woodyatt's revolver was wrenched from his hand and swung wildly on the end of its lanyard. But Zamerski was not as tall as his opponent and Woodyatt swung him round, his fingers gripping the hand that held the gun. As Woodyatt thrust at him, Zamerski lost his balance and teetered on the edge of the stream. The sun caught the water as it lifted in a wild splash, and glinted on a gun as it spun in the air to drop with a smaller splash alongside the floundering man who had been wielding it.

It was a chance to escape. '*Allez,*' Hugo yelled. '*Allez!*'

Woodyatt dropped into the car, which Dominique had held ready for his signal throughout. 'Go!' he shouted.

As Dominique let in the clutch, the Renault shot away with a screech of tyres and a cloud of dust, Woodyatt waving his thanks to the old Frenchman from the window.

As his quarry drew away, unharmed, Zamerski crawled from the river and dived for the gun the thin man had dropped. Hugo fired at him but, old soldier or not, his aim was poor and the bullet did no more than kick up the dust yards from Zamerski. As though irritated by a wasp, Zamerski turned and fired. His aim was better than it had been at Woodyatt and Woodyatt looked back in time to see the old Frenchman stagger at the impact, then, with a look of surprise on his face, Hugo sank down in the dust at the entrance to his workshop, red staining his shirt above his heart. Slowly he sagged to his right until he lay in a twisted heap, his features in the dust.

'Oh, God,' Woodyatt said.

Sickened, he signalled to Dominique to stop.

'No,' she shrieked. 'You mustn't go back! He'll kill you!' She was right. His job was to get Montrouge to safety not to look after the casualties of war.

'Heroes must also consider the order of things,' Montrouge observed, still remarkably unperturbed. 'Heroism without thought is pointless.'

'Shut your mouth, you ungrateful old bugger,' Woodyatt snarled in English. 'A man who owed you nothing has just died for you.'

Stopping as they reached the main road, Woodyatt and Dominique changed places then, swinging back into the main road, Woodyatt tried to rejoin the stream of traffic.

It wasn't easy.

'He'll be after us in a minute or two,' he warned.

The French deserters were still standing round their British lorry, chatting with each other and throwing ribald remarks at the passing drivers. They were continuing to smoke as if they'd never heard of safety precautions. It took some time to rejoin the stream of traffic and in desperation Woodyatt thrust the car into a narrow gap, scraping the wing of an oncoming Citroën so that the owner thrust out his head and started shouting.

As they moved forward and passed the lorry-load of petrol, in his mirror Woodyatt saw another car force its way into the traffic from the lane. Zamerski was on their tracks again, doubtless with another accomplice handy somewhere, waiting to be picked up. He heard a crunch and the scream of metal on metal and more shouts and guessed he, too, had forced his way into the column of vehicles.

The traffic was hardly moving and Zamerski was only a dozen cars behind. A door was flung open and Woodyatt saw that his pursuer had leapt from his car and was running towards them. He looked wet through and had blood on his face, and once again held a gun in his fist. Evidently he had decided to take a chance, fully expecting that in the climate of the times he could always claim he had shot a spy. As the car which Zamerski had vacated held up the traffic, the shouting started at once.

Wrenching the Renault's steering wheel, Woodyatt thrust the gear lever and jammed his foot on the accelerator to pull out. With the road crammed with vehicles it was difficult. There was another scrape of metal and he saw heads turn in the car in front and eyes glaring at him. At the same time there was a tremendous *whooomph* and he felt the car stagger under what seemed the blast of a bomb. For a moment he couldn't imagine what had happened then, turning, he saw the Bedford had gone up in a huge blossom of fire. Burning petrol, caught by the wind, was spraying in all directions in long offshoots of flame like the stamens of a fiery flower edged with black. As Woodyatt had been expecting for so long, one of the soldiers had got too near the leaking petrol with his cigarette.

Zamerski had disappeared, as though swept away by the blast or caught in the huge splash of fire. The only sign of him was his hat rolling along the ground in the breeze caused by the rush of air to the flames. The garage was burning, too, now, and there was another explosion as the storage tanks went up. The deserters, their clothes on fire, were screaming and trying to jump from the conflagration in the lorry. The driver and the garage proprietor lay in the road and a farmworker, his hair shrivelled, was trying to drag them clear.

Within minutes as the wind swept the flames along the street, the whole village was on fire. An amateur fire brigade with a small cart carrying hoses and a hand-pump arrived, but it was worse than useless. Round the garage was an inferno: the bodies on the ground and the man trying to drag them clear were no longer visible.

The whole village was burning from end to end with a brilliant brightness. The houses were also now enveloped in hard red and yellow tongues of fire that curled out of doors and through shattered roofs with a solid vicious strength. The heat was terrific. Every inch of roadway was covered with glass that had exploded from windows. As the air rushed in to fill the vacuum caused by the up-draught from the flames, it set up a tremendous wind that snatched at the clothes of the watchers.

It was hopeless trying to put the fire out and the locals stood gazing helplessly, clutching the few belongings they had managed to save. At the southern end of the village was a huddle of cars which had passed through to safety just in time. Their drivers and passengers had stopped to help. Behind them were those cars caught by the furnace; among them Zamerski's car stood tyreless and charred black, surrounded by clouds of stinking smoke. At the northern end, as the smoke drifted aside, grew another column of vehicles which could not pass, its number building up all the time as more and more arrived.

Woodyatt and his party were there until dark. Help arrived at last from neighbouring villages; the burned and injured, their skin livid and peeling, were helped to ambulances. One of the soldiers who was being carried away looked like burnt toast, with here and there a jagged strip of khaki cloth clinging by a seam, or a collar or a cuff, to the blackened flesh.

Woodyatt's own shirt had been burned when he had dragged an old woman from her house as it exploded into flame, and he had been given the checked shirt off her husband's back to replace it. He was sitting stony-faced at the side of the road as Dominique tried to apply ointment to his bright pink skin from the supplies she always carried with her.

'When will it end?' she asked with a tense desperation. Her face was drawn and her eyes were full of tears.

The opportunity to be rid of the red Renault was taken out of their hands and came sooner than expected.

They spent the night with other refugees in a barn outside the charred and stinking village of Marville. An ambulanceman had further attended to Woodyatt's burned shoulder and at last they had managed to fill the car's parched radiator. It was a good job, Woodyatt decided, that they hadn't very much further to go and that, with their pursuers gone, there was no longer the need to hurry so desperately. The dead had been taken away and they could only assume that Zamerski and partner had been among them, overwhelmed by the holocaust of fire that had destroyed Marville. Though at the expense of the villagers, the catastrophe caused by the deserters seemed to have saved them.

When they set off the following morning, the road had emptied and Woodyatt had a feeling that at last they were safe. They were tired, dirty and showing the effects of strain, but at long last the burden of fear had vanished. It was cooler now and a little rain made the day seem cold. Woodyatt's mind was busy. But for his skinned knuckles, it was hard to believe that he had actually struggled with their enemies. In the greater disaster of the fire, it was hard to remember the details of his own scuffle by the stream. Montrouge seemed as undisturbed as ever, though he must have been aware of the danger he had been in. Probably, Woodyatt thought, he was content to let others do the worrying. Perhaps he was even working out his defence for when he reached England.

Only Dominique, quiet and thoughtful, occasionally glancing at Woodyatt, made him realise it had all actually happened.

When the flames had died down and the confusion had halted, they had gone back to find Hugo. The old man was lying as they had left him and the flames had not reached his workshop.

He had no family. 'He was just an old soldier,' they were told.

In his sorrow, Woodyatt was still shocked that they had been traced so easily. It convinced him that the organisation seeking Montrouge was bigger than they had imagined.

The traffic seemed to have been directed away from the scene of the disaster and for a while they were alone on the road. Then, as they rounded a corner, they saw a large black Ford V8 saloon halted at the side of the road. As they approached, two men ran from behind it, dragging a small fallen tree across their path. Woodyatt recognised them at once as the city-suited men he'd assumed were Parisian gangsters seeking new hunting grounds. The next minute a pistol was stuck under his nose, as he was forced to stop.

As Woodyatt climbed out of the car he was relieved of his revolver. Then Montrouge was dragged from his seat and all their luggage and personal belongings followed. Dominique was the last to be ejected. Finally the familiar blonde woman appeared, staring sourly at the red Renault. 'Is that the best we can do?' she demanded.

'It's a car.' The man with the pistol peered at the fuel gauge.

'And it's full of petrol. Just get in and shut up.'

As the blonde climbed into the front passenger seat of the Renault, the second man piled their luggage from the Ford on to the rear seat and scrambled in beside it. As the car roared off, Dominique turned to Woodyatt, her face pink with rage.

'Why didn't you shoot them?' she demanded, her eyes sparkling with tears. 'They are a disgrace to France.'

Woodyatt was indifferent. 'Because,' he said calmly, 'they would undoubtedly have shot me first.'

'You shot the other man.'

'This is different. Perhaps we're well rid of the Renault.'

'You don't think we are still being followed, do you?'

'Nothing's normal in France at the moment. Perhaps Zamerski and partner somehow got a message to their friends even to the Luftwaffe – to destroy all red cars.'

'Could they identify us?'

'They could identify red cars. Their planes were low enough.'

'There is only one snag,' she pointed out. 'The car they've left has no petrol.'

Montrouge laughed. 'A problem, young man, I think,' he said.

Woodyatt glared at him. 'Stick him in the car,' he rapped. 'Stay with him. I'll find help.'

While Dominique was pushing the old man into the wide rear seat of the black Ford, Woodyatt went in search of his revolver which had been tossed into the bushes. He had been careful to note whereabouts it had landed and it didn't take him long to find it among the empty wine bottles and remnants of old picnics. He handed it to Dominique and gestured at Montrouge.

'It'll be up to you to see that the people who're looking for him don't get him.'

'Mother of God, do you expect me to shoot him?'

'Not him. *Them*.' He kissed her cheek. 'I'm off.'

She gave him a startled look and her fingers went to her face. She was still standing in the road, holding the revolver and staring after him, as he set off south.

It started to rain again and Woodyatt's thoughts were savage as he trudged on. Cars passed him occasionally but none of them stopped to offer a lift. His anger was directed against Pullinger; against France and its politicians; against French weather; against Dominique Sardier; above all against Montrouge. Everything about him: his cleverness; his intelligence; his sense of humour; his delight in tormenting

Woodyatt – all seemed to indicate he was whom Woodyatt believed him to be.

As the rain stopped, the wet road steamed in the sunshine that had broken through again. The countryside was well-wooded and lush but there didn't seem to be a house anywhere. Then, on a hill to his right, he saw a red-brick building approached by a lane. It looked like a small farm and he turned towards it. The gate was an iron bed-end held in place by wire. Beyond it he could see outhouses, a pigsty, chicken runs and what looked like a garage. An elderly woman was working at a vegetable patch. As he opened the gate with a clatter, she gestured at the sky.

'I think the rain has stopped,' she said, studying him. 'You look tired, young man.'

Woodyatt acknowledged the fact and, as he did so, he realised he hadn't slept in a bed for days.

'Perhaps you'd like to rest and take a glass of *prunelle?*'

Woodyatt nodded and smiled. As he entered the garden, the woman gestured at the cars that roared past from time to time on the road below.

'They've been at it for days,' she said. 'The Germans won't come here.'

Woodyatt wasn't so sure. 'I have a very old man with me,' he said. 'My car has been stolen. By men I think were Paris crooks. They left us one without petrol. Have you a car I can hire?'

The woman shrugged. 'There is a car. But it's not here. My brother's taken it to Saintes to collect supplies.'

'Perhaps I could have some petrol?' He tried to explain. 'I have to get my passenger to England. I can walk. But he can't. And he's important. If I could bring him here and let him rest a while, I could then get in touch with someone I know in Bray-en-Basse. Or the British Consul in Bordeaux who should be able to organise something.'

The woman smiled. 'We have petrol. We use it for the generator. I could let you have a little.'

Her name was Gonville and she was a widow. With her brother, she ran the smallholding for a living. 'We have only two bedrooms,' she said. 'They are occupied by myself and my brother. 'However –' she indicated the shabby building nearby ' – there is that. It was once a stable and before the war we made it into two rooms to offer to tourists.' She gave a wry smile. 'But this is not a popular area. There are no castles or chateaux to visit. Only fields and grass and, in the winter, mud. No one ever came except the occasional walker or cyclist, so we stopped bothering. There are beds and I can provide blankets. Perhaps you could make your old man comfortable there.'

Woodyatt could have hugged her.

Carrying a can half full of petrol, he set off back to where Dominique and the old man were waiting. As cars passed him, he remembered that the road swung in a wide curve to the East. Instead of following it, he cut across the fields to where the big Ford had been abandoned. As he trudged along in the afternoon heat, his mind was busy. He was wondering if he should head for the Spanish border or whether Darby would manage to arrange something for them. Bordeaux, he imagined, would be as chaotic as the rest of France.

As he reached the road again, he saw the black top of the Ford shining in the sun and instinctively began to hurry. Then, as he pushed across the sloping field, he heard a scream and raised his head. A man's shout set him running. Bursting through the hedge, he saw the Ford had been found by a group of four men, two of whom looked like the ones who had originally tried to steal the red Renault by the damaged bridge.

Dominique had her back to the car. She was flourishing Woodyatt's revolver and the men were clearly wary of approaching. They had split into two groups, one on each side of her and she looked baffled, wondering what they were going to do. Then, beyond them, she saw Woodyatt.

'James!'

As Woodyatt plunged forward, she pulled the trigger of the revolver. The report, harsh and staccato, echoed among the hills. It was hard to tell whom she was aiming at but the bullet whined past Woodyatt's ear. It startled the men by the car and, as their heads whipped round, Woodyatt emerged from the hedge.

His weight sent two of the men reeling, but the attackers were stubborn and came back. A whirling scuffle started and something hit Woodyatt over the right eye. In a fury he swung the petrol can as a weapon. It hit one of the men at the side of the head and sent him flying, then Dominique fired the revolver twice more and the attackers scuttled to safety. Still dazed by the blow over his eye, Woodyatt snatched the weapon from her. He almost had to fight her for it.

'For God's sake,' he snarled. 'Give it to me!'

The men had vanished and he took his fury out on Dominique. She was as edgy as he was and her retort was angry, but then she stopped dead and her expression showed concern. 'Your eye's bleeding.'

He lifted his hand to his forehead and saw there was blood on his fingers. 'It's nothing.'

She was calmer than he was and insisted that she should do something about it. She managed to persuade him to sit on the running board of the Ford and bent over him, her face close to his. 'It's split your eyebrow,' she said.

She managed to stop the bleeding and he apologised for the anger he'd shown. Lifting his head to look at her, he got the corner of her handkerchief in his eye. It made it water and he snatched out his own grubby handkerchief and started rubbing it.

'How splendid,' she said with a nurse's prim disapproval. 'What have you been using that for? Cleaning the windscreen? Dusting the floor? Wiping the oil from the engine? You'll probably get glaucoma and go blind.' She nodded towards the old man in the car. 'He's got a gun,' she pointed out. 'I think he has it now, on his lap.'

As Woodyatt approached, the old man's head lifted. He had made no attempt to leave his seat. 'Well?' his voice was calm and indifferent as if what might happen to him was a matter of no great moment. Woodyatt's face reddened. 'You have a gun!' he snapped.

'Yes.'

'Why didn't you use the bloody thing?'

'I might have hit Dominique. She was leaping about like a dog with fleas. There was plenty of time.'

Woodyatt stared at him angrily. 'Let me see it,' he said.

The old man held up a huge black revolver.

'That's a British gun.'

'In fact, it's American. Colt 45.' Again the hint of amusement came. 'I promise not to use it on you.'

The weapon was a monstrous thing. No wonder the old man had not been afraid of being kidnapped back at the bridge.

'British officers carried revolvers like that,' Woodyatt said. 'In the last war.'

'*And* before that. It's a little large but I have capacious pockets.'

'Where did you get it?'

'It was given to me.'

'By whom?'

'A German officer. In 1919. All he wanted was to be rid of it.'

'Redmond had one like that.'

'No wonder he didn't use it to kill himself.'

Woodyatt pounced at once. 'How do you know he didn't use it to kill himself?'

There was the faintest pause, as if the old man realised he had been caught in an error. Every time it happened, Woodyatt disliked him more. He felt Montrouge was crafty, cunning and devious, and too clever by half. Now the old man was even smiling.

'I heard,' he said.

Dominique had joined them and Woodyatt gestured at the revolver. 'Keep the bloody thing handy in future,' he said. 'And use it. The roads seem to contain the sweepings of all the jails of France.'

Dominique had listened to the exchanges silently, her expression worried. She could tell Woodyatt was still angry but she kept her eyes steady on his. 'I'm sorry for what is happening in my country,' she said quietly, trying to defuse the atmosphere.

'Forget it.' Woodyatt stopped dead. 'You called me "James",' he said remembering. 'When I arrived, you called me "James".'

'Yes.'

'Why?'

She avoided his eyes. 'I don't know.'

He grinned. 'It makes a change.'

Her eyes still held his steadily, her expression frank. 'Perhaps a change has taken place,' she said.

e i g h t

The petrol Woodyatt had brought was of low grade and their progress back to Madame Gonville's was slow.

She was waiting for them. Woodyatt explained that Dominique was Montrouge's niece and a nurse and was there to look after him. He wasn't sure that Madame Gonville believed him but she offered no objections.

The rooms over what had been the stables were spartan and tidy, though they smelled of mothballs and damp. Woodyatt decided to put Montrouge in the furthest of the two. 'I'll sleep on a mattress in the entrance,' he suggested.

Madame Gonville provided a rough and ready meal which they ate outside to the constant sound of distant traffic.

Montrouge was already asleep in the small room so they left him to it. His suitcase was alongside the bed where he could reach out and touch it. As Woodyatt discovered when he stealthily investigated, it was locked.

He had noticed that Madame Gonville had a telephone and he requested permission to use it. She seemed to wonder if he were a fifth columnist, but he agreed to speak in French so that she could listen.

Darby recognised his voice at once. 'Bring him here,' he said. 'I'll identify him. I knew him well. I'll contact the consul in Bordeaux. Ships are coming in. The bloody place is filling up with Brits coming from Italy, Majorca, Spain, the South of France. Especially now that Mussolini's joining the fun. I'll make sure we have boarding passes.'

It had grown hot again after the rain and the air was shimmering over the road. In the distance they could hear anonymous thuds and see a column of smoke rising.

In front of the house, the country sloped away in a series of folds, with clumps of trees and long lines of poplars. The last of the sun glinted on the river, and now that the traffic had stopped for the night, the area was quiet.

For the first time in days Woodyatt felt at peace with the world. They had a long way to go still but the heavy load of worry had lifted a little with the disappearance of Zamerski. Montrouge was out of the way and for the time being out of Woodyatt's mind, and Madame Gonville had provided enough from her garden to satisfy them all. She had killed a chicken, gathered fresh potatoes and beans, and produced a large flask of the harsh red wine of the district.

And for the first time almost, there seemed to be warmth between Dominique and himself. She kept looking at him strangely, her eyes gentle, as though trying to make out something about him that puzzled her.

'You were brave,' she said almost shyly.

'Not really.' He was smiling but she turned on him angrily.

'The English are such fools!' she snapped. 'Why should you risk your life in that way for two such ungrateful people?'

He touched her hand. 'Don't make too much of it,' he said quietly. 'It's no more than most men would do.'

'Not my Monsieur Maladroit,' she said. 'He wouldn't have.' Tears sparkled unexpectedly in her eyes. 'And I am not ungrateful,' she murmured. 'Not really. It is only that I have been so lacking in trust. It is since Monsieur Maladroit. It is a bad trait in me.'

The stable block was dark when they went inside and Montrouge was snoring quietly in the second of the two rooms. The other one contained a large bed and a sagging armchair. Dominique gave Woodyatt her usual quizzical, half-amused look at the situation into which they had been forced.

'Do you mind very much sharing a room with me?' he asked.

She gave a nervous little laugh. 'I've shared one before. And you'll remember I occasionally shared one with Monsieur Maladroit.'

There was a wash basin and, as she bent to her suitcase, Woodyatt took off the checked shirt and sloshed water on his face then stepped back to allow her to use it, too. As he turned, she was studying him.

'Your poor shoulder,' she said softly. She touched the livid mark where he'd been burned at Marville.

'It'll get better,' he said shortly.

There was a long silence before she spoke again. 'I hope you succeed in what you are trying to do, James Woodyatt,' she said.

It was the first time she had offered any encouragement whatsoever and he studied her, looking for the reason. She returned his gaze in her usual frank manner and he had a feeling she had indeed undergone a change of heart.

'If he's proved to be who I think he is,' he asked, 'what will you do?'

She shrugged. 'I was a nurse and I will continue to do what I can for him. I can't change overnight. What about you?'

What about him? Woodyatt considered. What were his plans? He didn't know. He hadn't expected the job of getting the old man to England to be fraught with so many problems, so many evils, so many unlooked-for disasters. When he had told the old man he was a brute-force Intelligence officer, he had meant that his part of the affair was simple, practical, and if necessary, a matter of straightforward organisation. He had to find Redmond,

219

identify him and take him to England. There had, however, proved to be occasion after occasion when he had had to rely on his own resources, his own ingenuity, nerve and cunning – and brute strength.

'If you need me,' Pullinger had said, 'contact me.' Well, he needed him now but, unfortunately, the whole German army was between them and communications had broken down. It had changed things a little. 'Take your time,' Pullinger had said. 'Just make sure you've got the right man.' But from a careful investigation of a forty-year-old mystery, it had become a rushed job to unravel an enigma-inside-a-puzzle-inside-a-catastrophe – and to boot involved a rescue from what Woodyatt felt sure were German agents. And by this time he didn't believe for one minute that even if he got Montrouge to England the best men that Pullinger could put on the job would ever get anything out of him. The simplest thing, he decided bitterly, would be to shoot the old bastard. That way, though the British wouldn't get him, neither would the Germans.

He looked up. Dominique was still standing quietly alongside him, waiting for an answer. Most of the time she was a sobersides, grave of expression and manner, as if loneliness had given her extra resources, but there was something else at that moment. It had been a terrible and terrifying two days and she looked tired. And there was also a tremulous uncertainty about her, as if she were afraid of herself and needed reassurance.

'We shall be with the Darbys soon,' Woodyatt said. 'They'll help. Darby knows why I'm here and he promised to contact the British Consul.'

She touched his hand. 'Those men who took the car. Were they the same men we saw in Marville.'

'No. I think *they* were caught by the flames.'

'Will the men who took the car come again?'

'*They* weren't after Montrouge.'

'Did they kill the old man at the hotel?'

'I don't think so. It was the others who did the killing. The ones we saw at Marville. They thought he was your uncle.'

There was a long silence then, 'I'm frightened. I said I wasn't, but I am. I'm all right when things are happening but afterwards – haven't you noticed?' She was begging for a little praise, a kind word.

As she had been talking, she moved to the wash basin. She had taken off her dress and was standing in her slip to wash. She was slender, with a graceful neck topped by a striking head. He noticed she was trembling in little shudders that shook her whole frame.

She turned, a towel in her hands, and caught his eyes on her. For a moment, she stared back at him, her glance unwavering.

'You have seen me without my dress before,' she pointed out sharply, scoldingly.

Realising he had been frankly admiring her, he turned away and busied himself with the blanket Madame Gonville had given him. He was reflecting that he ought to have been evaluating the secrets of what he believed to be a flawed old man in the next room rather than the shape of the attractive young woman in this.

She shrugged, her face rigidly expressionless, as if she were controlling her emotions with difficulty. 'It doesn't matter, anyway,' she said. 'Does that sort of thing ever matter? We're all made the same and we're not children. You are married –'

'Not any more.'

'Very well. You *have been* married. I had a lover – my little Monsieur Maladroit who dropped me like a hot cake when my mother became ill. We have both seen the opposite sex unclothed. We're adults and broadminded. There's nothing odd about this situation. It was forced on us and doubtless hundreds have had to adapt to it.' She was almost too matter-of-fact for comfort.

They were standing close together, their bodies almost touching, his eyes locked on hers.

'I'll sleep in the corridor outside,' he said quickly.

'No!' The word came out sharp and abrupt.

'All right.' He glanced about him and indicated the armchair in the corner of the room. 'I can sleep there.'

She gave him a confused look. In her weariness, she was desperately in need of affection and warmth. As her emotions welled up, almost suffocating her, her voice was beseeching.

'I'd rather you were closer than that.'

He shrugged and pulled the armchair across the room. As he stood alongside her, holding the blanket, she gave him a look of such despair he put his arms round her. As she leaned against him, her arms went round him, too, clinging to him. Tears were rolling down her cheeks now, blinding her, and she was shaking with the reaction to the events of the last two days.

'Take it easy,' he said. 'You've just had one hell of a time.'

'I don't think being in the chair will be enough,' she whispered.

He felt a pulse start in his temple and sensed his heart beating against the wall of his chest.

She was silent for a moment, almost as if she regretted what she had said. Then, as he gently took the towel from her, he heard her whisper – so low he could barely catch it – 'Please…'

nine

When Woodyatt awoke the following morning, Dominique was lying with her head against his shoulder, her hand on his chest. He knew she was awake, too, warm and drowsy like himself, preferring to forget the horrifying events they had lived through. There had been a hint of terror in her passion, as if she were clinging to a floating spar after a shipwreck. She had been hungry for the tenderness she had constantly denied herself.

She moved and he saw her looking down at him. Her expression was faintly puzzled.

'I'm sorry about last night,' she said, speaking softly so as not to disturb Montrouge.

Woodyatt smiled and she tried to make a joke of it. 'I said a prayer,' she pointed out. 'I felt God would understand.'

She was silent for a while. 'I expect you're disgusted with me,' she went on, the familiar stiffness returning.

Woodyatt's eyebrows rose. 'Am I?'

'Crying. Doing what I did. Inviting you into my bed. It was wrong. You have a wife.'

'That's over.'

She was silent for a moment. 'Is it?' she asked. 'I don't think anything like that is ever over. There are too many small things you remember, too many words that have been spoken, too many things shared. I still think of my Monsieur Maladroit. I don't wish to, but I do. Things remind me, and

223

it will go on until someone else comes along to make me forget them.'

What she said was true enough. Woodyatt's wife had gone but that didn't stop him remembering – sometimes with bitterness, sometimes with guilt, often with nostalgia and regret. But remembering, nevertheless.

'Most of the time it was difficult,' she admitted. 'His wife was suspicious and we had to make love in his car or in the woods. Often I didn't enjoy it. I got grit stuck to my bottom.'

He gave a hoot of laughter. She joined in reluctantly and he put his arms round her and pulled her to him. 'You're a cynic,' he said.

'I don't want to be a cynic,' she admitted quietly. 'But sometimes life takes a hand, doesn't it? I suppose really the affair was sordid. But to be in love is always to be a little unbalanced. Things appear clearer, different, sometimes more confused.' She was silent for a moment. 'The trouble was that I wanted more from my lover than he was prepared to give.'

'Optimists try again with someone else.'

'Are you an optimist?'

'I suppose so. But I wouldn't start again with the same woman. It would have to be real love.'

'When you married her, didn't you think then it was real love?'

It was an awkward point. She had a strange prickly gift of always introducing a jarring note into their conversation and he avoided answering, preferring to think how pleasant it was to be there with her beside him, her flesh warm against his. He turned towards her and kissed her. She responded enthusiastically.

'Cynicism wastes a lot of valuable time,' he said.

She smiled and was just lifting her arms to him when a sound from the old man's room brought them both out of bed at a run. Within two minutes they were looking as if they had been fully dressed and on their feet all night. As they headed for the door, their eyes met and she gave him one of the wonderful grins that made her so unpredictable, like a shaft of light through her stubborn sobriety.

'How nimble guilt can make one,' she said.

They left as soon as they could and almost immediately found petrol. For a long time they drove in silence. Dominique had hardly spoken and Woodyatt had a feeling she didn't quite know what to make of what had happened between them. Eventually, with the old man in the wide rear seat enjoying the sunshine that came through the window of the car, she stirred.

'I'm not really a loose woman.' She was back in her sober mood and the words came quietly. 'But so much has happened. It is still happening. Perhaps last night I was just tired.'

She became silent again and he waited, feeling she wanted to talk, as if she'd wanted to talk for years but had never had anyone close enough. Eventually she went on in a wondering voice, as though surprised at herself. 'Things are moving too swiftly. A lot of people are dying. It makes death seem closer.'

Her hand touched Woodyatt's and, as he took it, her fingers closed round his, tense as springs.

'I think,' he said, 'that at the moment a lot of people are thinking the way you're thinking. And a lot of people are behaving as we behaved. Because they're frightened or tired or lost or lonely. Life's suddenly become a bit difficult and different. Everything's different. Even morals, I suppose. There are other things that war produces besides death.'

Her head turned as she glanced at him. 'I don't know why I did what I did,' she went on, still speaking in a low voice so that the old man in the back of the car wouldn't hear. 'But I'm twenty-six and no longer a school girl and I suppose we're all a little desperate for warmth these days. There's so little of it. What we felt was not just passion. It was the comfort of shared sorrows.

He wished she wouldn't scourge herself so. But her face remained secret and enigmatic and she persisted with the lecture, as if she were determined he shouldn't escape.

'Loving's sharing,' she went on. 'And sharing's comfort.'

'Why do you dissect everything so?'

'Be quiet!' she snapped. 'I'm trying to tell you something. To me it was a reassurance. It made me feel that to someone I'm important. Because –' her voice shook ' – I am lost. I've been lost ever since you appeared, James Woodyatt. You took away someone I had begun to cherish. He doesn't exist any more. He's become a different man, a stranger, and I'm lonely again. I was lonely for a long time. After my Monsieur Maladroit left and my mother died, I was bitter and I hated being so. Then I acquired a relation, my only relation. He filled a gap and he was all I had. But now he's gone, too, because you've destroyed him.'

'I'm sorry.'

She shrugged. 'Oh, I don't blame you. But, you see, I am on my own again. I have no one to take his place. Perhaps it will be easier for me now that we have forgotten our good manners.'

Woodyatt, Dominique and their aged companion were silent as they ate at a small hotel. Like so many others, the owners were making money hand over fist from the refugees. They were near their destination now but, with the engine giving trouble, they were obviously not going to make it without another stop. By this time, not only were more cars beginning to run out of petrol, but their owners were also beginning to run out of money. There were constant hold-ups and some vehicles were towing others. A three-wheeled motor-driven cripple's chair was being pushed by an overloaded two-seater; the owner, a man with paralysed legs, sitting up in front.

They now began to pass through empty countryside devoid of hotels but eventually they found an old chateau, perched high above a river, which had been turned into a hotel. It had obviously been opened hurriedly to make money from the refugees, and the great hall had been made into a dormitory. Beds had been set up beneath the antlers, stag's heads and hunting horns: all of them black with grime. In the hall was a picture of the Battle of Sedan, showing glassy-eyed French soldiers holding tattered banners, with piles of dead Germans around them.

The owners were aloof and distant, survivors from another age living in a state of feudal splendour and poverty. Though they had been quick to put to good account the misery of the refugees, they obviously had little time for them. Their talk was stilted and reactionary, and they clearly felt France's troubles were due entirely to the Popular Front and International Jewry.

Woodyatt was able to obtain two rooms, one a small one beyond the other so that no one could reach Montrouge without passing through the larger one.

'Leave the light on,' the old man said as he stretched out on the bed. 'I am like Goethe. I don't fancy dying in the dark.'

He seemed more tired than usual and complained of being too weary to sleep. Woodyatt distrusted him and suspected him of working up some ruse to escape, but they eventually heard his breath become deep and steady. As they closed the connecting door, Dominique started removing her clothes with a blank face.

'We know what we are doing,' she said in a dogged way. 'We have decided we are neither of us innocents. We never were. And life teaches the impatience of the body and the impulses of the flesh.'

She sounded like a schoolteacher with a difficult pupil again and Woodyatt answered irritably.

'Dominique, we're about to go to bed together. We're not about to start a five-finger exercise on the piano.'

She stood before him, slim and white in the dusk, and he saw her eyes were wet. Her mouth was open, her lips trembling. In them he could see pain and, without saying a word, he gathered her in his arms. She didn't resist and leaned weakly against him. Then her arms went round him, clinging to him, and he could feel her shuddering in an emotion he couldn't fathom.

'Dominique – '

'Don't speak,' she said. 'It's best not for you to speak, best not for you to ask questions.'

As they turned the light out he reached for her.

'I would like us to make love,' she said. 'No. I would like *you* to make love to *me*.' She sounded like a sergeant in the WRAF. He felt her lips on his cheek. 'Good James Woodyatt,' she whispered. 'Kind, funny James Woodyatt. I am happier with you than with any man I've ever known. I am happy even here with you pawing me like a farm boy.' She gave a little laugh and moved closer to him. 'But we are such an ill-assorted couple and it is all so different from what I expected.'

He wondered what she meant and she went on slowly. 'I thought when I was very young that I would grow up and marry a prince. Later when I learned about things, I still thought that when I went to bed with a man it would be very romantic and the man I slept with would be my husband and I would love him very much. It would be beautiful like music and roses and perfume. But it isn't like that, is it? Monsieur Maladroit was not my husband. And neither are you. And we are in bed together not because I am in love, but because I need comfort and because we are in a war. And when you are in a war you must not waste time.' He heard her sigh. 'It's surprising how normal it becomes when everything else is abnormal.'

She was about to say more but he laid a finger on her lips. 'No,' he said. 'No more.'

She gave a little laugh. 'I always say too much,' she agreed. 'It is the teacher in me coming out. I feel I have to explain everything to myself as if I were my own most stupid pupil. But from now on I'll be forward and daring, and behave as an ardent lover with no worries about propriety or correctness. I no longer have any qualms of conscience. Perhaps I have no conscience. Certainly I have no fears any more.' She paused and gave a little laugh. 'Only that Monsieur Montrouge will wake up and catch us.'

The following morning there were no deep silences, no embarrassments, no self-accusations.

From the hotel wireless they learned that Pétain was about to hand France to the Germans on a plate. They'd heard rumours as far back as Fontainebleau that this would happen but had been unable to believe them. Now they seemed to be true. Stories of a terrible bombing of Paris came over but Woodyatt guessed they were all false, put out to salve the nation's conscience.

A rat of a man in a smart suit and tie had entered the hotel's breakfast restaurant and was delivering a tirade on the defiant speech Churchill had made when he had promised to continue the struggle. All France wanted was peace, he claimed. 'Let's get the war over,' he suggested loudly. 'And get back to calm.'

A fat woman kissed him in an excess of enthusiasm. 'The Armistice's about to be signed,' she crowed. 'France will be saved!'

Woodyatt noticed the look of contempt Dominique gave her.

Darby welcomed them with open arms. When they told him of their pursuers and what had happened at Marville, he seemed to consider that was the end of their worries. But he was obviously becoming nervous at the way events were going.

'Things have changed a bit since you were here last,' he said. 'The bloody Germans are going to have the whole Atlantic coast under the terms of the Armistice. The buggers will be able to set up submarine bases all the way from Norway to the Spanish border. We'll have to get out. St Nazaire and La Rochelle are due to fall anytime but so far there are still ships in Bordeaux. I've been down there and seen them. Find Redmond?'

'He's in the car. He's given nothing away. All I've been able to establish is that he drinks brandy and soda occasionally.'

'Well, we've got plenty of that.' Darby peered at the car. 'Who's the girl?'

Woodyatt explained and Darby grinned enthusiastically. 'Better wheel 'em in.' As his wife appeared, he turned to her. 'Got company, Daph. Our friend, Redmond. Should be an interesting encounter.'

Dominique was helping the old man out of the car. As he began to move up the path to the house, Darby frowned.

'He's changed,' he muttered.

As the introductions took place, Darby's frown grew deeper.

'This is Colonel Darby,' Woodyatt explained to Montrouge. 'An old friend of yours, I think.'

He had been hoping to trap the old man into a start of recognition but he ought to have known better. 'I've never met Colonel Darby before,' Montrouge said briskly.

'Colonel Darby was an acquaintance of General Redmond in South Africa.'

The old man gave a bark of a laugh. 'You don't give up, do you? I assure you – *and* Colonel Darby – we've never met.' The words were insultingly self-confident.

Darby's eyes were narrow. 'Does he know what happened?'

'He knows pretty well everything. He'll give an explanation if you care to go into it. But I shouldn't bother if I were you.' Woodyatt turned to Mrs Darby who was studying the old man minutely. Montrouge was staring back at her, a half-smile on his lips, the sort of half-smile any French gallant would wear as he rushed back to pick up some woman in whose face he had allowed a swing door to slam. But there was no hint of recognition.

'This is Mrs Darby,' Woodyatt said. 'Mrs Darby knew Redmond, too.'

'Really?' Montrouge gave a little bow but Daphne Darby said nothing, merely turning away to show them into the house.

Woodyatt turned to Darby. 'Well?'

Darby's face was dark and he was looking baffled. He made a frustrated gesture, like someone cheated of his prey.

'It's not him,' he said.

PART FOUR

Woodyatt's heart had sunk to his feet. Surely to God he hadn't gone to all this trouble for the wrong man! 'Are you sure?' he asked.

'No.' Darby ran his hand across his face. 'No, I'm not sure. Just doesn't look like him, that's all. But how can I tell? When I last saw him he was a man in his forties: young, virile, upright. He's an old man now. Voice is different. But old men's voices *are* different. Head seems to be a different shape, too, from what I remember. But heads change also, don't they? Skull stays the same but the flesh falls away and you can see bone structure you couldn't see before. Looked at his hand, too. Couldn't see any scar. I don't think it's him.'

Woodyatt was angry and began to outline all of what he considered had been attempts to destroy Redmond. Darby wasn't interested. Woodyatt suspected that at the last minute he had lost his nerve and hadn't the courage to condemn someone he wasn't sure about. As a result he was frowning heavily when Dominique appeared to say the old man was tired and was asking if he might lie down.

Darby turned, his expression worried. 'I'll show you his bed,' he said. He seemed to be in a hurry and anxious to be out of the room.

Daphne Darby appeared a moment later, with glasses and a brandy bottle. 'Have you arrested him?' she asked.

'Who?'

'Redmond. It *is* Redmond.'

Woodyatt was bewildered. 'Are you sure?'

'Of course I'm sure.'

'What makes you so sure?'

'The way he stands. The way he talks. The shape of his head.'

'Frank says it isn't him.'

'Frank didn't know him as I knew him.'

'How well did you know him?'

She eyed Woodyatt coolly. 'I was in love with him,' she said.

'Why didn't you tell me this before?' Woodyatt demanded.

She shrugged. 'You didn't ask. It is something I'm vaguely ashamed of now. And it's hurtful to Frank. He doesn't like to hear it.'

There was a long silence. 'No matter what Frank says,' Mrs Darby went on, 'it *is* him. I know. I was in love with him and love makes you clear-sighted. Not about character. God, no! But about the shape and colour of your beloved. Ask that girl you brought with you.'

'What do you mean?'

'She's in love with you. It's obvious.'

She gave him a shrewd look as if she knew exactly what their relationship was. 'Hers, of course, is different. It might get somewhere. Mine never did. But I had a terrible crush on him and I found it heartbreaking that no matter what I did he never noticed me.' She gave a little laugh. 'I know why now, after all that happened.' She paused, 'Frank and I weren't married then, of course, though I'd known him all my life. We grew up in the same village.'

'How did you get to know Redmond?'

She sat back in her chair, her eyes faraway as if she were looking at things she'd long since forgotten. 'I met him in Cape Town during the Boer War. I was eighteen. He was a good-looking man and women couldn't take their eyes off him. I know. I was one of them. The war was going badly at the time but there were a lot of handsome men about. Redmond was known as "Gorgeous George". And he *was* gorgeous. He really was – tall, strong, with a matinee idol profile. I was after a husband and I watched him a lot because he seemed a likely candidate.' She gestured towards the sitting room. 'What you've got there is Redmond.'

She paused then went on slowly. 'If he'd asked me to run away with him I'd have gone like a shot.' She gave a brittle laugh. 'Some hope! Thank God he didn't.' She laughed again. 'But then, he wouldn't have, would he?' She poured a brandy for herself and pushed the bottle towards Woodyatt. 'My father was a soldier, too,' she went on. 'When he was posted to the Cape garrison in 1898 he naturally took his family with him. I was seventeen when we left England and Cape Town was a good place to be. Garden parties. Races. Everything a young girl could want. I was having the time of my life.'

She paused. 'Frank was in Cape Town, too,' she said. 'On the staff. He had his eye on me even then but I'd grown up like a lot of girls in those days did, on a diet of romantic novels. He didn't seem handsome enough or dashing enough or sufficiently powerful and wealthy. I'd been spoiled. Then the war started and as you probably know, there was a series of disasters. Colenso. Magersfontein. Spion Kop. Ladysmith. Kimberley and Mafeking were besieged, and all the men they'd said were our best generals were defeated. They were all sacked and replaced.'

She gave another little laugh as if she were facing up to old terrors that didn't frighten her any more, terrors that in the present situation seemed only trivial.

'It doesn't sound much now,' she admitted. 'But it seemed important at the time. The Empire was in danger. Actually, the Boers could never really have kicked us out. There weren't enough of them. But a lot of people were scared stiff.

JOHN HARRIS

Then the reinforcements arrived, George Redmond with them. He was working in Intelligence at the time. He was all I wanted. Good-looking, already famous. Older, of course. But in all the books I'd read the heroines always married brave, famous older men who came as a relief after the irresponsible youngsters they'd first fallen in love with. He didn't look his age, mind you, and what was more he was unmarried. She paused. 'Or so we all believed at the time. Since he seemed to be free, I made a set at him. He totally ignored me. I couldn't make out why because I was pretty. Even generals usually managed to give me a smile. The fact that he didn't almost broke my heart. Until he moved north after the Boers, he was often at my father's house. He sometimes came uninvited and I thought it was to see me. Later – much later – I realised it wasn't me he was interested in. It was the gardener's boy. He was a Malay of about seventeen. It didn't mean a thing to me at the time, of course. It was only later I understood.'

'Did you ever meet him again?' Woodyatt was clinging to her words.

She lifted her glass. 'Chin chin,' she said, taking a swallow. 'Of course I did. In 1902, after we came home, I bumped into him at Ascot. But again he ignored me. It puzzled me because nobody treated me like that. He was with a man and a few days later I saw a picture of that man in a magazine. His name was Henry Cazalet. He was an actor. Then one day the following year I happened to go to Richmond to see an old nanny who'd gone to live there, and as I arrived I saw Redmond leaving a house further down the street. He got into a cab and vanished and I wondered whom he'd been visiting. And, of course, I jumped to conclusions because in those days men with money often set up women in discreet little villas. I was jealous enough to want to find out. I noted the name of the house and looked up the name of the occupier. It was Henry Cazalet.'

Mrs Darby became silent, her eyes far away again, the lines of disillusionment etched on her face. 'I was still young and silly, I suppose,' she went on slowly. 'And very innocent. By that time he was Chief of Staff to the reserve army and I saw him more than once in the area. With men. But while they might have been types who might have interested him when he was working in Intelligence, they hardly seemed to be the sort he would associate with as Chief of Staff to an army corps.'

Her face hardened. 'Then we read of his suicide in Paris. I was heartbroken. About two years later I read that Henry Cazalet had been arrested for gross indecency with another man. For the first time I began to get a glimpse of what it had all been about.'

She became silent again. Finishing her drink, she sloshed fresh brandy into her glass without asking Woodyatt if he wished to join her.

'Actually,' she continued, 'I didn't even know what "gross indecency" was. I made my brother tell me. I remember he went red and told me it was something I didn't need to know about. But I made him explain.'

'And Frank?' Woodyatt asked.

'He hates this part of the story.' Daphne Darby smiled. 'Eventually I married,' she went on. 'As I was expected to, and as I wanted to. A man called Marlowe. He was handsome, dashing and quite magnificent, and he killed himself hunting within a year. I married again quite soon afterwards. A nice man called Julian Winterton. Handsome again, of course, wealthy, all I wanted. Like my brother, he was one of the first to be killed in France in 1914.'

Daphne Darby's face wore a lost, bitter look as she continued. 'Then, late in 1916, Frank turned up again, minus a leg. He'd also married but his wife had gone off with another man. We fell into each other's arms. I needed comfort and he needed someone to lean on.

God! Woodyatt thought, it happens all the time. In every generation, in every war, people needed comfort.

Mrs Darby was toying with her glass. 'I was eternally grateful to him,' she said slowly. 'And always will be. I think he's grateful to me, too, though I'm not sure I've been good for him, or he for me. But that's the way things happen, isn't it? The Redmond affair ruined his career, of course, and he started to go for the bottle. He still does. Come to that, so do I. You'll have noticed. Two bad lots in the soup together, who didn't fit in with the old snobbish attitudes that started again after the war ended. Finally we saw this house and decided to chuck it all up and live here. It's not a very romantic story, but it explains why I know so much about Redmond.'

She shrugged. 'You have to remember,' she said, 'that, while to Frank he's someone he was intimately concerned with, he was still only someone he'd seen now and again. To me as a girl he was a dream, and I watched him like a hawk. I knew the cadence of his voice, every twitch of his eyebrows, every flicker of expression. I was in love with him. I knew what he looked like, the way he behaved, the way he moved, the way he stood, the way he held his head. The man you've got is Redmond.'

Woodyatt frowned. Daphne Darby was right, as Dominique had been right. People in love didn't forget. Despite her treachery, he could still remember every tiny thing about his wife with blinding clarity. He suspected he always would. It was obviously the same with Daphne Darby.

But how much could he trust her? After forty years how much did the memory retain accurately? He'd found that after many years things he'd known well differed when he'd seen them again. The steep hills of childhood became gentle slopes. Things that he had believed large were small. Women he had thought beautiful, he had realised, had never been so. How much could Daphne Darby really remember? And was she looking for revenge on someone, anyone, for what had happened? Did it colour her view? The bloody case, he thought, had more twists and dead ends than a maze.

Darby was clearly worried by the turn the war had taken. As they talked, Dominique sat alongside Woodyatt and he could feel her hand against his. Her face was expressionless and he remembered what Daphne Darby had said of her. She was enduring and resourceful and had helped with many of the decisions they had been forced to take. If only, he thought, she'd cease trying to be brave.

'I think we should be moving,' Darby insisted. 'There's fighting north of here round the bridges of Saumur.' He passed a hand over his face, as though trying to brush aside his gloomy thoughts. 'Christ, what a mess,' he growled. 'It said on the wireless that French soldiers rescued at Dunkirk are being sent back. The French government's demanding them, it seems, to form a new army to carry on the fight from the North African colonies. On the other hand, there are others who are coming back willingly. There are even a few enrolling in London.'

'For what?' Dominique asked.

'*Franc tireurs*. Agents. I don't know what they do these days. I'm out of date and out of touch.' He produced a map. 'The area the Germans want under the peace terms,' he said, 'is going to include this place. They're at Angouleme, Tours, Vichy and Lyon. But I'm told there is a gap north of Bordeaux that's still open. If we can get through we could be taken off tomorrow.

They all drank a little too much. Darby was suddenly uncertain of the future and it affected them all.

Mrs Darby had put Dominique in Woodyatt's room, but she made no attempt to draw close to him. He was aware of her unease and that she wasn't asleep.

'Are you awake?' she whispered.

'Yes.'

'After you've got your prisoner to England, will you be sent to the fighting?'

He thought about it for a while. 'The chances are that I'll stay in Intelligence,' he said. 'But I might be sent.'

It was some time before she spoke again. 'Colonel Darby said that many French people who've been taken to England are coming back. They're coming back to fight, to act as agents.'

'They must be mad.'

'Must they?'

'Would *you* come back?'

'You forget what they did to me.'

'They'd do it again. And worse. They'd shoot you.'

'Perhaps this time *I* could do the shooting.'

She lay stiff and straight alongside him, making no effort to move nearer. For a long time they lay in silence, Woodyatt staring at the moonlight streaming through the window. She seemed to be asleep at last and he wondered what had been running through her clever and complex mind. Then, hearing a small sound outside, he lifted his head. As he did so, Dominique sat up. They were still for a moment and in the silence they heard a creak on the landing.

'He's trying to slip away!'

They were out of bed in a moment, snatching at clothing. Montrouge was by the door. He was fully dressed, wearing his long overcoat and carrying his case. Woodyatt switched the light on and the old man froze. There was no sound from the room along the corridor where the Darbys slept.

'Where are you going?'

The old man shrugged. 'I'm not going anywhere,' he retorted. 'I am coming back. I *was* going but I have decided it might be wiser not to. There is a car outside in the road. It was not there earlier. I suspect, young man, that those pursuers you talked about so much have found us again.'

Woodyatt glanced at Dominique then he pushed the old man into his room and went to the landing window. Through the darkness he could just see a car. A match flared inside it as someone lit a cigarette.

Returning grim-faced to the bedroom, he faced the old man. 'Where *were* you going?' he demanded.

There was a moment's silence then the old man sighed. 'I grew tired of the questioning,' he said wearily. 'I decided to make my own way south. I changed my mind. With ladies and old men it's a privilege.'

'It's also imperative – if you're who I think you are.'

Montrouge shook his head wearily. 'Oh, young man,' he said heavily. 'Have you no idea how much you bore me?'

It seemed so unfeigned, such a natural reaction from an old man at the end of his tether, that it immediately started

Woodyatt doubting again. God, he thought, what if I've subjected the poor old bugger to all this humiliation and he isn't Redmond after all?

But then he remembered the car outside. Why was it there if this weren't Redmond? It seemed unbelievable that they were still being followed after all the disasters that had happened, that their pursuers had never been fooled and had picked up their track despite the disasters they had all faced. He thrust his doubts behind him. 'You'd not have got further than the end of the road,' he said. 'Were you thinking of pinching the car?' He watched as Dominique pushed the old man towards the bed. 'You made sure you had your case.'

'It contains my papers. One day I may write my memoirs.'

'They ought to be interesting.'

A ghost of the old man's smile appeared and Woodyatt became aware of a growing but grudging admiration for him.

He was a devious old bastard but he knew where he was going and he never seemed at a loss.

'I have plenty of stories to tell,' Montrouge said. 'What did you tell my niece when you first met her? That I was a French agent. For once, young man, you were right. I was posing as a French newspaper correspondent. There was nothing unusual in it. Half the London *Times* correspondents worked for British Intelligence.'

To Woodyatt this was just another new story that had surfaced. The old devil made them up as he went along. And they were all – every last one of them – too glib. He leaned forward, his eyes hot and angry. 'You ever heard of Mark Twain?' he asked.

'Of course.'

'He once said something about a liar. He called him "experienced, industrious, ambitious and often quite picturesque". I think it fits you.'

'That's your privilege.' The old man's expression changed and suddenly he seemed sly and calculating. 'There *is* something I can tell you, however. Have you ever heard of a German sympathiser in the top echelon of the British civil service?'

The words startled Woodyatt and he immediately decided they had been tossed at him to make him sit up and take notice. 'What about him?'

The old man smiled. 'I see you have. A Mr X he's known as.'

'Are you making a deal with me?'

'I seem to have no alternative. I need to get to England.'

'I've been trying to persuade you of that ever since I met you. What about Mr X? Do you know his name?'

'I saw letters addressed to him. His name begins with an "L". That's all I saw.'

'Where did you see these letters?'

'In the briefcase of a man called von Schalk. He was a friend.'

'And this is how you treat your friends? By going through their secret papers.'

'Do you want the name or not?' The words came out in an angry bark.

Woodyatt ignored the show of anger. 'We hear that Hitler intends to use our Mr X in any peace talks that occur,' he said.

The old man stared at him with glittering eyes. 'I would have thought the British were too stupid to ask for peace talks.'

'This "X". Tell me more.'

'He lives in Cheltenham.'

'Is that all?'

'It's all I know. If they can't work out from that who he is, they're slower than I thought.'

'All right. I have another question. Have you heard about rocket propulsion?'

'Of course I have.' The old man's head moved. 'They're obviously not as slow in England as I thought.'

'Flying bombs? Pilotless propellerless aeroplanes? We want to confirm they're a possibility.'

'Of course they're a possibility.'

'Tell me about them.'

'Argus Motorenwerke are behind them. The first jet propulsion was patented as early as 1907. Everybody was at it in the Thirties, with the Germans ahead on points.'

Woodyatt was listening carefully. 'A man called Schmidt developed a thing called the Schmidt duct,' Montrouge went on. 'It was a pulse jet. I expect your experts know as much about that as the Germans. Argus Motorenwerke produced their own Argus duct. It was then suggested that these ducts should be used to propel a flying torpedo. Just before the war started they were invited to submit proposals for a missile with a range of three hundred and fifty miles.'

'Are they going to use them?'

'If there aren't any peace talks.'

'I want provenance. Proof that this is genuine.'

'I knew Hermann Oberth, who developed the fuel. He lived only twenty kilometres from me. I also knew General Dornberger. He's been working on the project since 1932. I knew him when he was just an artillery officer with a technical background. He used to discuss his ideas with me.'

Dominique hadn't moved. Her eyes were fixed on the old man.

'What about the base for all this activity?' Woodyatt asked. 'There is no base. Just a few huts. It could grow bigger, though.'

'Where?'

'The Baltic coast. Pomerania. Near Rostock. Mecklenberg. Somewhere there. Try Peenemunde.'

'Never heard of it. Will Hitler invade Britain now he's got France?'

'He hasn't a navy.'

'He's got an air force.'

'You can't take over a country with aeroplanes.' It was a blunt professional opinion. 'I think he'd prefer it if Britain just capitulated. He admires the British Empire. He's a dreadful snob. He'd love to be invited to Buckingham Palace for tea.' The old man's sense of humour showed no signs of diminishing. 'But since Britain seems to have no intention of throwing in the sponge, he'll go into the Mediterranean instead.'

'The Mediterranean is Mussolini's sphere of influence.'

'He doesn't give a damn for Mussolini! This army they'll be rebuilding in England won't be needed to stop an invasion, but it *will* be needed in North Africa. He'll strike at Britain's friends. And being honourable, the British will be stupid enough to rush to their help. You should warn them, young man, to look to themselves. No more Polands. No more Norways.'

There was a long silence as Woodyatt digested what he'd been told. Montrouge seemed at last to have decided to come clean.

'What else?'

'He'll go into Russia.'

'Russia's his ally.'

The old man smiled. 'You really are naïve.'

'Surely he's read of Napoleon's disaster in 1812.'

'He considers himself cleverer than Napoleon. You'll also need to look further east than Russia.'

'There's nothing further east than Russia. Only Japan.'

The old man's eyebrows lifted. 'The Japanese are already servicing the German sea-raiders.'

'You'll be telling me next that Singapore's in danger.'

'That's exactly what I am telling you.'

247

'*Why* are you telling me these things? And who's this Zamerski type who's so interested in us? The type who's probably sitting in the car outside.'

Montrouge hesitated. 'A man I knew,' he said.

'What is he?'

'He's a German agent. He does their dirty work.'

'Gestapo? In France?'

'*The Germans are in France. Now!* The Gestapo will be here, too, before long.'

'And why is Zamerski after *you*?'

'A variety of reasons.'

'Tell me one.'

'The Jews.'

'What about the Jews?'

The old man paused. 'He's going to get rid of the Jews,' he said.

'Which Jews?'

'All Jews.'

'You can't get rid of a whole race.'

'Hitler can.'

'You can't get rid of millions of people.'

'*They* can. They will.'

'How, for God's sake?'

'Concentration camps. They have them already. I can give you names. Goebbels says they're just political reformatories. Don't you believe it. They'll become destruction camps. With experts who know how to use them. And there's always starvation. You've only to lock someone away and forget them and they disappear.'

'You're making it up.'

'You'll find I'm not. Jews. Communists. Catholics. Even Nazis who don't conform. I hope you haven't any Jewish relatives in Germany.'

Woodyatt stared unbelievingly at the old man. 'Is that why Redmond got out of Germany?'

'They had evidence against him.'

Woodyatt found himself grudgingly admiring again. You're a shrewd old bastard, he thought.

'And you?' he asked.

'I was rather busy at the time.'

'Doing what?'

'Getting my wife out of Germany. She was part-Jewish. I didn't love her or anything like that. Nor she me. But she had looked after me. I owed her something.'

There was an aching silence, and Woodyatt caught Dominique's puzzled expression. It was the very first indication they'd had that this old man in front of them had any feelings whatsoever. In the quietness, Dominique spoke.

'Were there any others you got out?'

'A few. Wealthy ones. What other kind ever escape?'

'How many did you save?'

'Not many. Three families. Twenty-two people.'

'Where are they now?'

'One family reached New York, I believe. One went to South Africa. One's in London.' The replies were flat and unemotional, as if they concerned something Montrouge preferred to forget.

'Was there anyone else involved?'

'One or two. One's dead. They shot him. Another's in a concentration camp.

'And the men who've been following you?' Woodyatt asked. 'All through France...'

Montrouge drew a deep breath like a sigh. 'Zamerski's men. They've been looking for me for two years.'

three

They locked Montrouge's door as they left. Their own door was left ajar.

'Did you believe him?' Dominique asked in a small shocked voice.

'Some of the time.'

'About the Jews? Catholics? People who disagreed? The people he saved?'

'We have only his word for them.'

'He wouldn't lie about a thing like that.'

Woodyatt could almost feel the disapproval oozing out of her. She was determined to believe Montrouge *had* helped the Jews to escape. It was as if it were the sign of redemption she had been seeking all along.

Neither of them spoke as they climbed back into bed. Woodyatt was silent for a long time, his mind weary with thinking, then he turned to her, looking for comfort. But she remained silent and, when he touched her, she made no response and lay as stiff and unyielding as a corpse. He kissed her cheek but she didn't even turn her head.

When he appeared downstairs the following morning the car in the road had vanished. Dominique was preparing a tray for Montrouge, giving it all her attention, as if it were a means of avoiding speaking to Woodyatt.

He told Darby about the car in the road over breakfast. The colonel was inclined to disregard it.

'It's nothing,' he said. 'There are some funny people about just now. Probably just resting on their way south.'

They finished breakfast in a fug of cigarette smoke and a confusion of road maps spread across the table with the cups and saucers, and ashtrays.

As Darby disappeared to fetch suitcases, Montrouge was sitting on a chair in the sun. 'Does that stupid drunk know what you're up to?' he asked Woodyatt.

His voice was harsh and querulous, with no hint of gratitude for the bed and the meals the Darbys had provided. The sympathy Woodyatt had begun to feel for him vanished at once. They were back to the old terms of distrust and dislike and selfishness.

'Yes,' he said shortly. 'He knows all right.'

'What you accuse me of?'

'That, too.'

'And what does he say?'

'He doesn't say anything yet.'

'Have you told him about last night?'

'No.'

'Why not?'

'His job's to identify you. My job's to let him, not to influence him by telling him that you're behaving with all the guilt of a cat burglar caught in the act.'

'He's a poor specimen. He's afraid of being involved.'

'He *is* involved, damn it,' Woodyatt snapped. 'He was involved as long ago as 1904. He was military attaché at the Embassy in Paris.'

Montrouge seemed startled at the information. 'He would know everything that happened then.'

'Yes'

'Yet he says nothing?'

'His wife says plenty. *She* insists you are Redmond.'

'How could she know?'

'She knew Redmond well.'

The old man was silent for a long time, deep in thought. 'Daphne Darby,' he said, groping into the past. 'I knew no Daphne Darby.'

'Her name at the time was Quennell. It was before she was married.'

'Quennell.' Was there a faint hint of wonderment in the voice, surprise that she remembered, that he remembered. 'Daphne Quennell.'

There was another long pause then the old man went on, almost, Woodyatt thought, as if he were vain enough to want to know what had been thought of him. 'What does she say?'

'That you're Redmond.'

'How would she know?'

'She was in love with him. She never took her eyes off him.'

The old man shifted in his chair, not looking at Woodyatt. 'She's as mad as the rest of you,' he growled.

When Dominique appeared, she was wearing a dress Daphne Darby had given her and had used make-up. The dress suited her and the make-up was skilfully applied.

Woodyatt complimented her on her appearance, trying to flatter her into a more conciliatory mood. She remained unyielding.

'Soon we shall have to say goodbye,' she said.

'What in God's name for?'

'You'll be going to England.'

'So, damn it, will you! You're part of the affair.' He paused. 'Come to that, you're part of me now.'

'I have no passport.'

'I can fix that.'

She looked at him and he saw her eyes were moist. 'Do you want me to come to England?'

'Of course I do.'

She still seemed doubtful and he went on quickly. 'I belong to a large family. You won't be short of friends.'

She continued to hesitate and he wanted to tell her what Mrs Darby had said of her. But that, he felt, with someone as independent as she was, would be the very thing to set her against him.

She touched his hand and he grasped her fingers. 'Things have changed, James Woodyatt,' she said. 'I don't think I'm the same person I was.'

As they'd been waiting, Darby had been making last-minute telephone calls to Bordeaux. 'They say there are a hundred thousand refugees there,' he announced. 'A lot of them Brits. You can't drive through for the crowds. Bordeaux's in a state of siege.'

He was still confident they could reach the quays, however. He had shown enough foresight to fill his car with petrol and stuff some cans of it in the boot, and there was more in his garage for the Ford. Other than that, he and his wife had made no attempt to pack much beyond clothing.

'What's the point?' Mrs Darby asked. 'We've lost our possessions before in hurried moves. "Pack and follow" was my life. There's a trail of our belongings all round the world.'

It was decided the Darbys should lead the way. As they set off the sky was full of black thunderclouds and it started to rain. There was the usual traffic, buses and cars with luggage, a few British army vehicles, all heading in the same direction.

Where the road joined the main highway, the usual colossal jam had built up, and a solitary policeman was struggling to sort it out. He was wearing thick woollen socks and sabots. As they halted, a motor bike festooned with parcels like a Christmas tree drew up alongside with a jerk. The pillion rider, a girl, fell off in a shower of packages. Climbing to her feet, she went up to the driver and gave him a clout to the side of the head that must have rattled his teeth.

'I do that every time we stop,' she shrieked.

A French officer appeared alongside the Darbys' car. He was wearing a row of medal ribbons. 'Will you permit me to see your papers?' he asked.

As they handed them over, he studied them carefully then handed them back and directed them on to a side road. Darby refused to go.

'That's not the way to Bordeaux,' he snapped.

'It's a diversion, Monsieur.'

'I don't believe it.'

The officer stared at him hostilely, then he indicated Montrouge who appeared to be asleep, his head on one side, his mouth open. Woodyatt and Dominique had opted to travel separately in the Ford.

'Who is this?' he demanded.

'The British ambassador's father,' Mrs Darby snapped.

The officer shrugged. 'Ah, *les Anglais,*' he said. 'Such humour. I know you well. I fought with you in 1916.' He indicated one of his decoration ribbons. 'I won this on the Somme. It is a British medal and was presented to me by General 'Aig himself.'

Darby jabbed at another of the ribbons. 'What's that one for?' he demanded aggressively.

The officer stared at him, red-faced.

'Well, go on! What's it for? Don't you remember? I know what *my* medals are for.'

The officer's hand moved to the pistol at his waist.

'Don't touch it,' Mrs Darby said quietly. 'I have one, too. Just under my handbag.'

The officer scowled and waved them and Woodyatt's Ford past. 'You will, of course, be stopped again at the bridge into Bordeaux,' he said, making an ostentatious note of the car numbers. 'Everybody is being stopped.'

A little further on, Darby halted his vehicle and, as Woodyatt drew up alongside him, he was questioning his wife. 'Where did you get a bloody pistol?' he was demanding. 'I got rid of mine years ago.'

'Don't be silly, Frank,' she replied calmly. 'I haven't got a pistol. But he wasn't to know, was he?'

Darby turned to look at Woodyatt. 'That chap was a phoney,' he said heatedly. 'That was no bloody British medal. Chinese, more like. Haig could never have given him that. The bastard's a fifth columnist.'

He was all for going back and telling the policeman what he thought of him but was finally persuaded not to.

'Don't be so bloody aggressive, Frank,' his wife said. 'It's not your war this time. It's not even your country. Perhaps he's not entitled to wear the damn medal but it wouldn't be the first time some poseur wore medals he wasn't entitled to and it wouldn't be the first time somebody said he was who he wasn't.'

She was looking at Montrouge as she spoke but the old man still had his head against the car window and looked as if he were asleep. Woodyatt could have sworn he saw his eyelids move, and wondered if he were afraid of Daphne Darby. She had pursued him as a young woman and perhaps he realised her eyes were sharper than her husband's.

At the suspension bridge outside the town, with the smell of the sea in the air, soldiers were examining papers. Around them were more remnants of the French army: a disorderly rabble of men – dirty, unshaven, lacking arms.

'No one,' they were told by an officer, 'is permitted to enter Bordeaux. There are already too many people there and there is no accommodation.'

'We have accommodation,' Mrs Darby lied. 'It's already booked.'

'I regret, Madame. Nobody can cross the bridge.'

'Suppose,' Dominique said sharply, 'we left the car and *walked* across the bridge. What would happen then?'

'I should be obliged to take action, Mademoiselle.'

'What sort of action?'

'My men have orders to shoot.'

'You'd shoot women?'

The officer, who was very young, flushed.

'Suppose,' Mrs Darby joined in, 'I were to leave the car here, and walk down the slope to the river. It's possible to swim across. I know because I've seen people swimming down there many times. Suppose I took my clothes off and swam across. Would you order your men to shoot at me as I did so?'

The officer's blush grew deeper and she linked her arm in Dominique's. 'Come along,' she said as they started walking. 'We're going across.'

She gestured at the cars to follow them and turned to the officer. 'We're *all* going across,' she insisted. 'If you shoot us, I hope you can square your conscience with God.'

four

Nobody stopped them. But at the other side was another officer who said no one was allowed into the city without a *laissez passer*.

'Where do I get that?' Mrs Darby was doing the talking now and they let her because she was a formidable woman and she was doing remarkably well.

The officer pointed to a building that looked like a school. It had a tricolour over the door.

Without argument, a tired-looking lieutenant handed over a *laissez passer* to cover the whole party. '*Pour aller et retour pour porter une lettre au Consul Brittanique*' was the reason it gave.

It didn't make it sound as if their journey was very important but it was signed with the officer's name and rank, with a large blob of sealing wax at the bottom to make it look official. It also bore the numbers of their cars and all their names.

As they moved into the outer suburbs of the city they had to pass through several barriers but nobody asked to see the *laissez passer*. Bordeaux was crammed with people, lorries, motor cars and bicycles, all bumping along the cobbled streets. There were cranes everywhere, like gigantic gallows against the sky, and what appeared to be hundreds of British all seeking ships. German aircraft seemed to be overhead all the time but no bombs fell and they learned at one of the shipping offices that they were dropping mines in the river mouth.

Trams were running along the quays and through the main thoroughfare, but the place was like a madhouse. There wasn't an inch of room anywhere and people were moving about like a crowd of depressed holiday-makers on a rainy day, staring with melancholy distress at the shop windows and the old houses.

They swarmed everywhere. Centres for refugees were advertised on every corner and the cars they saw had the number plates of half a dozen nations. Crowds were outside the churches, and the Place de la Comédie, a sad dignified centre where several streets met, was besieged by a rabble of terrified travellers. A theatre was being used as a temporary *Chambre des Députés* and people huddled in the portico hoping to find out what to do.

The Place des Quinconces, a large square open to the river, was packed with cars. A fair had been about to start and the site was marked by half-built pavilions. From the local paper they learned that the fighting at Saumur was over. The bridges had fallen, and the Germans were driving deep into Burgundy. There was a map of France with a line showing where they were, and another line showing how much of France they were demanding. It reduced the country to a quarter of its size, with no access to the sea except on the Mediterranean.

As they struggled down the main thoroughfare, they were held up by a policeman.

'*Le gouvernement*,' he said. 'A meeting in progress.'

They had to wait for half an hour until, from one of the buildings alongside, they saw men in suits and uniforms emerging. Among them were Weygand and Reynaud, both looking harassed, old and ill.

'The collapse committee,' Darby observed.

'Half the French Cabinet are here,' Dominique said bitterly. 'Together with their wives and mistresses.'

'The rich and the powerful,' Montrouge commented unexpectedly, 'will always survive.'

Further on they were held up again, this time by a procession of men with drums and trumpets who were led by a man wearing a sash of office and carrying a tricolour draped with black crepe. These marchers stopped at a memorial covered with names and dated 1914–1918. It had an angel with wings standing in a defiant attitude over a dying soldier, every bit of it plastered with pigeon droppings.

'Small men,' Dominique said coldly, 'honouring better men than they are.'

They were growing hungry and the café terraces were packed. But, as someone rose and left, they managed to crowd round a table and order a snack. The noise of voices around them was tremendous, and among the thousands of people in the city Woodyatt felt safe enough to relax.

Montrouge sat slightly apart, not facing the rest of the party, and it occurred to Woodyatt that he was trying to avoid facing the formidable Mrs Darby. She rarely took her eyes off him and whenever he did meet her gaze he looked the other way at once.

The waiter was young and handsome in an almost girlish way. He slipped swiftly between the tables, moving sinuously with lithe movements of his slender body. He was whistling gaily as he went, totally untouched by the tremendous tragedy taking place about him. The sun was hot and, in the atmosphere of panic that hung over the place, the air seemed stifling. A woman nearby was counting money on a table. A fat man was telling his neighbours that he had struggled all the way up France from the Italian border. A girl was weeping. She was extraordinarily pretty and Woodyatt found himself watching her simply because she was so good-looking. Darby was watching her, too, and so were most of the other men. Even the man complaining of his struggle up from the South of France and the husband of the woman counting her money.

Montrouge remained detached, indifferent to what was being said, as if he held the frightened middle-class people about him, and their conventions, in contempt. Woodyatt studied him. He looked surprisingly alert. This was no Pétain bowed down with age, he decided. Montrouge seemed remarkably fit, in fact, and he suspected that all the weakness, all the weariness he had shown, had been put on especially for his escort's benefit.

Woodyatt was beginning to suspect, even, that he was being used and had been for some time: exploited by Pullinger for revenge, and by the old man to gain safety. The truth of the situation, he realised suddenly, could well be that Montrouge was some rogue who was manipulating him for his own ends and his stories were merely offerings to confuse him, to make him feel the man he had with him was Redmond when in fact he was not.

One thing was sure. He had to get the old bastard to England in case he *was* Redmond. What he had told them was so startling it made Woodyatt's mission twice as grave.

He tried to push the old man to the back of his mind. There was enough going on around him to absorb his attention. The woman was still counting her money. The fat man who had complained of his struggle from the South had grabbed the waiter's arm. The boy was standing alongside him, faintly bored as the man questioned his friends on their choice. The girl was still weeping, sitting quietly alone, tears on her face, lost in desperate unhappiness, her beauty drawing every male eye to her. Was she weeping for a lost husband? A dead lover? A missing child?

Then, suddenly, Woodyatt realised that out of all the men on the crowded terrace only one had no eyes for her. It was Montrouge and he was looking at the handsome waiter. His eyes followed him everywhere he went, hungrily, lost in a sort of daydream.

They drove to the consul's office in silence. It was already under siege by dozens of people all wanting passes for British ships. It took them some time to fight their way to a man who stood behind a desk. He said the consul was due to leave and only a few clerks were remaining to handle the business. The hall of the consulate was full of luggage. Outside people who had petrol were loading their cars for the journey to St Jean de Luz and Spain. A train full of expatriate British had just left and those who had missed it were clamouring for another to be assembled.

'I must see the consul,' Woodyatt insisted and eventually they managed to get an interview. The consul looked worn out.

'I have your boarding passes,' he informed Darby. 'The problem is ships. There's nothing leaving tonight, though there may be something tomorrow. Try the docks. The passes will take you aboard any ship that's available. If nothing comes in – and perhaps nothing will, because the Germans have been dropping mines in the river – try Le Verdon.'

Woodyatt knew Le Verdon, but couldn't imagine it being a good port of embarkation. It lay on the other side of the River Gironde at the end of the long peninsula that pointed north like a spearhead towards Britain. It was well out of the German's reach but it was very small, and boarding ship would probably have to be done from boats.

'I'd advise getting there early,' the consul said. 'German aircraft are active over the river.'

With his help, Woodyatt got off a telegram to Pullinger demanding aid, stating where he was and that he had a man he believed to be Redmond.

Darby was unhappy about staying in the area of the town and wanted to head immediately for Le Verdon. They could hear aircraft about and he was afraid that a bombing raid might prevent them getting across the river.

'They've only to seal the entrance to the river,' he said, 'and nothing will get away.'

In the end they decided to seek a hotel outside Bordeaux but elected to eat before they left the city.

They found a large restaurant on the outskirts. As they sat down the radio began. *'Ici Radio-Journal de France.'* Everything came to a stop. The waitresses halted and conversation died. The first thing on the news was an announcement that the Cabinet had met; that the government had decided that power should be given to some man enjoying the respect of the nation, and that Marshal Philippe Pétain had been asked to assume the reins of government. As the name was spoken there was a gasp round the restaurant.

'God help France,' Montrouge said in a flat voice. 'It was said of him at the Ecole de Guerre that if he ever rose above the rank of major it would be a disaster.'

He was hushed to silence by the people around him and Pétain's voice came. He spoke with the wavering tones of a tired old man.

'By request of the Republic,' he said, 'I have today assumed the direction of the government of France.' A few of the worn clichés well-known to all politicians followed, then he went on that his heart went out to the army struggling against an enemy superior in numbers and equipment, and to the unhappy refugees who were crowding the roads. He finally ended with 'It is with a heavy heart that I say we must cease the fight, and last night I communicated with the enemy to ask if he is ready to seek with us, as between soldiers, after the conflict and with honour, a way to end hostilities.'

The dismal voice droned on until an ill-timed gramophone record played the 'Marseillaise', announcing to the listeners that '*Le jour de gloire est arrivé.*'

'The day of glory?' a disgusted voice said. 'This?'

'God help France,' Montrouge said again, his voice sharp with contempt. 'Poincaré decided, even in 1917 when Pétain was at the height of his fame, that he was a defeatist at heart.'

The packed restaurant had become still. The news had been totally unexpected. Then a man shouted, his voice crashing across the silent room. 'Vive la France!'

For a moment the cry was ignored, then a few people responded until finally the whole restaurant was at it, yelling as hard as they could, in defiance, relief or sheer misery.

Dominique remained motionless, her face stiff, but there was a strange exalted glow in her eyes, as if she had suddenly seen some light in the darkness.

Woodyatt sat in silence. Not long before, Reynaud had said it didn't matter if the whole of France were captured; the fight would continue from North Africa. And now had come this humiliating surrender. As they left, hurriedly scrawled placards announcing the new government were already appearing on the street.

They headed for the outskirts of the town. Darby was leading, driving fast and moving dexterously in and out of the other vehicles. Woodyatt tried to stay on his tail but at the first traffic lights a string of cars from a side road slipped between them.

Somehow defeat didn't seem possible. There was no visible bomb damage and – apart from the crowds, the overloaded cars and the occasional weeping woman no sign of despair. It looked more like an overcrowded holiday season than anything else. The shops they passed were packed with goods, clothes, cakes, chocolates, perfume, wines – though the *tabacs* all seemed to have notices outside to indicate they had sold out of cigarettes. From time to time they passed ambulances carrying the wounded, but they couldn't tell whether they were victims of air raids or evacuees from the battles in the North, brought to Bordeaux by sea.

Eventually they cleared the town and found themselves in sandy country wooded with pines. There were a few other cars and the noise of the engines prevented them hearing the aircraft. Almost before they were aware of it, Woodyatt heard the rattle of guns and a *whoo-oosh* as an aeroplane passed low overhead.

'For God's sake,' he snarled, 'I thought the bloody war was over!'

Drawing into the side of the road, he halted the car under a group of pines and they scrambled out. Montrouge refused to budge. Woodyatt didn't argue. He dragged the old man roughly from his seat and, with Dominique on the other side of him, they ran for the side of the road. Pushing the old man down, Woodyatt put his arm round the girl and together they lay on the ground, surrounded by other people, all yelling with fright. Dominique made no sound, lying half-beneath Woodyatt, her cheek against his.

A stick of bombs burst a little further along the road then the howl of engines died. Woodyatt rose to his feet and pulled Dominique after him, leaving Montrouge to follow. Somewhere ahead, someone was wailing and he realised that one of the bombs had fallen on the road. A car was on its side burning and a group of people were staring at it. A woman lay a little further along, silent and still beside her bicycle. Then he saw Daphne Darby and the expression on her face set him running.

Darby lay at her feet and she had taken off her coat and placed it under his head. There was blood on his face and in the thick grey hair.

Dominique knelt and felt his pulse, then she crossed herself and lifted her face to Woodyatt's. Daphne Darby understood. She drew a deep breath and her body stiffened.

Bending down and covering her husband's face, she rose tiredly. 'We'd better get on our way,' she said. 'I wonder if you'd be kind enough to offer me a lift.'

five

A group of British soldiers in a lorry offered to bury Darby. The sandy soil was soft and the job was quickly done and one of them erected a crude cross on which they wrote his name in pencil. 'Albert Francis Cummings Darby.' No more.

The soldiers also offered Mrs Darby a lift to Le Verdon. She looked at the wrecked car, and then unhappily at Woodyatt and Dominique as if she felt she were abandoning them. Woodyatt helped her into the lorry.

'There's nothing more you can do,' he said. 'I've got a statement from both you and Frank. They don't agree but that's by the way.'

Her eyes wandered to the Ford where the old man was again sitting, surrounded by luggage. 'It *is* Redmond,' she said. 'I *know*.'

Woodyatt didn't argue. He gave her his address and told her how to contact him through Pullinger at the War Office. 'It might be necessary to answer a few questions,' he said.

As the lorry drew away, Dominique's fingers touched Woodyatt's and he drew a deep painful breath. It was already late and they had to continue their search to find somewhere for the night. There was a hotel near St Laurent, off the main road, Norman in style with yellow-washed walls in which bare beams were criss-crossed. It was in an area of sandy soil through which grew sparse grass that was broken by clumps of pine trees and tough-looking bushes of broom. It was clearly a waste of time trying to get a room. The lobby of the hotel was crowded and there were piles of luggage everywhere. The chairs and settees were all full of sleeping people.

The proprietor was permitting travellers to wash in the hotel. There seemed to be hundreds of them, almost all British, their cars drawn up anyhow among the trees. Scattered rugs, cushions and abandoned suitcases showed where earlier refugees had camped out.

They were able to obtain a meal but it had been hurriedly cooked and the wine was poor. The proprietor shrugged. 'There are so many, Monsieur,' he explained.

He promised to let them know if news of a British ship arrived. 'I have a contact in Le Verdon,' he said.

Dominique helped the old man back to the car. He had eaten a good meal and, Woodyatt had noticed, had polished off a brandy and soda very smartly. They got him established in the rear seat of the Ford and made themselves a bed from the abandoned rugs and cushions around them. As soon as Woodyatt lay down, Dominique moved close to him. She did it in her usual cool, deliberate manner, as if she needed his warmth, even the physical contact with him, but resented having to be in any way dependent on him.

She was silent for a while then she spoke in a grieving whisper. 'Poor Mrs Darby,' she said. She shifted restlessly and turned to look at him. 'Are you in love with me, James Woodyatt?' she demanded. She sounded as if she were asking a dull pupil if he understood where Africa was.

'I think so.'

'That is how I feel. You have brought me back to life and I shall always be grateful for that. And for what you have done for me. And my uncle,' she added. 'Are you still determined to take him to England to be questioned?'

'Yes.'

She sighed. 'Nothing surprises me any more,' she went on quietly. 'Not you. Not France with her failures. Not me, with mine. Not my uncle, with his. Nothing is perfect. Everything is flawed in some way.' She kissed him fiercely. 'Which is why you must always understand, James Woodyatt. I'm not someone who fits into a slot, a pattern, a type. I'm me.'

In the distance they could hear occasional shots and all around them quiet discussions were going on about what to take and what to leave.

'Bugger the suitcases,' one angry man was saying. 'The thing is to get aboard a ship. Suitcases will impede us. One bag. No more.'

A woman was wailing that she was having to leave her wedding dress behind while another was complaining that the silver she had packed so carefully had been lost. In their panic and haste, a lot of them were showing the triviality of the lives they had lived. Suitcases were being left half-open on the ground with clothes hanging out, together with picnic baskets, even trunks, some of them still full.

The sky was clear with the hint of a moon. As he watched the clouds, unexpectedly and from nowhere Woodyatt remembered Zamerski and the car in the road by the Darby's gate. Sleep suddenly became impossible as he realised he had dropped his guard. After following them across half of France, their pursuers would hardly be likely to give up until all the British had left. They could well be among the shadowy figures moving among the trees.

He climbed to his feet quickly. His mind was still racing when he heard a telephone ringing in the hotel. Soon afterwards, he saw lights go on in the reception area and a figure moving down the steps. It approached one of the cars and he heard a door slam. Then there was a shout.

'It's arrived! It's off Le Verdon now!'

As the proprietor of the hotel had predicted, people started running from the hotel immediately and began to climb into cars. Engines started and in the semi-darkness of the summer night voices were raised.

'Wake up! For Christ's sake, wake up! It's arrived!'

Within minutes the first car moved off. It lurched over the uneven ground beneath the pines, it's headlamps lighting up the shapes of those people scrambling in or out of other cars, tossing in rugs, suitcases and baskets. In no time, more vehicles began to jolt past.

Dominique was bent over Montrouge, her hand on his forehead. 'I think he's got a temperature,' she said. She was grave and quiet and there was no indication that the old man meant anything to her.

Woodyatt stared at the old man, puzzled by him as he always was. He had a feeling he was playing possum. He was a tough old bastard, he thought, from a harder generation than his own. Despite his age, he had survived the struggle from Paris better than many younger in years.

Woodyatt refused to be put off. 'Get him up,' he said.

By this time the hotel had emptied of people. The last groups of British were hurrying out in ones and twos, carrying their belongings, and the number of cars had already dwindled considerably. Montrouge still seemed to be feigning sleep and in the end, irritated beyond measure, Woodyatt shook him hard. He came to life and struggled to sit upright in the back of the car. For a brief moment he looked his age and Woodyatt felt as if he were being a bully.

'We're moving,' he announced.

'Is Hitler at our heels?' The old man had recovered quickly and spoke with a wealth of sly humour that made Woodyatt feel again that Montrouge had the full measure of him. He had sensed more than once that Montrouge enjoyed the panic among the British, most of whom had until now enjoyed life in the South of France away from the cold and damp of England. Their complaints seemed to amuse the old man.

All the cars appeared to have gone now. Some distance away the starter of a last one could be heard whirring, until eventually, as the battery died, it grew fainter and fainter and finally stopped. Soon afterwards three or four people moved through the semi-darkness carrying suitcases. All round the black Ford cars had been abandoned because of mechanical faults or lack of petrol; scattered among them were numerous thermos flasks, clothes, shoes, cast-off suitcases, and bags. One huge bow-topped black trunk stood wide open nearby, with what looked like a set of green velvet curtains dripping from it.

The old man was complaining about the earliness of the hour, but far too briskly to be convincing. Somewhere in the distance, they could hear shooting short bursts as if coming from a machine gun, then, closer, occasional shots, as if enemy agents were among the pine woods trying to stir up panic.

The old man was out of the car at last, stumbling about in the half-darkness.

'Old men's bladders,' he growled, 'aren't quite so accommodating as younger men's.'

Woodyatt and the girl stood in silence, looking at each other as he moved away from them. Then Woodyatt woke up to the fact that Montrouge had drifted off out of sight. He whirled in alarm. Despite Darby's reassurances about the car outside the house, he had never accepted his explanation, but weariness and the nearness of safety had caused him to relax his alertness.

It was just light enough to see and, desperate and furious, he picked his way among the general debris. He was growing angrier with every second. Then, turning, he saw that the old man, a bulky figure in the half-darkness, had returned to the car and Woodyatt realised he had somehow passed him in the half-light. As dawn broke it became possible to pick out the line of the hotel among the trees. Then he saw that Montrouge and Dominique had been joined by another man. In the gathering light it was possible to discern the gun he held and the bright blond hair of Zamerski. He was alone. There was no sign of the thin man and Woodyatt saw that his left hand was heavily bandaged, no doubt from burns sustained at Marville.

Here he was, and they had probably been followed ever since the episode near the bridge outside Bordeaux. The French officer with the doubtful medals had obviously been another of Zamerski's men trying to force them on to a side road where they could be picked up. Woodyatt surmised that he had directed Zamerski after them and provided the numbers of their cars.

'Your name is Montrouge?'

Woodyatt stopped dead, his ears pricked to hear a confession.

'Is it?' The old man sounded remarkably cool.

'I've been looking for you a long time.'

'I've noticed.'

Zamerski stared at him and Montrouge shuffled in the long coat he wore. His hands were in the pockets, hugging it to him against the dawn chill.

The very next instant a shot rang out and Woodyatt saw the old man was holding the ancient revolver. There was a hole in his coat that was still smoking a little.

'In war,' Montrouge said to him, 'you have to make up your mind at once. Hesitation will be the death of you, though I have to admit you did well at Marville.'

The shooting had been witnessed by no one save themselves. The hotel was silent and they were far enough away among the clumps of broom not to be seen. In the distance they could still hear bursts of firing.

'That was quick,' Woodyatt said. No wonder the old man had never been very perturbed.

'I always was quick,' Montrouge pointed out.

'So I was told. And a good shot.'

'That, too.'

'Especially since you had it in your pocket.'

'It was no trouble really.' They were speaking in English and for a moment Woodyatt thought the old devil sounded more English than he had ever sounded French. Montrouge smiled. 'I think we'll make a soldier of you yet,' he said, taking charge as if he had been used all his life to command. 'But we're wasting time. Don't you think we should get rid of that?'

He pointed with the revolver at Zamerski's body. 'Murder's murder, after all, even in the middle of a defeat.'

Woodyatt frowned as he stared about him, then Montrouge's voice came again. 'The trunk, young man. The trunk.' He gestured briskly at the huge bow-topped black trunk with its load of green velvet curtains. 'In there, with the curtains on top. Secured and strapped up, I imagine it will be a day or two before anyone thinks of looking inside.'

Angry with himself for losing the initiative, Woodyatt dragged the body to the trunk, then Dominique joined him and together they got the head and shoulders over the edge and pushed the rest of the body after them. It slid away to the bottom in a particularly sickening way.

The old man appeared alongside them. He had put the revolver away and was gesturing with his hand. 'If you look carefully,' he went on calmly, 'you will notice near your left foot a bunch of keys. I suggest you try them.'

Feeling slow-witted, Woodyatt picked up the keys and found the one that fitted almost immediately. Strapping up the trunk, he locked it and pushed the keys into his pocket without thinking.

'If I were you,' Montrouge said. 'I think I would throw them away.'

He seemed to have come remarkably to life. Woodyatt glared at him then, swinging his arm, he flung the keys as far from him as he could.

'Excellent,' Montrouge commented. 'That's the way to do it.'

'You seem to know exactly what to do,' Woodyatt said savagely. 'I suppose you've been in one or two shady affairs before.'

Montrouge smiled. 'You can't live to my age, young man,' he pointed out, 'without defaulting somewhere. We all have our guilty little secrets, don't we?'

s i x

The land was like the hollow in a vast dune, with vineyards and pine trees and a road that ran arrow-straight the whole length of the peninsula. Gradually it began to be more sandy and wooded and there was a strong smell of the sea. Then they left the woods behind them for open country, immense stretches of sand lay ahead of them. The wide mouth of the river was dotted with ships at anchor, large liners and small merchant ships, some of the flags Dutch, some Belgian, some French, some British. On the other side of the river was Royan, an Edwardian resort of no great beauty but at that moment shining in the sun, the church on the hill pointing like a finger to the sky. Reaching Le Verdon, they passed the memorial on the Pointe de Grave, erected to the memory of the Americans who had landed there in 1917 as they came to the aid of France.

Despite his title, the naval control officer was a British businessman from Bordeaux. Waiting to board were British soldiers, an RAF intelligence group, two or three wounded and a crowd of civilians. Cars were parked everywhere.

They learned that a launch was to take them out to a ship at four p.m. so they had lunch at a restaurant near the American memorial and afterwards Dominique insisted on going into the church nearby. 'I would like to say a prayer for Colonel Darby,' she announced.

'You could say one for us too,' Woodyatt suggested.

'I have been doing that for some time,' she said primly. When they arrived at the water's edge people were struggling up with their luggage. Most of them had been too lazy, too arrogant or too stupid to leave before, and now they were behaving badly and making things worse for those whose presence there was not of their own doing.

They emptied the Ford of its luggage and Montrouge climbed out. Hoping to see inside his case, Woodyatt placed it to one side. 'I'll carry it.'

'No!' The old man grabbed the handle. '*I* will.'

People were boarding the launches from a small stone quay, everybody pushing and shoving angrily. Forcing his way through, Woodyatt edged to the front.

'Here! You lot!' a man with several chins and an expensive accent called out. 'Where do you think you're going? We were here long before you.

A naval lieutenant at the top of the steps that led down to the launches was shouting over the heads of the queue. 'You might as well settle down for the night,' he yelled. 'There'll be no more after this one.'

As Woodyatt appeared, he pushed him back. 'Take your turn, old boy,' he said sharply. 'Everybody takes their turn.'

'I have a man here who must get to England.'

'Sorry. *You* can go. You're in uniform but there are no special favours for civilians.'

'He's needed in England.'

'I've heard that one before.'

The lieutenant's manner infuriated Woodyatt and he waved Pullinger's documents. 'You'd better take a look at these,' he said. 'Or it will be God help you, believe me.'

The lieutenant turned. He was still trying to be authoritative but he took the papers. Flipping through them, he read the signatures and his face stiffened. For a while he was silent then he looked up. 'All right,' he said, making no apology. 'Let's have you.'

Montrouge was pushed through the crowd by Dominique.

'Who is he?' the lieutenant asked. 'My instructions are that everybody taken on board has to have a good reason. We're getting some funny types through. They're already sending back French who were picked up at Dunkirk and don't fancy roast beef and Yorkshire pud. Who's the girl?'

'She's his nurse,' Woodyatt snapped. 'If you open your eyes you can see he's old and needs one. And, as it happens, she's my wife.'

As they went down the steps to the launch, Montrouge was at Woodyatt's side. 'Young man,' he murmured, 'I begin to see that you might yet have a future in the army.'

As they took their places in the launch, Dominique was sitting quietly beside Woodyatt.

'You told him I was your wife,' she said.

Woodyatt was still angry, with Montrouge, with the lieutenant, with the whole French nation and, for no reason at all, with her.

'You could be,' he retorted.

'But I am not.'

'Then we'd better make it so as soon as possible.'

She was silent for a long time. 'Is that supposed to be a proposal?' she asked.

'Yes.'

'It's a very odd one.'

'There've been odder.'

'We barely know each other.'

'We've known each other for years.'

With her hands in her lap, her eyes directed towards her feet, she took the steam out of Woodyatt's anger. His temper began to cool and, as his heart stopped thumping and his breathing slowed, he looked at her and grinned. 'We've done all the things lovers do,' he pointed out.

'Yes,' she agreed. 'We have.' She looked at him, her eyes full of mischief.

'Since we're discussing it – ' Woodyatt pressed the point home ' – it's quite possible that what that naval twit said is right and they are sending French people back to France. Whether they like it or not. They wouldn't send an English wife. It can be done quickly at a Registry Office. You could always divorce me later.'

She looked at him, her eyes gentle, and he went on, stumbling a little. 'I wouldn't hold you to it. It would be a means of being safe.'

She had turned her head away but now her eyes lifted and unexpectedly she gave him one of the wide flashing grins that always devastated him when they appeared.

'I think I just caught the smell of burned boats,' she said.

They were put aboard a destroyer and, despite the naval man's insistence, nobody asked to see their papers or sought their identities. After a while the ship began to move and she brought up alongside a British passenger liner named the *Coniston*. The liner had a dirty yellow line painted round her to indicate she had been degaussed against the magnetic mines the Germans had been dropping in the river. The sailors who helped them up the long ladder were Lascars. They were polite and helpful but they seemed amused that the pukka sahibs to whom they'd always had to show subservience were being herded like coolies. The ship had come from East Africa via the Cape of Good Hope and Sierra Leone and she had normal accommodation for a hundred and fifty passengers. There were already between five and six hundred aboard and more were expected.

There were no cabins free because they had been snatched up long since but they settled for a deck chair on the boat deck for Montrouge and a seat on the planking for themselves. As the old man sat down, he placed his suitcase alongside him and called Woodyatt's attention to a steward moving past with glasses on a tray.

'I think the bar's open,' he said in English. 'So B and S wouldn't come amiss.' Suddenly he seemed to have thrown caution to the wind and become indifferent to what he said or how he said it.

More people came aboard until it was almost impossible to move. Woodyatt thought he saw Daphne Darby on the deck below but then he lost her again in the crowd. An aeroplane appeared overhead and somebody said it was Italian.

'They haven't declared an armistice yet,' he explained.

A bomb was dropped but it came nowhere near them. And suddenly it didn't seem to matter. They were in the hands of the navy, that traditional haven for thousands of weary soldiers and refugees over the centuries. Woodyatt found a great burden of responsibility had fallen from his shoulders. All he had to do now was leave it to the seamen. All the accumulated strain of the last few days had vanished and a sense of luxurious security flooded over him.

There was still the sound of aeroplanes about but none were visible. The story aboard the ship was that the Italians were determined to push the French to the limit from the South to get all they could before their German overlords told them to stop.

Other ships arrived and dropped anchor. The British government had obviously mounted a major rescue attempt for troops cut off from the North and British passport-holders trying to get out of France. French, Belgian and Dutch ships lay among them.

'That's a Norwegian,' a sailor standing at the rail by Woodyatt said. '*Stavanger*. She was in Southampton when I was there last year. Collier. Six thousand tons, built on the Tyne.'

The ship was a big lumpy flush-decker, painted as black as the cargoes she carried.

'Built on the Isherwood system,' the sailor continued. ''Stead of her ribs being arranged vertically from keel to deck, they run horizontally from forward to aft. Strong. Sensible, o'course, because she spends a lot of time in icebound waters. That's why she has that heavy stern. It goes down well below the waterline. They don't build 'em like that any more. Insurance companies think they're too dangerous.'

He offered Woodyatt a cigarette. 'She came in here carrying coal,' he went on. 'Around ten thousand tons, I reckon. But they commandeered her, coal and all, to take people home. They must be short of ships after Dunkirk.'

Up ahead a mat of small boats was clustered round another ship and more were arriving all the time from the shore.

'I suppose now,' Montrouge said amiably, 'you can sit back with the feeling that everything will be taken care of from London.'

He was lying comfortably in his chair as Woodyatt and Dominique squatted on the deck.

'That's about the idea,' Woodyatt said equably.

'And I suppose they'll do the same as you and assume I'm this fellow Redmond you talk about.'

'I think they will.'

Montrouge smiled. 'British Intelligence was never very good.'

He seemed to feel he could handle anything that was thrown at him and Woodyatt smiled back, curiously at ease with him for once.

'It's learned a lot since your time,' he said cheerfully. 'They already know more than I know. More than you know, too. They have several thick files about you.'

'It would need fingerprints, and prints weren't in general use when Redmond disappeared.'

'True,' Woodyatt agreed. 'But when he was a young soldier, he made the mistake of allowing himself to be interviewed by the French anthropometrist, Alphonse Bertillon. He measured Redmond's head, his fingers, his foot, his forearms. Had you forgotten?'

Montrouge was silent for a moment. 'Bertillon was a fool,' he snapped.

For the first time he seemed shaken.

Woodyatt smiled. 'In addition, they have very careful records of every known mark on his body. Darby made them.'

'Darby drank.' There wasn't the slightest indication of sorrow for Darby's death.

'He was no fool, all the same. He collected every bit of information on the Redmond affair there was. Every bit.'

'British Intelligence was never that thorough.' Montrouge suddenly sounded lame and hesitant.

'Darby wasn't working for Intelligence,' Woodyatt pointed out. 'He was working for himself.'

The *Coniston* still hadn't moved when darkness came, and they began to hear a chorus of complaints. They were the same complaints they had heard ashore and they came from the same people. Why weren't the authorities doing more for their comfort? Why weren't they taking steps to move them to safety? The grumbling went on long after dark.

Montrouge was fast asleep in his chair, as indifferent, it seemed, to the complaints as to the chilly breeze off the sea. He was swathed in the long overcoat, his head down in the collar.

Woodyatt could still hear aircraft in the sky and there was an occasional thump and now and then a short burst of machine-gun fire. Whatever had been decided about France, the war with Britain hadn't finished.

It was impossible to sleep. The deck was hard and there was the constant coming and going of people as uncomfortable as themselves. Always there was someone tripping over their feet or stumbling against them as everyone moved restlessly about the ship in the dark. Dominique slept with her head against Woodyatt's shoulder. His arm was round her and he could feel the warmth and softness of her breast against his hand.

He awoke to find there was already light in the sky. It looked as it had when they left the hotel at St Laurent, and he wondered if anybody had bothered to examine the trunk yet.

Dominique stirred and her head lifted. She caught his eyes on her and smiled, pushing at her hair.

Behind them they could see smoke rising ashore from burning buildings beyond Royan. The wind was off the land and depositing a layer of fine dust and ash on the *Coniston*. The river was beginning to come to life and over the water they could hear the clang of ships' bells and the higher sound of engine-room telegraphs. The Norwegian collier, the *Stavanger*, which had been lying further downstream, was already underway and heading slowly towards them. As they became aware of the smell of cooking coming from somewhere aboard the ship, Woodyatt scrambled to his feet.

'I think I'd better try to find some food,' he said.

Rations were already beginning to run out on the overcrowded vessel but he managed to bribe his way to a tray containing cups of tea and a plateful of buttered toast. The sound of aircraft was still in the sky as he returned to where Dominique waited with Montrouge. He had just reached them when, high up, faint and silvery, like midges in the sun, he saw a group of planes heading towards them from the direction of Royan.

'Better eat while you can,' he advised.

He swallowed the tepid tea and watched Dominique do the same, then they stuffed their mouths with the toast and placed the tray on the old man's lap. He seemed startled at their hurry. As he began on the toast, the guns on the destroyer nearby opened fire with a crash that almost split their eardrums: the harsh racket of pompoms mingled with the crash of heavier weapons. Lewis guns from smaller craft and the rattle of rifles joined the barrage. The planes were nearer now and the destroyer was going astern; the boats which had been alongside her cast adrift. On board the *Coniston* men were pushing screaming women through doors into companionways leading from the deck. Trays, cups, saucers and plates had been dropped and were crunched under hurrying feet.

The bombers were nearer now and every ship in the river mouth suddenly seemed to be moving. The destroyer was tearing away at speed and another liner, which had been surrounded by a mat of boats, was already heading north to the sea. There was a crash and a roar from forward and somebody yelled that the captain had slipped the anchor. Woodyatt could feel the throbbing of the ship's engines and realised they were moving.

'Full ahead!' Even above the noise he heard the bridge order.

The tide had been on the turn and ships had been lying all ways so that they were moving in every direction imaginable. Among them, the *Stavanger* had increased to full speed and was moving quickly towards the sea. The bombers were almost overhead now. There were three waves of them coming down in shallow dives as the *Coniston* began to work up speed. Huge waterspouts rose as the bombs fell in the river mouth, the water dropping back across the deck of the moving ship. The screams and shouts intensified, but they seemed to have escaped damage.

Then, as the last aeroplane passed beyond the bow of the ship, Woodyatt saw the stick of bombs it had dropped, hanging in the air above them, poised for what seemed an age, growing larger and larger as they fell.

Guns were hammering all round them and they saw a piece break off the wing of the aeroplane. As it fluttered down, the plane disappeared across the river, struggling to maintain height. Everybody's eyes were on it and only a few of the passengers were watching the bombs. Woodyatt saw a line of splashes beside the ship and felt the thump of the explosions. He was drenched by the collapsing waterspouts. Then as the last bomb landed somewhere just below the overhanging stern, he felt the deck leap beneath his feet, under an explosion that jarred his spine and made his teeth feel loose.

seven

At first the *Coniston* seemed to have escaped damage. There was no sign of wreckage and no one had been injured, and it seemed there was nothing to do but continue towards the sea.

Then Woodyatt realised the ship was swinging wildly and, as several members of the crew hurried past him towards the stern, he gathered that the bomb had jammed the rudder and the ship was out of control.

There had been no sign of fear from Dominique, only a movement nearer to Woodyatt. Montrouge had risen to his feet from the chair. Woodyatt watched him put his cup and saucer down on the deck, fascinated by his slowness and calmness. It was as though he were trying to show people younger than he was how to behave in the face of danger.

Now that the aeroplanes had gone, the passengers were crowding back on deck from the companionways, trying to see what had happened. Someone yelled from the bridge.

'Go astern! Go astern!'

The engine-room telegraph sounded and the ship shuddered as the engines were thrown into reverse. The shout had not been directed towards the *Coniston* herself though, but towards the *Stavanger*, which was still roaring up at full speed towards the open sea.

With her ten thousand tons of coal aboard, she was right down to her load mark with only a few feet of freeboard between waterline and deck. Someone aboard had spotted the swinging *Coniston* and Woodyatt saw a furious froth of water under her overhanging stern as her engines were put into reverse. The *Coniston*'s siren boomed and the *Stavanger*'s roared in reply. But because of the bombing, both ships had been moving to full speed and in the distance available there was no stopping them. The *Coniston* was slowing but, under the dead weight of her cargo, the *Stavanger* still moved swiftly forward, impossible to halt in the distance available.

'Go astern!' The cry came again from the *Coniston*'s bridge.

Watching with fascinated horror as the ships drew closer, Woodyatt remembered what the sailor had told him the previous evening. He had no experience whatsoever of ships, but he could see that sharp upright bow drawing closer to where he stood. The thought that passed through his mind was that it was like an immense cold chisel.

Her siren shrieking a pointless warning, the *Stavanger* struck the side of the bigger vessel like a gigantic steel wedge. There was no shock to send everybody reeling, none of the scream of tortured metal Woodyatt expected. The collision produced nothing more than a slight jar as the collier's bows bit into the side of the *Coniston* and a fireworks display of sparks as steel ground against steel.

As the pointless screeching of the sirens stopped, Woodyatt heard a command from above him. 'Warn all hands. Get the boats ready.' Then – to the *Stavanger* – 'Keep going ahead on your engines! For God's sake, keep her bows in the hole!'

Instinct warned Woodyatt they were now in real danger and he looked round to see Dominique standing quietly alongside him, waiting to be told what to do. Even Montrouge seemed to be aware that for once his magnificent calm wasn't going to help. The steel stem of the Norwegian ship had sliced into the *Coniston*'s side like a hatchet. Despite the apparent slightness of the collision, the huge bows had cut a gap that had opened the liner from deck to double bottom, a hole like the mark of an axe had appeared in her hull – a horrific wound over twenty feet deep and fifteen feet wide.

Despite the attempt to remain in place with her engine full ahead, the *Stavanger* had drifted off in the current and the *Coniston,* the hole unplugged, was filling with water at an alarming rate. It was as if she had been torpedoed. Despite all the safety precautions that had gone into her building there was nothing that could withstand that terrible wound, and she was already beginning to list. Like all passenger vessels, her side was lined with portholes and most of them were filled with faces. The lowest were not far above the waterline and because of the heat, most were open and many of them had scoops out to produce a little breeze.

At first, chiefly through lack of nautical know-how among the passengers, there was no alarm but, as the ship lurched once more, the air became filled with the screams of women and the shouts of men. It was still early in the morning and many of the passengers had not yet left their cabins. Some of those in the lower berths on the starboard side where the *Stavanger* had struck could have had no knowledge of what was happening before the incoming water had swept over them.

As men and women began to claw their way through the listing passageways, the boat deck began to fill with those who were panic-stricken. Woodyatt wrenched open a chest of life jackets and grabbed an armful. Immediately they were snatched from him by frantic hands and he had to dive into it again. He got one on Dominique even as she was securing the one they had forced on Montrouge. They were old-fashioned and cumbersome with square blocks of cork that made movement difficult.

The boat deck was swarming now as passengers formed into groups that got in the way of the crew struggling against the increasing list of the ship to swing out boats. Because of the confusion in the river mouth after the bombing, no other ship seemed to have noticed what had happened to the *Coniston* but, as she lurched again, Woodyatt saw the destroyer's bow swing in their direction.

Montrouge gave Woodyatt a thin smile. 'This is a situation you hadn't bargained for, young man, isn't it?' he said. 'But what a splendid opportunity for nobility. Women and children first, of course. The British have a rare taste for martyrdom.'

Struggling through the crowding masses, Woodyatt forced his way to a boat. He pushed Montrouge ahead of him, feeling that if he were saved, someone would deal with the problem of who he was. He still had his suitcase with him.

Moving was difficult and the list had increased the gap between the boat and the side of the ship, so that the boat's crew were having difficulty holding it in place.

'For Christ's sake, get him in!' someone yelled.

They managed to scramble the old man aboard.

'Now you!' Woodyatt pushed Dominique forward.

'I'll stay with you.'

'Get in! Don't argue!'

She was still begging to be allowed to stay when someone dragged her into the boat and it disappeared in jerks down the side of the ship. Her face was agonised as she stared up at Woodyatt. Standing by the rail, he watched the boat cast off the falls that held it to the ship like umbilical cords. The men manning the oars were a scratch lot of saloon crew and passengers and they were having difficulties. Oars clashed and strokes were missed but the boat slowly drew away. As it left, there was another swirl of people to the rail from the port side where the list was making it impossible to launch the boats. They were shouting and trying to find places and, for a moment, Woodyatt thought he saw Daphne Darby among them again. Then one of the two-ton steel boats on the portside which, due to the angle of the ship, had been dangling inboard over the heads of the men struggling to launch it, broke free and thundered across the deck. It swept away crew and screaming passengers and crashed into the rails on the lower side of the ship, taking them and the people huddled against them into the sea.

The ship's engines had thudded to a halt as the steam failed, and more gear crashed across the deck as the list increased. Then, as the ship lurched again, Woodyatt saw the great black and green funnels swinging over in a vast arc. He grabbed for a handhold as he saw people sliding across the deck. One of the heavy deck chairs struck him in the side, throwing him down and knocking all the breath out of him. As he rose, the ship lurched once more and he was flung against the cleat of a davit.

The thump of his body against the iron stanchion sent a shock of pain through him. He tried to grab for another handhold but his arm suddenly wouldn't work. A swinging block hit him on the head and he felt himself falling. As he hit the river, it seemed solid and sent a shock of pain through his injured arm and side. He swallowed a lot of water but then his head emerged and he gasped for air. Despite the warm weather the river was icy enough to take his breath away.

He was in a patch of oil and tried to swim clear but a shaft of pain ran through his arm and he found he couldn't move it. He tried to lift it to look at it but it was impossible and the pain made him gasp. An oar floated past and he managed to get his good arm across it. He had come to the surface in the middle of a yelling mass of people who had been flung into the sea like himself and who were all now thrashing about in the water. From them came a terrible cry and, looking up, he saw the ship's funnels slap against the surface of the river, sending a surge of water rolling away.

He had heard that a sinking ship could carry swimmers down with it, so he kicked his way to a clear stretch of water. Black with fuel oil but supporting his injured arm with the aid of the floating oar, he managed to fight his way from the terrified survivors reaching out to grab at him.

The dying ship had left hundreds of people struggling for their lives. All round Woodyatt there was the moaning sound that came from the drowning passengers. Then he saw a boat just ahead of him and began to fight his way towards it. The oarsman were disorganised, those on one side pulling in short bursts, those on the other resting on their sweeps so that the boat was going round in circles. Looking back, he saw the ship lying on her side, the deck like a huge man-made cliff, with the water roaring down her funnels.

For a while she hung motionless, lying lower and lower in the water with every minute, almost as if she were a sandcastle on the beach facing an incoming tide. He could see a man walking down her hull, and people struggling in the water to free themselves from the aerials and rigging trailing over her rails. Then she gave another lurch and in seconds there was nothing but a whirlpool in which the bodies of both living and dead were swirled around with numerous spars and pieces of timber and an upturned boat. As she disappeared there was a moan of despair from hundreds of throats. The survivors standing on the ship's side had been swept away by her final plunge and the vast wave that roared along her frame.

Still struggling towards the nearby boat through red waves of pain, Woodyatt became aware of a voice he knew calling his name and realised it was Dominique's. As the boat's side loomed above him, he let go of the oar and lifted his good arm. A hand came down and grasped his wrist and he was heaved upward and over the side of the boat with a swift roughness that made him shout with agony. As he was dragged aboard, half-fainting, he realised that the hand that had saved him had been Montrouge's and he noticed through the pain that it was surprisingly firm and strong. As he flopped into the bottom of the boat, exhausted, he was conscious of Dominique holding his head in her lap, and found himself looking up at Montrouge.

'Not quite as you expected,' the old man said cheerfully. 'The wrong man's doing the rescuing. But it seemed to be an emergency. I tried to be aware of the dignity of a British officer.'

The oarsmen were still disorganised so that the boat moved in haphazard zigzags. Then Montrouge barked a few orders and they began to make headway. The destroyer came tearing up and stopped almost dead as she reversed engines and went astern. Her sailors dived into the sea and started swimming to drowning people. Then the *Stavanger* loomed up alongside and they were dragged aboard, cold and exhausted. For some the shock had been too great and several of those lifted to the collier's decks were already dead. The crew, a starveling lot, gave what they had to help, offering clothes, blankets and food. The captain produced a bottle of whisky and began to dose the wretched survivors.

Tablecloths and curtains were found to cover half-naked men and women. Dozens of people crowded into the engine and boiler rooms to find warmth, and women, shaking with cold, tried to dry their nightdresses, in many cases their only garment.

Soon afterwards the destroyer came alongside and, as soon as the survivors were transferred, she swung to face north and lifted her bows to full speed. A naval surgeon and sick-berth attendants came round, dosing people and putting broken limbs in splints. A lot of the survivors were covered in oil and the destroyer's deck was as slippery as a skating rink. Below, it reeked of blood, chloroform and fuel oil.

Going round the coughing, groaning masses, the doctor stopped at Woodyatt. He was huddled on the deck, twisted with pain. Dominique was holding him, crouched over him, her cheeks wet with tears.

'Good God,' the doctor said cheerfully. 'You're in a mess, old fruit.'

It appeared that in addition to a broken forearm, the crash against the projections on the *Coniston*'s davits had left Woodyatt with a broken shoulder blade, two broken ribs and a cut head. The doctor got one of the sick-berth tiffies to organise splints and gave the patient a shot of morphine. As he felt himself slipping into unconsciousness, Woodyatt looked at Dominique. Though she had not been in the water, contact with survivors had left her wet through, bedraggled and daubed with oil. She seemed the only sane person in a world gone mad.

'Montrouge,' he said. 'What happened to him?'

'He's aboard. I saw him. He even still has his case.'

'Make sure,' he said as he slipped into oblivion. 'Otherwise we've just wasted our time.'

eight

When Woodyatt came round he seemed to be almost entirely covered in plaster. Those parts of his body which weren't covered in plaster were swathed in bandages. He could remember nothing of the journey home except Dominique's arms round him and her tears falling on his face, and, as the ship had come alongside a jetty, somebody saying, 'Make way. This man's injured.'

His first thought was for the job he'd been doing and he looked round for Dominique. There was no indication that she had ever been there and the nurse who appeared had no knowledge of her.

'Where am I?' he asked.

'In hospital,' the nurse said. 'You've been here for two days.'

'Where in hospital?'

'Falmouth. We're the nearest point to where you left France. Everybody was brought here.'

'My home town's Truro.'

'My aren't you lucky!'

'Do you think you could get in touch with someone for me? My mother and my chief in London.'

He was just drowsily trying to organise his thoughts when his mother turned up. She was trying to put on a brave face in front of her battered son.

'Thank God,' she said, tears filling her eyes. 'We're all together again. I was worried sick with both my boys in

France. But Tom's regiment got away and he's safe. And guess who else has turned up.'

'Who?'

'You remember Nicole? Nicole Maury.'

'Of course. I saw her. In Metz.'

'She's here, too. In London. She wrote to me. She escaped and she wondered if you had. Poor child, her husband was killed. That was what decided her. I wrote back to say she must stay with us and to come at once. She's a very pretty girl and very intelligent. There was a time when you were very fond of her and I rather hoped, in fact – '

Woodyatt interrupted the excited chatter. 'Where's Dominique?' he asked.

'Who, dear?'

'The girl who was with me.'

'I didn't know there *was* a girl with you.'

Woodyatt got her to ring the bell behind the bed and when the nurse came he repeated the question.

'Everybody from the *Coniston* was taken to a centre in the town,' she told him. 'Apart from such as you. The worst injured were brought here. The slightly hurt went to the outpatients' department or the Cottage Hospital. The rest were sent to the Mount Pleasant Hotel to be identified, listed and given clothes.'

'And then what?'

'I think they were allowed to go home.'

'I'm looking for one who didn't have a home in this country.'

The nurse didn't turn a hair. 'Foreign refugees would be claimed by representatives of their country.'

'This one was French.'

'Then the French Embassy, some Free French organisation, the Anglo-French Society – somebody like that. They'd have claimed him.'

'It's not a him. It's a her.'

The nurse cocked an eyebrow and smiled.

'Important, is she?'

'Yes, she is.' Woodyatt weakly beat the bedclothes with his fist. 'For God's sake,' he said. 'She shouldn't have been sent away.'

'Why dear?' his mother asked. 'Are you fond of her or something?'

'That's not the point. Find her, Mother. Find out what happened to her. Her name's Sardier. Dominique Sardier. She'd probably give an address in Dreuil, Picardy. I've got to find her.'

Faintly bemused, Woodyatt's mother looked at the nurse, shrugged and set off for the town. She returned about two hours later, looking worried. She had been to the Mount Pleasant Hotel. 'She *was* there,' she said. 'But she's not there now. Though they said they thought they could trace her. They have her name. Is she all that important, dear?'

'She knew everything I was doing in France.'

'What *were* you doing in France? I thought you worked in London.'

'I was sent on a job. A secret job. She worked with me. She has to be found.'

'Well, I'll do my best but I can't imagine... Does she speak English?'

'Not terribly well. We always spoke French.'

'Well, I suppose that was the reason she disappeared. Apart from a few like us, nobody in this country *ever* understands a foreign language. I imagine the poor girl was trying to give her message and all they could think of was that she was asking for a change of underwear.'

With his mother gone, there wasn't much to do except read the paper. The nurse fixed him up a stand and laboriously he managed to turn the pages on his own. She had taken a fancy to him and fussed around him, all hearty good cheer.

'Feeling better?' she asked.

'No,' he said. 'Much worse.'

'Don't despair. There's a lot of life in you still.'

The newspapers were full of what had happened. France had gone and so had Norway and Denmark, while Italy had come in on the Germans' side. The whole of Europe from North Cape to the Mediterranean was against Britain now, because Franco in Spain was no friend, and men like the ancient Pétain, and Quisling in Norway, whose names had become synonymous with treachery, were helping the Germans to make sure there would be no reverses. But, at least, the British now knew where they stood. With their backs to the bloody wall, Woodyatt thought wryly. It had finally dawned on the newspapers that cricket scores, theatre criticisms and the latest fashions weren't really important any more. War, they had at last noticed, was different from peace and you couldn't just go on behaving in the old way. The columns were suddenly full of exhortations to roll up sleeves, to work harder, not to despair, to look the enemy firmly in the eye. Having found a brand new set of slogans that sounded exciting, the politicians were giving it everything they'd got. Out of the lot of them, only Churchill seemed to make sense.

England was in trouble. Bad trouble. Germany was very much on top, with half Europe at her feet, and it was going to take a long time for the Allies to claw their way back even to equal terms. It was going to be a long war; and for the French it was going to be awful.

Later in the day the nurse woke him to say there was a man to see him. For a moment Woodyatt thought it might be Redmond, but immediately dismissed the idea as pure fantasy.

'Colonel,' she informed him. 'Name of Pullinger.'

Woodyatt was looking forward to the fray. 'Wheel him in,' he said.

Pullinger looked pleased with himself and it was obvious why within seconds. 'Hannah sends her regards,' he said. 'We're going to get married. It's the sort of thing you do in wartime.' He didn't show a lot of concern for Woodyatt's condition. 'What happened to you?' he said.

'I got knocked about a bit when the ship sank.'

'Thought you'd be cleverer than that. I gather you got your man.'

'I got him to the destroyer that brought us to England.'

Pullinger gestured irritably, his good temper vanishing. 'Did you bring him *home*?'

'On the contrary. He brought me home.'

Pullinger's face changed again. 'What do you mean by that?'

'Bit ironic, isn't it? I didn't save his life when the *Coniston* disappeared. He saved mine.' Woodyatt tried to explain. 'He was on the destroyer. I know he was. So he must have been brought ashore in Falmouth. He had a suitcase with him – judging by the way he hung on to it, I reckon he has it still. It's full of papers. As a newspaperman I wouldn't mind poking inside it myself. I bet there's plenty there to set people thinking for weeks ahead, to say nothing of a few names that might startle them. He gave me the identity of your Mr X, by the way.'

Pullinger's eyes lit up. 'He did? Who?'

'He lives in Cheltenham and his name begins with "L".'

'Limboury,' Pullinger said immediately. 'It can only be Limboury. Sir George Limboury. Known to the juniors as "Cheltenham Charlie". I always thought he was a bit of a shit. Well, that's a help. We'll ask him a few sharp questions. What else did you get out of him?'

'A few things. The Germans *are* working on pilotless aircraft and rockets, and have been doing for years. They're well advanced.'

'We knew that. When do they start operating?'

'They don't. After what's just happened, they'll be feeling they won't need them. They'll be expecting us to chuck our hand in.'

'Well, for your information, we're not going to. What about *him*? We need to talk to him.'

'Yes, you do. He had a lot of interesting little titbits you'll be interested in. He said you'd need to watch Singapore.'

'Singapore's as safe as houses.'

'He didn't seem to think so. So you'd better get on with finding him. He'll have a lot to tell you. And there are people who are very eager to get their hands on him.'

'Nazis?'

'They were unpleasant enough to be Nazis.'

'Right.' Pullinger became brisk and energetic. He almost rubbed his hands in his eagerness to get on. 'Where is he?'

Woodyatt smiled. 'God knows. That's up to you. I know he's here, so you'd better start looking for him.'

Pullinger gave him a look of sheer hatred. 'You mean you didn't hang on to him?'

'I was rather preoccupied at the time. Isn't he on the list of survivors? He ought to be.'

Pullinger hurriedly began to thumb his way through a bundle of papers in his hand. 'There's no bloody name here,' he said eventually, 'that could conceivably be his. What did he call himself?'

'Well, it wasn't Redmond and it certainly wouldn't be von Rothügel. Is there a Montrouge?'

Pullinger furiously turned sheets of paper. 'Nobody of that name.'

'He must be around somewhere. The survivors were all gathered together to be cleaned, fed and clothed.'

Pullinger's face reddened. 'I understand one or two of them were allowed to slip away,' he admitted.

Woodyatt gave a bark of laughter. It hurt but he enjoyed it. 'I bet they were,' he said. 'And he was among them. I think you've lost him, so you'd better start making enquiries. And while you're at it, you'd better also look for a girl called Sardier. Dominique Sardier. Age twenty-six. French. Address in Dreuil, Picardy. Chestnut hair. Good-looking.'

'Who's she? Some bit of fluff you picked up en route.'

'She's his niece by marriage,' Woodyatt snapped. 'His only relation. She led me to him and she was with me all the way to Bordeaux and on to the ship. Is she on that list of yours?'

The name was there.

'Then find her,' Woodyatt said savagely.

'I'll find her,' Pullinger was suddenly in a hurry as he thought he scented his quarry. 'I expect they whipped all the French nationals to London. That's where the Free French have set up headquarters. They're checking all their people for us. A lot of people arrived from Dunkirk, and there may be a few among them who're working for the Germans. It was a splendid opportunity to get their agents into England.'

'She's not a bloody agent!'

'All right! All right! But they have to do their job. There are some who don't want to stay in England, some who're better sent home. We're making sure they go.'

'I'll hold you responsible if she's lost,' Woodyatt said furiously. 'You've got to find her.'

'Why?'

'She *found* him for you, damn it!' Woodyatt emphasised the words as though Pullinger were stupid. 'Hasn't it occurred to you yet she's one of the few people besides me who can pick your bloody Redmond out of a crowd?'

Woodyatt's mother arrived almost as Pullinger vanished. She was tremendously excited.

'I've found her!' she said at once. 'She's at some sort of centre for the French in London. I spoke to her on the telephone. It wasn't easy because, of course, after Dunkirk the whole of the South of England's full of people trying to make contact with each other.'

Woodyatt gestured impatiently. 'How was she?'

'She seemed very angry.'

'I'll bet she was. What did she say?'

'All she wanted to know was how you were. It seemed important.'

'Find her, please. Get her away from London. Take her home.'

She leaned over to kiss him. 'It sounds most romantic.'

'Being chased across France by the Germans wasn't romantic, Mother.'

Mrs Woodyatt remained interested. 'Did you rescue her?'

'Sort of. Just look after her until I can get out of this bloody place. Buy her some decent clothes. She'll need them. She's lost everything and I expect they've stuffed her into some bloody awful old cast-offs that make her look dreadful. And she doesn't really look like that at all.'

'You sound very impressed with her.'

'She stood up to being shot at and bombed. To say nothing of being tortured for information. That's always impressive.'

His mother's face set. 'I'll do what I can for her. I'll get them to put her on the overnight train. I'll tell them I'm her aunt.'

Woodyatt was expecting Pullinger to reappear but it was his mother who returned first. She looked serious.

'She won't come,' she said.

'Why not?'

'She said she had things to do. But she also said she'd never forget you. *Never.* That sounds nice.'

It also sounded ominous. 'What else?'

'She said she had to see someone to safety. Because of a promise.'

'Did she say who?'

'We had quite a long conversation, and we were able to understand each other quite well. But she wouldn't tell me.'

'Is she coming here then?'

'She said that after she'd finished what she had to do she didn't know what would happen. I think she wants to go back to France.'

'What!' Woodyatt tried to sit up but the pain threw him back on the pillows. Into his mind came the conversation he had had with Dominique at the Darbys'. He knew what she intended. It was the sort of headlong thing she would do, and he suddenly realised why she was so willing to accept Montrouge, whoever, whatever he was. They were two of a kind. Despite everything, despite all she'd said, despite all her support, she had probably never really been convinced of the old man's guilt.

He lay back on the pillows as his mother left, his mind on Dominique. The thought of her almost choked him. He knew he would never see her again and he missed her, even the foolish little stiffnesses that had been melting more and more with every day.

He was still brooding on what his mother had said when the nurse bustled in.

'Letter for you,' she said. Hand-delivered. Small boy on a bike. Said he'd been given ten shillings to see it arrived.'

The letter was properly addressed to 'Captain James Woodyatt' at the hospital. The absence of a postmark and the use of the boy on the bicycle made him wonder if it were from Dominique. He was just about to open it when Pullinger appeared and instead he stuffed it under the pillow.

Pullinger announced proudly that he had found Dominique.

'You needn't worry,' Woodyatt said coolly. 'My mother got there before you.'

Pullinger looked faintly indignant, as though someone had been beavering away at his job behind his back.

'Oh, well,' he said. 'Never mind, I suppose we'd better concentrate on finding your bloody Redmond now.'

'Not *my* Redmond,' Woodyatt reminded him sharply. 'But *yours*.'

Pullinger gestured angrily. He had made some progress. Unable to identify the old man from the list of the *Coniston's* survivors, he had tried a new angle and asked for all their ages. From that, he had discovered that an old man who had refused to give his name had been taken to the Cottage Hospital suffering from exhaustion. Probing further, he had learned that although this character had seemed on the point of death, during the night he had managed to get out of bed and, finding clothes belonging to another patient, had collected his suitcase and left.

Woodyatt gave a yell of laughter. 'By God,' he said, 'it certainly sounds like him. All the time I was with him, he feigned exhaustion and the weakness of old age. But it was all put on. There was nothing weak about the way he yanked me out of the sea. The bugger was as brisk as a kipper. He was saving his energy for now. Where is he?'

Pullinger gave him a bitter look. 'He's vanished,' he said. 'We've asked at all the obvious places. YMCA. Missions to Seamen. Salvation Army. Church Army. Everywhere we can think of.'

Not for the first time, Woodyatt felt a sneaking regard for the old man.

'Is he Redmond?' Pullinger asked.

'I'm almost sure.'

'Proof?'

'There isn't any. There's no proof at all that it's him.'

'But *you* think it is?'

Woodyatt remembered Brigadier Witkins who had refused to be jockeyed into an agreement or a denial. It seemed the most honourable course to follow his lead. All that had happened, everything that had been said, could easily be explained by some simpler twist. After all, Montrouge was sufficient of a mystery man to have been mixed up in all sorts of shifty things. None had ever been explained and now it seemed they never would be.

'I don't know,' he said.

'You must have an opinion.'

'Yes. I have.'

'Right. Let's have it.'

'He could be. On the other hand, he might not be.'

'You call that a bloody opinion?'

'It's the best I can offer. That suitcase of his could hold a million delights for you, I'm sure. But you haven't got it, have you? And the delights it contains might have nothing to do with our friend Redmond.'

'Of course they have.'

'Have they? Or do they concern a Frenchman involved in shady deals, smuggling, drugs, theft, blackmail. You don't know and neither do I. He's probably just a petty swindler wanted by the police.'

For the first time it occurred to Woodyatt that Montrouge really might have been no more than a clever crook. He even began to suspect he'd been out-manoeuvred all along the line by a more cunning man. Instead of Woodyatt getting Montrouge to safety, Montrouge had got *himself* to safety and had used Woodyatt to provide the means. Woodyatt's arrival in Paris had been fortuitous because Montrouge had already been trying to find a train out. Having been offered a surer means of escape, after a period of resistance to make Woodyatt more keen, he had snatched at it. He had doubtless spent the journey making plans for another escape when he arrived in England. Even the late Zamerski's interest in him could be explained. He could have been someone Montrouge had swindled; someone on the shady side of the law; someone anxious to rub Montrouge out because of some treachery or high-priced financial deal.

Perhaps the old bastard had been using Woodyatt all along! Perhaps he had even used Dominique? Perhaps he had not been her uncle at all, but had listened as carefully to her as he had to Woodyatt, and then seen in her an unquestioning faithful helper.

'It would explain his desire for anonymity just as well as the treachery theory,' Woodyatt pointed out to the baffled Pullinger. 'Perhaps at this moment, he has plans to lift the crown jewels or raise a mortgage on Buckingham Palace. There are always suckers.'

'Don't be a bloody fool! It's proof we need, not half-baked theories.'

'Right. Find the suitcase and if it doesn't contain loot or bearer bonds, or something like that, I'll think again.'

Pullinger's face was pink with rage and Woodyatt was feeling weary, now, from the pain of his injuries and in his heart of hearts he didn't really believe his new line. 'Montrouge did like brandy and soda,' he offered. 'And he had a British revolver circa 1904. *And* he was a dead shot with it and wasn't afraid to use it. It's only a hunch but everything about him made *me* feel he was Redmond.'

For Pullinger's benefit he went on to describe the arguments and the conversations he had had with the old man: including the things Montrouge had told him about the base on the Baltic coast, about the Jews.

Pullinger's face changed. 'You can't kill off a whole race,' he insisted.

'That's what I said. He said the Nazis *could*.'

'What about Darby? Did he meet your Montrouge?'

'Yes, he met him.'

'What did he say?'

'He said he wasn't Redmond.'

'For Christ's sake – !'

'But he'd been drinking a lot for a long time and he wasn't very certain of a lot of things.'

'He knew Redmond,' Pullinger snorted. 'Personally.'

'He didn't recognise him.'

Pullinger tugged at his lip, angry and disappointed.

'On the other hand, his wife thought differently.'

'I met her once. Went off the rails, I heard. Drank a bit.'

'She was still drinking a bit,' agreed Woodyatt.

'Not sure she was good for Darby.'

'She was a damn sight better for him than a lot of people who claimed to be his friends. And she thought our man was Redmond.'

'How would she know?'

'It seems she knew him better than Darby. She once set out her stall to marry him. She was once in love with him. She followed him everywhere. She knew Redmond well.'

'It's a long time ago.'

'Women don't forget. People in love don't forget.' I will never forget, Woodyatt thought.

Pullinger drew a deep breath. 'Where are they now? Perhaps we can test their memories.'

'You'll have a job. Darby's dead. I saw him buried. His wife's probably dead, too. I thought I saw her on the *Coniston*.'

Pullinger studied the list of survivors. He shook his head and lifted a face to Woodyatt that suddenly looked defeated. 'Well,' he growled, 'Wherever the old bugger is *we* haven't got him and he's free to do the dirty on us again if he wants.'

'He won't want to do the dirty. Not on anybody.'

'How do you know?'

Woodyatt was certain. It was the one thing he'd been certain about for a long time.

'For one thing,' he pointed out, 'he's too old. I reckon he's fit enough but he no longer moves fast enough. For another, I don't think he has the wish to. He's had it. He's finished.'

Pullinger was doubtful. 'He could contact a German agent over here,' he said. 'They have them. They reckon one was responsible for the sinking of the *Royal Oak* at Scapa Flow last year.'

'He won't contact any German agent,' Woodyatt pointed out. 'They were too keen to remove him from the scene.' He described the attempts Zamerski and his friends had made. 'He doesn't want the Germans,' he said. 'Not any more. But he also doesn't want *you*.'

'Why not? Conscience, do you think?'

'Not a bit of it. I don't think he'd know what a conscience was if he met one on the stairs. Every word he spoke seemed to indicate he had no regrets for what he'd done. *And there's no proof.*'

'We'll get that when we find him. We'll check all the old people's homes, hostels, the YMCA – '

Woodyatt shook his head. 'Save your breath. He won't be in any of them. He's cleverer than that. He must be to have done what he's done, to live the life he's lived for so long in so many places. You'd have to check every hotel and boarding house in the country, and even you haven't the resources for that. You're too late. He went and went fast. He was on his way the minute he arrived in England and nothing was going to stop him. Not even good manners and a thank you for the help he received.'

Pullinger was frowning, angry and humiliated. With good reason, Woodyatt decided. After all his careful planning, he had been made to look as big a fool as his father had forty years before.

'Where would he go?' he demanded.

'America?' Woodyatt offered. 'If what he's got in that suitcase is what I suspect it is, they might well be interested in it. *They're* going to have to face the Germans, too, before long and they'd probably be glad to pay for what he's got.'

'*I* want him,' Pullinger snapped. 'Not the Americans. We'll watch the ports.'

'They have an embassy,' Woodyatt pointed out gently. 'And they're neutrals. They'd find a means of smuggling him out. In any case, it might not be America. He might have gone to Ireland. He's probably calling himself O'Reilly now. Or even Redmond again. Isn't Redmond an Irish name? You'll never find him.'

'I'm sure we will.'

'No.' Woodyatt smiled. 'He has someone with him whom I suspect will be equal to anything you can produce.'

'We have some pretty bright people.'

'But none with the same sense of purpose.'

'Who is he?' Pullinger asked.

'It's not a he. It's a she. It's Dominique Sardier.'

'Is she a bloody turncoat too?'

'No!' Woodyatt countered. 'She's not. But she claims he's her uncle and she feels she must see he's safe.'

Pullinger scowled. 'We'll find her and find out where she took him.'

'It might be more difficult than that. She's gone to join the Free French.' And Woodyatt drew a deep breath. Knowing Dominique, he knew she had meant what she had said. But as he pictured her disappearing into the darkness of God alone knew what future, he knew her promise to return depended on just too many things to be worth much. 'You'll never find her,' he said. And, he thought to himself with a certainty that was rock-hard, neither will I. Perhaps it was as well. People didn't change as they grew older. They just grew more so, and God help anybody who had to contend with Dominique Sardier in her old age.

The thought of her as an old woman amused him and he managed a smile. 'She wants to go back to France,' he went on. 'She wants to hit back. She'll insist that they hide her. And they will. She's good at insisting. And that means our friend, Redmond, whoever – whatever – he is, won't be found either. Because he doesn't want to be. He doesn't care

what you think of him. He hasn't cared what people like us have thought of him most of his adult life. He is his own man. And he has the means to be. He's got enough money, I gathered, to see him through what's left of his life in comfort. He has funds in Switzerland, in France, here in England.'

Woodyatt lay back on the pillows, exhausted. 'Anyway,' he said, 'What's it matter? Forty years is a long time. Nobody remembers him now except a few die-hards like you. Nobody else is even interested. They've got bigger and better traitors these days. Like Quisling in Norway and Pétain in France – and doubtless a few, like your Mr X, who'll turn up here in England. There's no inclination to look for an old man who might or might not have been a turncoat in wars that took place before the turn of the century.

Pullinger's face was set and angry and Woodyatt went on, almost enjoying himself. 'What everybody's thinking of at the moment,' he said, 'is winning this war – or, more likely just now, simply surviving it.' He shook his head. 'You've had it. Those people who signed all those papers for me, all those high-ups you mustered to back you, they've disappeared. They've been swept away in the chaos – replaced by better, younger, cleverer, braver men who are likely to show more initiative than they ever did. And if they weren't swept away – ' Woodyatt shrugged ' – they'll have bigger things on their minds now.'

Pullinger was silent for a moment or two then he nodded and rose. His face was expressionless. 'You're probably right,' he said sharply. 'Perhaps I'd better get on with the war.'

Patting Woodyatt's sound hand, he gave a stiff smile, turned on his heel and walked swiftly from the ward.

As he disappeared, Woodyatt lay still for a while, his mind working, then, remembering the letter that had arrived, he fished it out and tore it open.

It wasn't from Dominique as he had hoped and he was conscious of a desperate disappointment. It was unsigned and very short. 'Tell Pullinger he's as slow as his father,' was all it said. 'It was nice knowing you.'

John Harris

China Seas

In this action-packed adventure, Willie Sarth becomes a survivor. Forced to fight pirates on the East China Seas, wrestle for his life on the South China Seas and cross the Sea of Japan ravaged by typhus, Sarth is determined to come out alive. Dealing with human tragedy, war and revolution, Harris presents a novel which packs an awesome punch.

A Funny Place to Hold a War

Ginger Donnelly is on the trail of Nazi saboteurs in Sierra Leone. Whilst taking a midnight paddle in a canoe cajoled from a local fisherman along with a willing woman, Donnelly sees an enormous seaplane thunder across the sky only to crash in a ball of brilliant flame. It seems like an accident... at least until a second plane explodes in a blistering shower along the same flight path.

John Harris

Live Free or Die!

Charles Walter Scully, cut off from his unit and running on empty, is trapped. It's 1944 and, though the Allied invasion of France has finally begun, for Scully the war isn't going well. That is, until he meets a French boy trying to get home to Paris and so what begins is an incredible hair-raising journey into the heart of the French liberation and one of the most monumental events of the war. Harris portrays wartime France in a vividly overwhelming panorama of scenes intended to enthral and entertain the reader.

The Old Trade of Killing

Set against the backdrop of the Western Desert and scene of the Eighth Army battles, Harris presents an exciting adventure where the men who fought together in the Second World War return twenty years later in search of treasure. But twenty years may change a man. Young ideals have been replaced by greed. Comradeship has vanished along with innocence. And treachery and murder make for a breathtaking read.

JOHN HARRIS

THE SEA SHALL NOT HAVE THEM

This is John Harris' classic war novel of espionage in the most extreme of situations. An essential flight from France leaves the crew of RAF *Hudson* missing, and somewhere in the North Sea four men cling to a dinghy, praying for rescue before exposure kills them or the enemy finds them. One man is critically injured; another (a rocket expert) is carrying a briefcase stuffed with vital secrets. As time begins to run out each man yearns to evade capture. This story charts the daring and courage of these men, and the men who rescued them in a breathtaking mission with the most awesome of consequences.

TAKE OR DESTROY!

Lieutenant-Colonel George Hockold must destroy Rommel's vast fuel reserves stored at the port of Qaba if the Eighth Army is to succeed in the Alamein offensive. Time is desperately running out, resources are scant and the commando unit Hockold must lead is a ragtag band of misfits scraped from the dregs of the British Army. They must attack Qaba. The orders...take or destroy.

'One of the finest war novels of the year'
– *Evening News*

TITLES BY JOHN HARRIS AVAILABLE DIRECT
FROM HOUSE OF STRATUS

Quantity		£	$(US)	$(CAN)	€
☐	ARMY OF SHADOWS	6.99	11.50	15.99	11.50
☐	CHINA SEAS	6.99	11.50	15.99	11.50
☐	THE CLAWS OF MERCY	6.99	11.50	15.99	11.50
☐	CORPORAL COTTON'S LITTLE WAR	6.99	11.50	15.99	11.50
☐	THE CROSS OF LAZZARO	6.99	11.50	15.99	11.50
☐	THE FOX FROM HIS LAIR	6.99	11.50	15.99	11.50
☐	A FUNNY PLACE TO HOLD A WAR	6.99	11.50	15.99	11.50
☐	GETAWAY	6.99	11.50	15.99	11.50
☐	HARKAWAY'S SIXTH COLUMN	6.99	11.50	15.99	11.50
☐	A KIND OF COURAGE	6.99	11.50	15.99	11.50
☐	LIVE FREE OR DIE!	6.99	11.50	15.99	11.50
☐	THE LONELY VOYAGE	6.99	11.50	15.99	11.50
☐	THE MERCENARIES	6.99	11.50	15.99	11.50
☐	NORTH STRIKE	6.99	11.50	15.99	11.50
☐	THE OLD TRADE OF KILLING	6.99	11.50	15.99	11.50

ALL HOUSE OF STRATUS BOOKS ARE AVAILABLE FROM GOOD BOOKSHOPS
OR DIRECT FROM THE PUBLISHER:

Internet: www.houseofstratus.com including author interviews, reviews, features.

Email: sales@houseofstratus.com please quote author, title and credit card details.

TITLES BY JOHN HARRIS AVAILABLE DIRECT
FROM HOUSE OF STRATUS

Quantity		£	$(US)	$(CAN)	€
	PICTURE OF DEFEAT	6.99	11.50	15.99	11.50
	THE QUICK BOAT MEN	6.99	11.50	15.99	11.50
	RIDE OUT THE STORM	6.99	11.50	15.99	11.50
	RIGHT OF REPLY	6.99	11.50	15.99	11.50
	ROAD TO THE COAST	6.99	11.50	15.99	11.50
	THE SEA SHALL NOT HAVE THEM	6.99	11.50	15.99	11.50
	THE SLEEPING MOUNTAIN	6.99	11.50	15.99	11.50
	SMILING WILLIE AND THE TIGER	6.99	11.50	15.99	11.50
	SO FAR FROM GOD	6.99	11.50	15.99	11.50
	THE SPRING OF MALICE	6.99	11.50	15.99	11.50
	SUNSET AT SHEBA	6.99	11.50	15.99	11.50
	SWORDPOINT	6.99	11.50	15.99	11.50
	TAKE OR DESTROY!	6.99	11.50	15.99	11.50
	THE THIRTY DAYS' WAR	6.99	11.50	15.99	11.50
	THE UNFORGIVING WIND	6.99	11.50	15.99	11.50
	UP FOR GRABS	6.99	11.50	15.99	11.50
	VARDY	6.99	11.50	15.99	11.50

ALL HOUSE OF STRATUS BOOKS ARE AVAILABLE FROM GOOD BOOKSHOPS
OR DIRECT FROM THE PUBLISHER:

Hotline: UK ONLY: 0800 169 1780, please quote author, title and credit card
details.
INTERNATIONAL: +44 (0) 20 7494 6400, please quote author, title,
and credit card details.

Send to: House of Stratus Sales Department
24c Old Burlington Street
London
W1X 1RL
UK

Please allow for postage costs charged per order plus an amount per book as set out in the tables below:

	£(Sterling)	$(US)	$(CAN)	€(Euros)
Cost per order				
UK	2.00	3.00	4.50	3.30
Europe	3.00	4.50	6.75	5.00
North America	3.00	4.50	6.75	5.00
Rest of World	3.00	4.50	6.75	5.00
Additional cost per book				
UK	0.50	0.75	1.15	0.85
Europe	1.00	1.50	2.30	1.70
North America	2.00	3.00	4.60	3.40
Rest of World	2.50	3.75	5.75	4.25

PLEASE SEND CHEQUE, POSTAL ORDER (STERLING ONLY), EUROCHEQUE, OR INTERNATIONAL MONEY ORDER (PLEASE CIRCLE METHOD OF PAYMENT YOU WISH TO USE)
MAKE PAYABLE TO: STRATUS HOLDINGS plc

Cost of book(s): —————————— Example: 3 x books at £6.99 each: £20.97

Cost of order: —————————— Example: £2.00 (Delivery to UK address)

Additional cost per book: ————— Example: 3 x £0.50: £1.50

Order total including postage: ——— Example: £24.47

Please tick currency you wish to use and add total amount of order:

☐ £ (Sterling)   ☐ $ (US)   ☐ $ (CAN)   ☐ € (EUROS)

VISA, MASTERCARD, SWITCH, AMEX, SOLO, JCB:

☐☐☐☐☐☐☐☐☐☐☐☐☐☐☐☐☐☐☐☐

Issue number (Switch only):

☐☐☐

Start Date: **Expiry Date:**

☐☐ / ☐☐   ☐☐ / ☐☐

Signature: _____

NAME: _____

ADDRESS: _____

_____

POSTCODE: _____

Please allow 28 days for delivery.

Prices subject to change without notice.
Please tick box if you do not wish to receive any additional information. ☐

House of Stratus publishes many other titles in this genre; please check our website (**www.houseofstratus.com**) for more details.